A
CRACK
IN THE
SEA

ALSO BY H. M. BOUWMAN

The Remarkable & Very True Story of Lucy and Snowcap

Owen and Eleanor Move In

A Tear in the Ocean

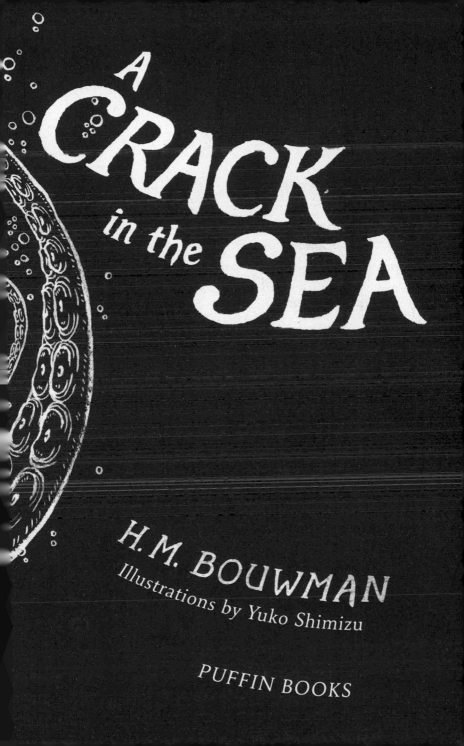

A CRACK in the SEA

H. M. BOUWMAN

Illustrations by Yuko Shimizu

PUFFIN BOOKS

PUFFIN BOOKS
An imprint of Penguin Random House LLC
375 Hudson Street
New York, New York 10014

First published in the United States of America by G. P. Putnam's Sons,
an imprint of Penguin Random House LLC, 2017
Published by Puffin Books, an imprint of Penguin Random House LLC, 2019

THE LIBRARY OF CONGRESS HAS CATALOGED THE G. P. PUTNAM'S SONS EDITION AS FOLLOWS:
Names: Bouwman, H. M., author.
Title: A crack in the sea / H. M. Bouwman.
Description: New York, NY : G. P. Putnam's Sons, [2017]
Summary: "Pip, a young boy who can speak to fish, and his sister Kinchen set off on a great
adventure, joined by twins with magical powers, refugees fleeing post-war Vietnam, and some
helpful sea monsters"—Provided by publisher. | Includes bibliographical references.
Identifiers: LCCN 2016008734 | ISBN 9780399545191 (hardback)
Subjects: | CYAC: Fantasy. | Adventure and adventurers—Fiction. | Kraken—Fiction. | Sea
monsters—Fiction. | Slavery—Fiction. | Refugees—Fiction. | BISAC: JUVENILE FICTION
/ Fantasy & Magic. | JUVENILE FICTION / Action & Adventure / General. | JUVENILE
FICTION / Historical / General.
Classification: LCC PZ7.B6713 Cr 2016 | DDC [Fic]—dc23
LC record available at https://lccn.loc.gov/2016008734

Design by Annie Ericsson. Text set in Maxime Std.
The interior illustrations were done in ink on paper.
The cover illustrations were drawn in ink with digital color.
This is a work of fiction. Names, characters, places, and incidents either are the product of the
author's imagination or are used fictitiously, and any resemblance to actual persons, living or
dead, businesses, companies, events, or locales is entirely coincidental.

Puffin Books ISBN 9780399545214

Printed in the United States of America

10 9 8 7 6 5 4 3 2 1

This book is for the other cousins: Isabelle, Grace, and Cole. And for Camille: fantastic child. And Mikayla, who fits in perfectly; and Kaitlyn, who is now stuck with us all. And especially, Ruhamah and Sophia: you traveled so far to come to this family, who loved you before we ever met you; and we love you more each day.

AS WITH TRUE STORIES, *Venus's story has no beginning. As with fantasy, her tale weaves through everything.*

The book about her—this book you are holding in your hands right now—will open with Kinchen and Pip and, soon enough, Caesar. We'll arrive at Thanh much, much later. Because it is sometimes the nature of books to tell things in what seems to be the wrong order.

Don't forget Thanh. He's coming. And Venus: will be here all along.

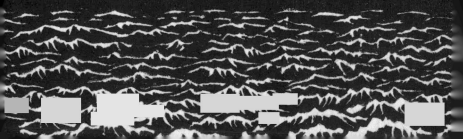

PART ONE

Kinchen (and Pip)

Tathenn. Summer 1978.

WHEN KINCHEN came back from milking the goats, Old Ren sat up in bed and told her that Pip was gone. He'd been taken away by a very polite Raftworlder—one of the Raft King's guards—down to the governor's house for afternoon tea.

"Afternoon tea?" Kinchen asked. It was the first thing that came out of her mouth, but certainly not the real question. What would the king of Raftworld—or their island's own governor, for that matter—want with Pip? He was just a boy, only eleven. And on top of that, everyone in town thought he was slow-witted, "not all there," as she'd once overheard a townswoman say, fake-delicately.

(Kinchen had bumped into that woman and fake-accidentally caused her to drop her bag of apples. *No one* talked about her little brother that way. At least not in front of her.)

Old Ren coughed, his unusually pale face even whiter than usual. His cold had prevented him all week from leaving the house, and today he hadn't even left his bed. "Afternoon tea," he confirmed. "And no, I don't know why. Right after you left for the goats. The guard said they needed him—not anyone else, just him. And that he'd meet the Raft King at tea."

"I don't understand," said Kinchen. Already, though, she was finding her shoes for the trek into town. She'd have to go after him. Pip wasn't stupid—he *wasn't*—but he was odd, especially with people. He needed her help; he always would. She grabbed the dishrag and scrubbed at her face and hands. Probably it would be good to be presentable if she was going to attend a governor's tea.

Ren shook his head. "I offered to come along. But the guard said no, just Pip."

She stood in the middle of the room, shoes in hand, and stared at Old Ren. Their grandfather for all these years. The only adult she trusted completely. What was he telling her?

He leaned forward in his bed and coughed once more, holding her eyes with his. "Pip has gifts that no one else here has. Gifts with water. And the Raft King, who lives on the water, has no such gifts. My guess is that they want to consult Pip. They have a favor to ask him, someone they want him to talk to."

Kinchen nodded slowly. That made sense. She stooped to pull on a shoe.

"You aren't invited," Ren repeated.

"I'm going."

Ren nodded and lay back down on his pillows, pulling the covers back over his chest. Years ago he'd told Kinchen that he'd seen her personality clear and sharp, right away, the moment he'd adopted her—when she was three and Pip was two. And knowing her as he did, Ren never stopped her if she had her mind set on something. It was, in Kinchen's opinion, one of the many good things about Old Ren.

One shoe still in her hand, Kinchen studied him. "Are you going to be okay? I'll be back as soon as I can. With Pip," she added firmly.

"I'd go with you if I could."

Kinchen knew then that Ren was worried. He wasn't just letting her have her way; he was anxious about Pip.

But he didn't say any more about that. "You be careful. And try to be polite. I'll be fine, child. I'm just going to take a nap." He closed his eyes, and his face suddenly looked gray and immobile, like a statue of himself.

She slipped on her other shoe and left, running down the hill and through the woods toward town.

KINCHEN RAN. She was very fast, but Pip and the Raftworld guard had quite a head start on her—probably more than an hour. Had the guard purposely arrived after she left the house? No, she wasn't going to assume this was some kind of conspiracy. That was crazy. She was just going to find Pip and keep him from feeling lost and alone. Help him out. She put her hand up to her forehead almost without thinking and felt the coarser patch of hair that started at her temple and fell down the side of her face—the white stripe that she'd bleached into her dark hair, like a skunk's tail. No matter how hard he tried, Pip couldn't recognize faces, not even Kinchen's. He couldn't identify the governor or the Raft King or anyone else in town on sight, but with the stripe at least he'd always know his sister.

As she ran, she thought about what the Raft King might want; information from the fish made sense. After all, the water was wide, and Raftworld perched on it.

This world—the second world, as they all called it—contained few islands, and not all of them were fit for habitation. The Raftworlders lived on their enormous raft and moved from place to place, following the good weather and always searching for a place to call their own. And Kinchen's people—the Islanders, as they were usually and simply called—lived on the main island of Tathenn and the little Colay islands that swung away from it in a string. Altogether, they called their land simply: the Islands.

Tathenn, where Kinchen lived with Old Ren and Pip, was the seat of government for the Islanders, so naturally when Raftworld visited—which they did, every decade or so—they came to the big island. As was their custom, they had sent a bird ahead to announce their arrival. And two days later they'd arrived, and everything on the island was put on hold for a week or more of celebration while they were in port. So much partying and music and food.

And so much trading: trading of cloth and baskets and books and paper (from the Islands) and beads and jewelry and fishing implements and clockwork devices and hydraulic machines (from Raftworld). And trading of food, and of stories and songs and news.

And exchanging of people. Traditionally, a few people

from Raftworld would decide to stay on the island; and a few from the Islands would elect to join Raftworld. These were volunteers, and they were celebrated for their choosing, for some people were simply happier living on land, and others happier at sea. In practice this exchanging meant that although the Raftworlders looked different from the Islanders—their dark brown skin and tightly curled hair contrasted with the Islanders' medium-brown skin and straight hair—there were, after all these years of trading, some darker people on the islands and lighter people on the rafts. And with marriages and the having of children, even more mixing. Sometimes you couldn't tell for sure if someone was a Raftworlder or an Islander.

And since they were all here by accident and because of others' schemes, they'd decided long ago to make peace with one another. When they met, they met in friendship.

Last time Raftworld came to visit, Kinchen and Pip were both too young to remember it. Nine years ago, shortly after Ren had adopted them: Kinchen had been only three and Pip two.

When Raftworld finally returned four days ago, Old Ren had reminded Kinchen and Pip of all the history between Raftworld and the Islands, especially the friendship part. And he said there would be all kinds of goings-on in town for the Islanders to participate in.

"Maybe Pip should stay home," said Kinchen. Her little brother, sitting at the table in their common room, hunched deeper into his book, so that only his spiky black hair stood up behind it.

Old Ren looked up from threading a needle. He was across the table from Pip, rebinding an old book for the town library. It was an early handwritten manuscript, almost two hundred years old, from before they'd invented a press, and the smell of old paper hung in the air.

"Because of the—the *issue*. With him in crowds. With faces. With people," Kinchen said.

Pip scrunched down even farther. Only the very top of his hair showed.

"He should go." Ren inserted the needle into the pages he was binding. "At least to hear the stories. You could tag along with him, keep him company if he likes."

Kinchen frowned. She wanted Pip to be safe and not to be embarrassed or do something foolish—which meant he should stay out of crowds and away from people.

"You'll both be fine," said Ren. "And the storyteller from Raftworld is stellar."

But now? Now Pip was gone, and he'd be scared and he wouldn't recognize anyone and who knew what would happen?

Ren had said not to worry. But when he'd told her to be polite, she'd seen something flicker across his face. He'd glanced at her, his eyes pale blue and wide, and she'd stood shoe in hand and seen the fear there. She ran.

2

WHEN KINCHEN reached town, she headed down the back street directly for the governor's house. She didn't see anyone. Music and laughter rang from the dock area: crowds of Islanders there yet again, trading and eating and mixing with the Raftworlders, who wouldn't go back to Raftworld until late at night—and then would return again by small boats early the next morning.

She paused only for a second as she heard a particularly loud voice call out, "Tell us another one!" The Islands didn't have an official storyteller, but Raftworld did—an old man with special gifts at remembering and making stories. Heeding Ren's suggestion (though with reservations on her own part), Kinchen and Pip had lain on a dockside shed roof just yesterday and listened to the storyteller as he stood in the market, a crowd around him, and told tales. True stories, made-up ones, stories from this world and from the one before. The old Raftworld storyteller, dark-skinned like most Raftworlders and with thick white hair pulled back in a tie, had a deep, magical voice, and listening to him was like being inside a dream. Kinchen would have loved to hear more— and she knew Pip felt that even more strongly than she did.

At the kitchen entrance to the governor's big house, she hesitated, then slowly cracked open the door. Usually the cook—a terrifying person named Prissy who did not want her clean and efficient kitchen interrupted, ever—stood at the back window chopping and stirring, and would have hailed anyone who ran up to the back door. But today no one was there. *Ah.* Kinchen remembered a booth she'd spotted from her perch on the shed roof yesterday. A couple of Raftworld mechanics had brought several new clockwork and hydraulic kitchen devices—including something called a "beater" (which Kinchen suspected, based on the name alone, would appeal to the governor's cook) and a new type of small bread cooker. Prissy would certainly be trying out these items as much as possible before making a trade for them.

Perfect. Kinchen didn't even need to dream up an excuse for being at the governor's house—not yet, anyway. She slid in the side door, removed her shoes to be polite, and slipped through the kitchen, resisting the urge to irritate Prissy by rearranging the hanging pots or crumpling the neatly folded towel on the counter.

The governor's house was not enormous. It was merely larger than the other Island homes, because the governor held a lot of meetings there—often in a large, airy room next to the town's library of historical manuscripts, which took up most of the rest of the ground floor. Kinchen had been in the house many times, to pick up or drop off books for Ren to repair.

It took only a moment to be sure that no one was home.

She even ran upstairs and checked the bedrooms. Back in the kitchen, she paused. *Where?*

The kitchen window was open to the back garden, and through it drifted faint voices: people at the pond behind the house. Frowning, Kinchen went back outside, shoes in hand, and sneaked quietly down the path to the pond. As she drew nearer, she could hear the governor's low, smooth tones intermingled with a deeper voice, a man's, Raftworld-accented—less nasal than the Islanders—and speaking English, the language used for trade.

But she couldn't hear Pip.

Sure enough, the governor and the Raft King (in a deep purple cape, easily recognizable as she drew near) stood with their backs to Kinchen, watching the pond. It wasn't anything special, just a swimming hole fed by a creek that led from the sea. Occasionally a larger fish would find its way in from the bay, but mostly the creatures were small and quiet. Toddlers were brought here, where there was no tide or undertow, to learn swimming in safe waters.

Kinchen crept closer, working herself behind a bush. She wondered what the adults were doing—and where Pip was. She feared . . . yes, there he was. Sure enough.

In the middle of the small deep pond, Pip floated, face-down, completely still and spread-eagled like a drowned child.

He was talking to the fish.

The Raft King and the governor stood on shore, watching. "We have someone with a water gift, too," the Raft King said. "But she doesn't float. She sinks." A tall, muscled man with big shoulders, he wore wide Raftworld-style pants under his impressive cape. His curly black hair was closely trimmed to his head.

"Well, every gift is different." The governor, her gray top and leggings dull next to the king's clothes, shrugged as if these kinds of gifts didn't make much sense to her. "He's the only one we have right now like this. And his adopted grandfather," she corrected, "but the old man has only a little magic, I'm told. And he's too feeble to use it."

"This is exactly what I needed to see," said the Raft King. "Exactly the type of person I was hoping you'd have. Is he really talking? If so, this boy is what I need."

"When he's old enough, we'll definitely offer him the opportunity to go with you," said the governor in a bland, cool tone. "Now. Let's discuss the volunteers and our trading deals."

"I don't want any volunteers."

"What?" The governor's voice rose. And Kinchen could understand her surprise. There were always volunteers—both to go to Raftworld and to join the Islanders, grown-ups traveling from each direction. "We have a perfect fourteen this year, seven men and seven women, all adventurous—"

"I don't want them. Raftworld is overcrowded. We don't have room." The Raft King put his hands on his hips and nodded toward the pond. "I want this boy, with his gifts. Only this boy."

"But—you just want to consult with him, right?"

"I need to take him with me." The Raft King's voice sounded strained. In the distance, Pip hung motionless in the water, facedown. Kinchen felt frozen as well—what could the Raft King mean?

"What?" the governor said again. She stepped back from the water's edge, away from the Raft King. "We don't allow children to volunteer—and I'm not sure he *would* volunteer anyway. His sister wouldn't let him. Nor his adopted grandfather."

"*Adopted* grandfather?" The Raft King turned toward the governor, and Kinchen could see his strong features in profile. He did not see Kinchen, so intent was he on the governor's words.

"Their parents died when they were only toddlers. One after the other. Old Ren volunteered to take them in. He's— he's different."

She didn't go on, but she didn't need to. The Raft King had evidently heard of him. "The albino."

Ren wasn't albino—his skin tanned every summer, and he said he'd once had brown hair. But he was awfully pale. No one knew where he'd come from or how he'd come by such a strange complexion. He'd been around for ages, living alone in the hill caves for as long as anyone could remember. Alone until Kinchen and Pip's parents died, when he came down from the caves and volunteered to take them in. Even though it was clear that Pip was awkward with people, always looking at them like he didn't know who they were (and before it was known he had a gift), Ren had volunteered anyway. And Ren loved Pip right from the start; he didn't think Pip was stupid. It was, thought Kinchen, another of Ren's great qualities. He thought his grandchildren were good the way they were.

"Yes, the albino. That's the one," the governor confirmed.

"So the boy doesn't have any real family."

"He has his sister. And Ren."

"But I mean, family who would object to him going off. This is a big opportunity for him, you know. What does he have *here* to look forward to?"

"Not much," the governor said. "He's bright enough with math and literature and *things*, but with people . . . well, he's odd. Mostly he talks to fish, I think."

"Exactly. So we take him off your hands."

"I see what you're saying. But the fact is, we Islanders don't trade people unwillingly. I can't give you this boy. He'd have to volunteer, and he's not likely to."

The Raft King's voice thinned. "It's what's best for him."

"I'm sorry." The governor sounded like she was reluctant to say no—but saying *no* nonetheless. Firmly.

The Raft King's voice grew suddenly firmer, too. And threaded in it was a note of something else. Fear? "I *must* have this boy. You don't understand, you people with your islands. We need this child." The Raft King took a deep breath. "He can lead us to our own land."

"What? How?" The governor sounded genuinely interested. Kinchen was, too—how in the world could Pip help the Raftworlders find their land? And what was *their land*?

She thought the Raftworlders had always lived on Raftworld, ever since they'd arrived here in the second world. That was the story, anyway.

The Raft King looked out over the pond for so long, it seemed like he wasn't going to reply. And when he did, he didn't answer the question. "State secret. But this boy is the key." The governor took a breath as if to speak, but the king cut her off. "And until you give him to me, there will be no more trading, no nothing. We're the only two nations in the world, and we won't be friends, not without the boy."

The two adults stood in silence, staring out across the water. Pip still floated facedown, but now his arms, instead of drifting off to his sides, were gesticulating downward, as if he were waving slowly at someone at the bottom of the pond, or petting something beneath him in the water.

Why wasn't the governor saying no to the Raft King? Who cared about Raftworld anyway? And how dare the Raft King say so casually that he would take Pip away? And how could Pip survive without Kinchen's help?

Finally the governor cleared her throat and said, in a small voice that sounded like a shrug, "You can have him. For a visit only."

That was when Kinchen leaped out from behind the bush, eyes blazing.

At the same moment on the little deep pond, schools of fish leapt high into the air, small and quick, over and over, hundreds of them bubbling up like a pot at high boil.

3

Pip floated facedown.

He made sure to float at the surface, because he knew the Raft King wanted to see him, to see at least some of what he was doing. And anyway, Pip couldn't sink more than ten or twelve feet deep without his head aching—like most people, he assumed, except that most people had to come up for air. And he didn't.

And most people couldn't talk with fish.

He also stayed at the surface because—just a little bit—he wanted to show off. After all, his ability with sea creatures was the only interesting thing about him, the only thing that he was especially good at. Kinchen, always protecting him, kept him away from people, so he'd never before had an audience. And it felt good to have an audience when he was doing something right.

He hung motionless in the water and sent out thoughts. For talking to fish, thinking wasn't enough; you had to think *with direction*. Otherwise they couldn't hear anything you said. It had taken him time to figure that out. Talking with fish wasn't just something you *did*, no matter what people seemed to think. It might be a gift, but it wasn't simply given; he'd had to practice it.

His thoughts flowed outward in rings. *Hello? Who's there?* Eventually the fish began to arrive, returning the greeting and nudging one another as they congregated below him. Pip recognized some of them—those who swam back and forth from the bay near his house to this protected inland pond. Some of these fish he'd never seen before; but they'd all heard of him. Their thoughts swirled around him. *The boy. The human who can talk.* The fish jostled in the water.

As the sea creatures gathered, Pip studied them so he'd recognize them the next time he saw them. Fish were easy. They all looked like themselves. Individual and special, with their own markings and their own movements and their own quick way of flashing thoughts and their own sparkle.

Not like people, who—no matter how long Pip studied them—all looked the same to him. He could tell people apart by approximate age and size and length of hair and body shape, and sometimes by skin tone, if they were far enough off the medium-brown norm. But stand two average kids next to each other? Or two women? Or two old men? And it was over. Lucky for him Ren was so pale; and lucky too that Kinchen bleached the stripe in her hair for him. It was always a relief to see that hair and know that his recognizing work was done.

One of the fish he knew twitched upward to him, and

Pip reached down to stroke her smooth, cool back. She was a young bass who called herself Flicker. *We arrive here for a super-secret meeting of fishy minds and we still can't escape you.* She nipped his hand gently as she thought at him, and he grinned.

I'm a fish spy; it's true.

Why the visit? Does this have to do with the giant raft? Flicker threaded herself through his dangling legs not unlike a cat. The other fish shivered into a pack, and he could hear their thoughts, wondering why he had come to the pond.

No, nothing is wrong. At least, I don't think so. The Raft King—the human in charge of the giant raft—he thought it was interesting that I could talk to you all, and he wanted to see it. Pip struggled to keep his thoughts from sounding smug or bragging. *He wanted to see me talk to fish.*

Why? asked a minnow, and all the minnows echoed, *Why? Why? Why?* Their thin, wavery thoughts flashed through the water together.

The bass's thoughts, deep and clear, drove through the clatter. *Do the humans need something from us? What do they want?*

I don't know. There must be something the Raft King wanted—beyond just a simple show of Pip's gift—but Pip didn't know what it was. And he realized now, he'd been so excited to show his gift, so thrilled to be asked, that he hadn't wondered what else the Raft King might want. *I'll find out when I go back up. Meanwhile . . . ?*

Fine, we'll do a trick for your little human friends. If fish could roll their eyes, Flicker would be doing it now. Her thoughts had that fake-grumpy quality to them that Pip adored about her. *What do you want?*

Something happy. And impressive. Could you—could you all jump at the same time? Into the air?

4

KINCHEN KNEW who was making the fish leap: Pip, of course. Pip, not realizing what a pond full of jumping fish might look like to the king—not realizing that it might look like he was floating in the middle of a feeding frenzy or something—

"Amazing," said the Raft King. "The fish obey him. Yes, I need this boy." To Kinchen, still standing where she'd jumped out of the bushes, he said, "You are . . . ?"

The governor said, "This is the boy's sister—the one I was telling you about."

"He's not going anywhere with you," said Kinchen.

The fish finished jumping and the pond's surface stilled. Pip's head popped up as he began to swim toward shore. He didn't look at the three people on the beach. It almost seemed like he'd forgotten about them, but Kinchen knew he hadn't. He just didn't know what to say or how to act around people—people not her or Ren. And knowing Pip, he'd probably already forgotten who these people were. Or at least forgotten which was which.

"He's not going," she said. "He lives here, on the Islands, with me and Old Ren, and he's not going with you."

The Raft King ignored her and called to Pip. "Good job. You made them leap?"

Pip shook his head no as he walked up onto the beach. Then he shook his head even harder, like a dog, and the water flew out of his short hair until it stood up in black spikes all over his head.

"It wasn't you?" asked the governor in surprise.

"I didn't make them. I asked them." Pip glanced toward the pond.

"That's what I meant," said the Raft King.

Pip frowned as if he didn't understand. And Kinchen could feel herself getting exasperated. This kind of misunderstanding was exactly why he couldn't go places in public, why he should stay away from crowds. He didn't know how to talk to people at all. He said, "But if you *meant* that—"

Kinchen said, "We need to get home, Pip. Now."

Pip looked as if he'd just noticed her for the first time. "When did you get here?"

She didn't answer. "We're leaving," she said to the Raft King. She narrowed her eyes at him and then at the governor, trying to give them each equal glare time.

The Raft King coughed. "Of course. Of course. I'd never make someone visit Raftworld—just *visit*, that's all—if they didn't want to. My apologies. But do let me offer you tea first. A Raftworld blend—very special. The governor and I were going to have some." He gestured toward the mansion, and Kinchen could see a small table just outside the back door, set with a teapot and cups and plates. She must have rushed past it earlier.

Pip's face lit up, his shock of black hair around his head looking (as usual) like a dandelion gone to seed. His big brown eyes were even wider than usual and seemed to take up his whole face.

"Fine," Kinchen said. "One cup of tea, and then we go home."

The Raft King straightened his purple cape across his shoulders. "Excellent. Pip, is it?"

"Short for Pippin," said the governor.

"No it isn't," said Kinchen.

"I'm just Pip," said Pip. His name was short for the very old-fashioned name Philip, as Pip well knew. But Kinchen didn't correct him.

"Well, Just Pip," said the Raft King in a jolly voice. "Walk with me and tell me more about talking to the fish. Since you're not sailing with me, you'll need to tell me all about it now." The two of them walked ahead toward the house.

The governor turned to Kinchen. "I would never allow anyone to be forced to go. Especially a child." She emphasized the last word a tiny bit, as if to suggest that Pip was even more a child than typical, as if he needed even more protection than other children. Which, Kinchen thought, he did.

Kinchen frowned. "What about the trade agreement? What about *the only two nations in the world won't be friends anymore*?"

The governor said, "I'm sure he didn't mean it." But she didn't look sure.

5

PIP WAS, he admitted to himself as they walked toward the mansion, disappointed not to be going to Raftworld for a visit. Because it sounded like that's what the Raft King had wanted, and that would have been an adventure. On top of that, he was angry that Kinchen had arrived to save him. He didn't *need* rescuing; he was pretty sure of that. And anyway, if he did, why couldn't he save himself? He would have just said, *No, I don't want to go to Raftworld.* Kinchen didn't need to do that for him.

But *would* he have said no?

On top of everything, he felt guilty about being mad at Kinchen. She took care of him. She protected him. And when he said or did dumb things, she covered for him. He shouldn't be mad at her. He shouldn't.

As they walked toward the tea table, the Raft King talked, and when he paused for a response Pip realized, too late, that he hadn't been listening. "Uh . . ."

"I understand," said the king, patting his head. "So you've known this about yourself all your life."

"I—I guess," said Pip. Then he realized the Raft King was probably asking about the talking to fish. "I mean, yes. I knew since the first time I put my head under the water. My grandfather was teaching me to swim."

The Raft King chuckled. "I'll bet your grandfather was surprised."

"He said he didn't need to teach me swimming anymore." He felt a brief surge of pride. It had taken Kinchen years to learn to swim, and even now, though she was a strong swimmer, she wasn't nearly as comfortable in the water as he.

They reached the table. The governor and Kinchen lagged behind, talking. Kinchen was angry; Pip could tell because of the way her fists clenched and unclenched as she walked. Pip sighed. She was probably scolding the governor for letting Pip show his gift to the Raft King.

He turned back to the Raft King just in time to see him reach into a chest pocket on the inside of his robe and bring out a small packet. "Oh. It's for the tea." The Raft King added the powdery contents of the packet to two cups and poured the tea over them, stirring the powder and the tea together with a spoon. Into the other two cups he simply poured tea.

"Why . . . ?"

"I figured you kids would want a little sweetener. Raftworld tea can be bitter until you get used to it." The Raft King winked. "I doubt your sister will even notice that I added it."

But if the tea was bitter, they could just add honey . . . which was sitting on the table in a jar. Why add powder from a packet in your robe? Looking up at the Raft King's unremarkable face, a face he'd not recognize again if he saw the king five years from now—or five minutes from now—Pip knew that the Raft King was covering something up. And he was making up a stupid lie because he thought Pip was too dumb to catch on. He wasn't even bothering to come up with a good story.

Pip nodded, thinking all these thoughts, just as the governor and Kinchen arrived. Kinchen looked calmer, and the governor looked relieved. "Tea sounds wonderful just now," she said.

The Raft King handed her one of the unpowdered cups, taking the other for himself. "Could you and I talk business for just a moment or two more? While these two drink their tea?" He handed Kinchen and Pip their cups, one after the other. "Drink up, kids."

The governor shrugged, as if unsure about leaving Pip and Kinchen alone.

"We'll be fine," said Kinchen. "I'll take care of Pip." She patted his back like he was a toddler.

At that moment, Pip decided to let her drink the tea.

He decided to drink his, too. The king wouldn't actually poison them. But if there was something going on, he was going to be a part of it.

6

WHEN KINCHEN woke up she couldn't remember where she was or why. Her mouth tasted like sheep's wool, greasy and fuzzy at the same time. And bitter. She thought about sitting up, but somehow her brain felt like it needed to stay lying down. Slowly she tilted her head and studied her surroundings. She seemed to be lying on a bed, on top of a quilt dyed in stripes of green and blue—the official colors of the Islands. The walls of the room, too, were green and blue, bright and clean: one of the governor's upstairs rooms. The windows stood open to let in a breeze and a bright late-morning light.

Too bright. She tilted her head the other way. A dresser, bare but for a slip of old-fashioned birch-bark paper lying importantly in the center. She squinted, but couldn't see what it said from her angle—and didn't feel like getting up yet. Between the dresser and the door, on the floor, lay a bulging burlap sack, securely tied at the top with boating rope. Her own shoes hung above the sack on a wall hook. She lifted one heavy foot toward the ceiling and stared at it, feeling stupid because she couldn't figure anything out. Her foot was bare. And somewhat dirty.

Yes, dirty. She searched her memory, foggy, for a clue. Her feet were dirty because she'd been gathering the goats and milking them, and she'd been barefoot, and then she'd shoved on her shoes and gone to find Pip—

Pip.

She flipped her head around the room again, grimacing at the sudden, sharp headache.

Pip was not there.

Everything flashed back to her, Pip at the pond and the tea afterward, and she sat up, head spinning. Had she fallen asleep? No, she must have gotten sick. The last thing she remembered was the tea. The Raft King's tea, whose bitterness still rested on her tongue.

The paper on the dresser was a note; she could see that now. She'd have to stand to reach it. Slowly she slid her legs to the side of the bed. She had to walk only a few steps to the dresser, but she didn't know if she could make it.

Of course she could. Taking a deep breath, she lunged for the dresser. She didn't walk so much as she fell with forward motion, grabbing the note on her way to the floor.

At first the letters on the page didn't look like anything, just scrawls that kept going in and out of focus. She breathed deeply, wiped her sweaty forehead, and gazed around the room, letting her head clear as much as it could. The bag on the floor was even bigger now that she sat across from it— almost the same size as she was.

Kinchen studied the paper again and was relieved to find that she could remember how to read. The scrawls shaped themselves into letters and the letters into words. But the words didn't make sense.

Dear Kinchen,

You've been here all night, sleeping off your sudden illness. I hope you will feel better upon waking.

Meanwhile, your guardian, Mr. Ren, has not even bothered to come to town to look for you and your brother. It is clear to me that neither you nor Pippin are well-cared-for children, and I am now convinced that Pippin at least would be better off where he can learn a trade and be taken care of. The Raft King has offered to adopt him—even after learning about his limitations in interacting with others. This is the best offer he might ever receive—a life fit for a prince, really. I know that you will not want to hold him back from such a wonderful opportunity. I know that you will want the best for your brother.

You may, if you wish, continue to live with Mr. Ren. You are old enough to make that decision for yourself. If you feel, as I now do, however, that he is not a competent caregiver, I will be happy to find you acceptable housing in town. You'll be able to attend school. (It's yet another example of your guardian's thoughtlessness that he has never sent you.)

Do let me know your thoughts on your future housing. Meanwhile, please try to be happy for your brother's good fortune.

The Raft King has left you a gift. He wouldn't say what it was, just that it would amply compensate your grandfather for any lost help around the house or fields. It's in the sack.

With respect,
Clarissa Flans-Daughter,
Governor

IT FELT like hours, but was probably only minutes, that Kinchen sat with the note in her hand, trying to take it in. Then she crumpled the paper into a ball and dropped it on the floor between her feet. Her heart raced and the bitter tea rose in her throat and tried to come back up. She swallowed hard.

She hadn't gotten sick, that much was clear. She'd been poisoned—she and probably Pip, too—by the Raft King. All to steal Pip away from her. To take him somewhere where she couldn't protect him.

Well, she'd only been knocked out one night. Pip was probably lodged on the giant raft by now, but Raftworld was still sitting just outside the harbor. Kinchen could borrow a rowboat (with or without permission; right now she didn't care) and get out there easily in an hour or two. Blast—she would *swim* there if she needed to. Raftworld wasn't slated to leave for several days yet. There was time to get Pip back, to rescue him.

No time to waste, though. Pip would wake soon, and he'd be scared. He wouldn't recognize anyone, and he'd act weird, and everyone would think he was an idiot and then, as usual, he'd stop talking and confirm their conclusions. And they'd treat him like he was not normal and he'd feel terrible. She needed to find him.

Just then the door opened. The governor poked her head in, saw Kinchen on the floor, and stopped short. Her thick black hair, barely streaked with gray, was pulled back in a tight knot, as always—very professional and governor-like— but her face didn't look like the face of someone in charge. It looked fallen in, like a landslide, and she seemed much older than usual.

"You jerk," said Kinchen.

The governor sighed. "You have no idea how much of a jerk," she said, and she eased into the room and sat on the floor across from Kinchen. "You read my note."

Kinchen kicked the crumpled paper toward the governor.

"I thought you'd see reason in the morning—but if you didn't, you'd have time to go out to Raftworld and retrieve Pippin."

"Pip."

"Yes. Pip." She lowered her head and twisted her hands together. "But I've been bamboozled. And I've bamboozled you, too. You have to believe that I didn't intend to. I thought—still think—that I was doing the best for Pip. Giving him an opportunity to shine. But I also thought you'd have a say in the matter when you woke up, and if, after reading my letter, you still felt he should live with you"—Kinchen glared, and the governor faltered, then continued—"you could make that choice. I didn't mean for him to be stolen away."

Stolen away? "What do you mean?" Kinchen felt almost like she couldn't breathe. *Stolen away?*

"Raftworld is—gone."

Kinchen stared at the governor. Nothing made sense. "They're not supposed to leave until next week."

"I know! But they left sometime during the night. Without the fourteen volunteers. Without finishing the trading deals. Without the big send off party. They just left. We went out to the harbor this morning, and they were gone. The Raft King swindled me—swindled *us*. And I think he did it so that he could take Pippin—Pip—with him."

The governor's words were sharp and clear, like a shard of good gypsum stone. No: like a skinning knife. Every word cut into Kinchen. She wasn't sure she was breathing.

The governor continued. "I meant what I said about your guardian, about Old Ren, and I'm concerned—"

"He's sick. He couldn't get out of bed."

The governor blinked.

"That's why he didn't come looking for us. He's the best grandfather ever. He loves me—and he loves Pip."

The older woman blinked again. Then, in a low voice: "I'm sorry, Kinchen."

Kinchen did not answer. She was concentrating on not

crying—or exploding. She needed to focus, to find something to do to fix all this. "Send out a ship to find them."

"You know we can't do that," the governor said gently. "We don't have seafaring ships, only fishing boats. Raftworld is far out of our waters by now, and we don't know the world out there. All our seafaring folk . . ."

"Have joined Raftworld."

"Yes. Over the years. It's—it *was*—a good system." She took a deep breath. "I'll call together some of the former Raftworlders—the ones who joined us last time."

"Almost ten years ago." Kinchen couldn't keep the scorn out of her voice. As if they could help.

"They knew the Raft King—long before he became king. They at least can tell us something of his personality, his desires."

"From ten years ago."

She sighed. "Yes. But it's the best I can do right now. Kinchen, I'm sure Raftworld will return. After Pip is done—with whatever it is they want him to do. They'll bring him back."

Kinchen refused to nod, refused to let this woman off the hook. "Just go. Please."

The governor sat for a minute, then rose gracefully—despite her age—and brushed off her long tunic. "I'll keep in touch. Don't forget your sack." Then she stepped out through the door and was gone.

Kinchen sat for a few minutes more. She felt frozen. But she had to move. She had to get back to Old Ren, who must be worried. And he was sick—what if he needed something? She stood up and reached for her shoes, then sat back down to put them on. She shook her head to test it. The fuzzy sheep's wool feeling still lingered in her mouth, but her head felt much clearer. Okay. Go back to Old Ren and then figure out how to rescue Pip. What else?

Don't forget your sack.

The sack. Her prize for losing her brother.

She stared at it, only a few feet away from where she sat. Big, lumpy thing. The Raft King had said it was something to help around the house or barn, did he? It was probably a clockwork of some kind; the Raftworlders were known for them. A floor cleaner or timekeeper or something. Like that would make up for the loss of a brother.

She was tempted to give the bag a big kick and leave it there for the governor to deal with. Yes, that seemed about right.

She stood up, steadying herself, not sure she could kick something right now without toppling but determined to try. Angry.

She pulled back her foot.

The bag sighed.

7

AFTER IT sighed, the bag trembled.

Kinchen reached into her vest and pulled out her knife.
What kind of clockwork had the Raft King left her?

There. The bundle twitched again. She took a step toward it.

The sack froze. Then it shuddered another shudder, almost as if something inside were waking up.

Something. But what?

Kinchen's heart thrummed inside her throat; she could feel it knocking like it wanted to leap out of her mouth. She shook herself. *Not me,* she told herself. *I'm never scared.*

No, she was definitely scared.

Whatever it was, she couldn't leave now, not knowing. Kinchen took a deep breath. With her knife, she cut the rope that bound the bag shut, yanked the top open, and peered inside.

It was—

A boy. Or maybe a girl—hard to tell in the dim interior of the bag. Smaller than Kinchen. Dark-skinned, like Raftworld people tended to be. More than that she couldn't see. Whoever it was, he or she lay on its side, bound and gagged, peering up at her, huge brown eyes blinking rapidly in the sudden light.

The Raft King's clockwork trade was a person.

8

KINCHEN'S MIND raced. Not only was the clockwork in the sack a person, but it was a person who probably hadn't volunteered to be traded. Maybe, thought Kinchen, it was a person who could explain what was going on. Maybe a person who could help her find Pip.

The person shifted and stared up at Kinchen; realizing that she'd been pointing her knife into the sack, Kinchen slipped it back in her vest. Then she opened the sack all the way and eased it down.

The person was a girl—at least, if the braids were anything to go by. Dozens of long black braids. A *little* girl? Younger than Kinchen, anyway. Thin face.

She was probably hungry, thirsty. Maybe hurt.

"I'm going to cut the cords off you. Hold still."

The girl nodded and waited until Kinchen had cut all the rope and loosened the gag before she sat up and rubbed her wrists and ankles. She swallowed several times.

"Well," she said. Her voice cracked like she hadn't used

it in a while, but it cleared as she kept talking. "He gave me a sleeping draught. I didn't expect that." She swallowed again. "Jumping jellyfish, my mouth tastes like a sour desert."

Kinchen nodded. "I don't have any water, but we can get some downstairs. Do you know where you are?"

"Generally speaking. On the big Island, yes? That's what I asked for, anyway." The girl looked unconcerned, even chipper. "But I have to say, I think it was a little unfair to drug me to sleep. I wasn't going to put up a fuss." Then she grinned. "I'm Caesar. Are you Kinchen? He said you'd be my adopted sister."

"Who said?" But Kinchen already knew the answer.

"The Raft King, silly. I'm the volunteer." She paused. "You *were* expecting me, right? In exchange for *your* volunteer?"

"There wasn't any volunteer."

"Sure there was! I was traded for *someone*." She stood up shakily. "Can we get that water you promised and then talk about it? I'm about dead of thirst."

Kinchen stood, too, blocking the door. They'd talk about this *now*. "There wasn't any trade. Your Raft King stole my brother. My little brother."

"A kid?" She shook her head, eyes big. "Nah."

"You think I'm lying to you? Pip's only eleven—he needs me to take care of him. He's not old enough to be a volunteer. And anyway, he *didn't* volunteer. The Raft King drugged him and me—and stole him. *Your* Raft King," she added spitefully.

The Raftworld girl tensed, hand at throat. Small and thin, she looked like she was made of wire; and she vibrated like a strung bow. Her braids angled crookedly down her back, and some of the shorter hairs had worked their way out of the braids and fanned out from her head in a fuzzy halo—reminiscent of Pip's own thatch of hair. Against the light, it was hard to make out her features.

"I didn't know," she said. "I didn't. Or I would never have agreed."

Kinchen snorted.

"I *didn't* know."

Maybe that was true—she was stuffed in a sack, after all. "Let's get some water. Then we'll go home to my grandfather and make sure he's okay. Then you'll tell me how to find Raftworld."

The girl, Caesar, nodded slowly. "And maybe some food, too?"

AS THE GIRL drank from the kitchen faucet, Kinchen asked, just to see if she'd heard right, "Your name is . . . Caesar?"

"Yup." She wiped her mouth with the back of her hand and smacked her lips. "That was *perfect. Amazing.*"

"Caesar is a boy's name," said Kinchen. Immediately she was embarrassed—maybe this person *was* a boy. Maybe braids were what boys on Raftworld wore—how would she know what crazy things they did there? ". . . Are you a boy?"

She giggled. "I'm a girl. My name is Caesar. For real."

"A boy's name."

"Says who? If a girl has it, it's a girl name." She tipped her head to the side. "Is Kinchen a made-up name?"

"It's just old," Kinchen said defensively.

"Old-fashioned is nice. It's a fantastic name." Then: "What's your age?"

"Twelve. You?"

The girl flashed a grin. "Twelve." Kinchen must have looked doubting, because Caesar said, "Am too. I'm just short for my age."

"Why—why did you volunteer? I thought only adults could do that."

She grinned and gestured to the sink. Kinchen was glad to bend and drink; maybe she could wash the drug's bad taste away.

"I'm an exception. The Raft King wanted to get rid of me."

Kinchen brought her head up, mouth dripping. "Why?"

"I wouldn't help him." She shrugged. "He wanted me to go walking out into storms and look for something in the water—a doorway or something." She said *doorway* like it was a question. "He said it was for the good of Raftworld. But it's not for the good of Raftworld to go chasing storms—we sail *away* from storms. The Raft King and I had a big fight about that, and then he said I could either help him or I could go. So I went. I mean, it's not like there was any good reason to stay—" She broke off. "I just didn't think he'd drug me first. I kind of thought I'd be part of the ceremony—you know, part of the exchange of volunteers. And there would be a party and food and all that. How many volunteers were there, anyway? Besides your brother, I mean," she added.

"None." Kinchen wiped her mouth off. She'd had enough. "There were supposed to be fourteen. But Raftworld left without them. What do you mean, *walk into storms and look for a doorway?*"

"We were kind of yelling at each other by that point. Well, *I* was yelling. So the king didn't spell everything out exactly, but I have a theory about the doorway. And going out into storms . . . I have a gift with the sea." Then, seeing Kinchen's expression, she said, with a sudden flash of light across her own face, "Your brother does, too, doesn't he?" She pursed her lips. "Maybe that's why the king took him."

Caesar and Pip had similar talents, that much was clear. And maybe Kinchen could get more information out of Caesar—to save Pip from whatever the Raft King planned. But first: Ren. "Let's get going."

Caesar grinned. "Yes, let's."

They left town and walked along the path toward the cliffs—the same path Kinchen had run down only the day

before. The thin, underused trail led only to Old Ren and
Kinchen and Pip's house. Once in a while the town's schoolteacher visited (and made sure Kinchen and Pip were learning), and a few times a year someone else would venture out
to see them, but other than that: nothing. So the path was
barely visible, appearing and disappearing into the under-
growth as you followed it.

When they reached the jagged, low cliffs that led toward
the big bay, Kinchen slowed down to give Caesar a sense
of the land. "The bay out there—it's known for having
strange fish." Then she stopped. Pip had spent a lot of time
at the bay, but he didn't often tell her about it; some things
he kept to himself. "Is your gift to talk . . . with . . . ?"

"No," Caesar said. "That's part of why the Raft King was
okay with getting rid of me. My gift wasn't exactly what he
wanted. I just walk. The fish don't talk with me."

Kinchen nodded. Maybe Caesar could go out into storms
(whatever that meant), but it hadn't been enough. The Raft
King had wanted Pip instead.

She continued the tour. "Our house is ahead." She gestured to a small cabin just visible above them, at the base of a
steep hill—almost a mountain, really. "In the cliff behind our
house are a bunch of caves. There's a story that the founder
of Raftworld came to Tathenn once and lived in one of those
caves, with her puppy . . ." But she'd forgotten the rest of the
story. She wasn't very good with history.

Though Caesar had been drooping, now her hungry face
came to life. "You mean *Venus* lived here? That's amazing!"

She studied the mountain as if she could pick out the cave Raftworld's founder had lived in. "You'll have to show me her home. Tomorrow?"

Kinchen laughed. "No one knows where the cave is. Anyway, it might not even be real. Just a story."

Just then, away up the hill, Old Ren stepped into the doorframe of the cabin. He straightened his back with one hand and waved to them with the other. Kinchen sighed with relief. Ren was up and moving around. He was feeling better.

Caesar gasped. "Who's THAT?"

Kinchen waved and walked faster. "Old Ren. We live with him."

"He looks *so creaky*. He's the ancientest person I've ever seen."

Kinchen squinted. Ren certainly was old, with his long white hair and hunched back. Sometimes she didn't notice exactly *how* old; other times—like when he was sick—she studied his wrinkled face and his gnarled hands and how slow he moved, and she worried.

"And he's so *pale*. He looks like bones. Like all his color is drained out of him. What's *wrong* with him?"

"That's just the way he is," said Kinchen stiffly. "He said he's always been white-skinned. He said he's a throwback to the English who crashed here a couple hundred years ago."

Caesar wrinkled her nose in confusion. "You mean he's two hundred years old?"

Kinchen frowned at those dark brown eyes. How could Caesar possibly be twelve? She was such a baby. "That would be crazy, wouldn't it? He *looks like* the English. That's what I'm saying." They passed through the raspberry brambles— Kinchen lifted a particularly long branch off the path so that they could pass through—and stepped into the yard in front of the house. "You're out of bed," she said to Old Ren. She meant more with those words than she could say.

"And well." He winked at her and lifted his pale face to the sunshine.

Kinchen gestured to the girl beside her. "This is Caesar. From Raftworld. This is my adopted grandfather, Ren."

They nodded to each other, and then Kinchen said, "It's about Pip."

He said, "I already know. Prissy came out late last night. She was stirred up about it all. Upset for you. But we'll fix it." Then to Caesar he said, "So you must be the trade in the big sack?"

"Clockwork trade," said Kinchen, before Caesar could answer. "That's what I thought she was, anyway, until the sack moved."

"How'd you know about me?" Caesar asked.

"Prissy read the note." Ren grinned, looking almost like his healthy self. "Did you meet her? The cook? She's terrify-ing if she isn't on your side. The governor will not be eating well for a long time."

They weren't talking about what was important. "How are we going to fix it?" asked Kinchen. "Pip."

"We'll walk to town later today and row over to Raftworld." He stretched his back, groaning a little. "*You'll* row."

He didn't know yet—not all of it. Kinchen said, "Raftworld left late last night. With Pip."

Ren's grin dropped off his face. "Ah." He leaned back against the doorframe as if he'd suddenly deflated. "I—was not aware of that."

"No one knew until this morning, when they weren't there anymore."

He nodded his head slowly, thinking. "Well. Now I need to sit down. And we'll discuss this. Make plans."

INSIDE, KINCHEN set the pot on the stove for tea and rummaged in the cupboard for food. There wasn't much. There never was; they generally had enough, but no more than that. She found some raspberries in a bowl, and then Ren said, sitting heavily on a cushion on the floor, "Prissy brought us some stew. It's on the back hotplate." And sure enough, in a sealed pot on the back of the stove, cold vegetables sat in a thick brown sauce. Kinchen lit the burner.

Caesar put her hands on her hips. "For your reference from now on: I don't want to be known as *the clockwork trade*. Maybe we can come up with some new way to introduce me to all your friends. How about . . ." She trailed off, thinking. "The Astounding . . . The Amazing . . ."

"We'll come up with something." Ren's craggy face assembled into a half smile—but not the grin of earlier. He gripped Kinchen's shoulder as she leaned past him to place bowls on the table. "We'll come up with something." And his words were a promise that made her feel just a little better.

At supper, Caesar ate more than half of the stew. Maybe, Kinchen thought, she was so small because she was half starved. The way she was inhaling food, she'd take care of that problem quickly enough.

"I need to find a job," said Caesar finally, licking off her spoon. "Where can I look for work?"

Ren sat back on his cushion. "What?"

"I live on Tathenn now. And I don't have any relatives to take care of me. So I need a job." She clattered her spoon to the table, lifted her bowl and licked it clean. "The sooner the better, right? Might as well settle in. Is there any dessert?"

Ren motioned to the cupboard, and Kinchen brought out the raspberries. Caesar took a handful and popped several berries into her mouth.

It was like she wasn't even concerned about Pip. Kinchen took the spoons and bowls to the sink, setting them down just a little harder than she meant to. "I need to find Pip. I was hoping you'd care enough to help."

"Kinchen," said Ren. His voice had a warning in it.

Caesar sat up straight. "Of course I care."

"Tell me how I can find Raftworld."

Caesar ate the rest of the berries in her hand, all in one bite, then answered with her mouth full. "You can't."

Before Kinchen could protest, Caesar swallowed and amended her statement. "Not by yourself, anyway." She tapped her chest and took another handful of berries.

"You'll help me find Raftworld? *Can* you find it?"

She shrugged. "I can *try*. I'll help you look, and you're

more likely to find it with me than without me. I do have an *amazing* gift with the sea, after all."

At least Pip didn't brag about his magic all the time. "You use the word *amazing* an awful lot."

"Of course."

"I can help," said Old Ren quietly. "I can help you find Raftworld." They turned to him, Caesar bright-faced and Kinchen in surprise. Kinchen knew Ren had some magical gifts—though he always claimed his were shallow, weak things compared to Pip's gift (and apparently Caesar's). Kinchen didn't see how her grandfather could locate Pip. She'd thought Ren's main talent was being really, really old.

"You can find Raftworld? How?"

"I have a friend—I think he can take you there. Or at least partway there." He narrowed his eyes at Caesar as if he were studying her. "If my friend can take you close and point you in the right direction, you can go the rest of the way, yes?"

She nodded, grinning. "Sounds like you have good magic."

"And so do you," Ren said. "My gifts are small, but I have several. One is that I can sometimes see gifts in others." He stood to make the tea.

"That's why he adopted us," said Kinchen. "He could see that Pip had gifts, too." She hadn't meant to say it; the words just popped out.

Ren frowned down at her. "How can you think that? I adopted you because you needed me, and it seemed to be my job to take you in. And because I loved you immediately."

She could feel herself flushing. Ren rarely talked about love. She muttered, quickly, "I love you, too." Then she cleared her throat. "But you could see that Pip had gifts."

He nodded. "I could. But that's not why I adopted you." Then he said to Caesar, "If you have a gift for the sea, and the Raft King wants someone with a gift for the sea, why didn't he keep you?"

"My gift wasn't exactly what he wanted. And I wouldn't help. Anyway, I thought I might as well come here as stay there." Her last sentence trailed off just a little, and Caesar finished the raspberries in silence. Ren strained the tea.

Kinchen sat and thought. It seemed like everyone had gifts except her. She knew that in truth, magical gifts were extremely rare and only a few people on the Islands had any gift at all. But it didn't feel that way. She'd been living all her remembered life with two people who had magic—and now a third, and she the only one without.

"Here's what I want to know," said Ren, returning to the table with the mugs and setting them down before Caesar. "What does the Raft King want with our Pip? And if we find him, can we bring him back home?"

"I don't know about the second question," said Caesar. "But I know the first. He wants to find a doorway. And he thinks Pip can find it."

"Why Pip?" said Kinchen.

"What kind of doorway?" said Ren. He began to pour the tea.

"Pip can talk to fish, yes? Well, the Raft King thinks the fish know how to get to the doorway. He says there's something—like a gate, or a portal—and the fish can find it." She shrugged. "I don't know why he thinks the fish know anything."

Ren nodded slowly like that idea made sense. He poured a second mug of tea and tilted the teapot over the third cup.

Caesar continued. "And he wants to find the doorway because he wants to go through it. Into the first world."

Ren dropped the teapot.

It fell only a few inches, onto the table, and it didn't break. But hot liquid sloshed all over, and Kinchen jerked back to avoid getting spattered. "I'm sorry, child," he said mildly, and he took a towel and wiped the table.

The two girls watched.

"Pip was stolen," said Ren, as if he'd never dropped the teapot. "I can't go across the globe after him—I'm still re-covering from being ill. You girls should find Raftworld and Pip." He turned to Caesar. "Maybe, also, you can return to your own country if you like, and not be forced to find a job here." His mouth twisted in a half smile.

Caesar smiled back, a real smile—not her flashing-like-water grin but an open and lingering happiness. She had a nice smile, thought Kinchen, full-lipped and crinkly at the edges. Her thin face and high cheekbones seemed to re-arrange into something lean and warm rather than starved and pinched. Her eyes glowed in her dark clear skin like twin planets.

"So. How do we do it?" Caesar rubbed her hands together. "And is there any more food?"

"WHAT FRIEND?" Kinchen asked Old Ren, when it seemed like Caesar was filling up—and slowing down. "What friend of yours can help us?" Kinchen didn't know Ren had any friends. There were the schoolteacher and a few others who visited them once in a while. But not *friends*. Not people who could drop their lives to transport you somehow to Raftworld, or at least near enough to it for you to get the rest of the way yourself.

Ren studied his now-empty mug, his face more lined than ever. Then he looked up and smiled at Kinchen. "Believe it or not, he's older than I am."

She felt her eyes narrow. There was no one older than Ren. Surely.

"Let's go meet this man," said Caesar. She'd finished the last crumbs of the goat cheese and crackers Kinchen had brought out after the raspberries, and she leaned back on her cushion and patted her stomach. "I could still eat," she mused to herself.

"Yes, let's go," said Kinchen. There was no fresh food left in the house.

"We'll not find my friend until dusk," said Old Ren. "But it might be good to think until then."

"Think?" asked Caesar. "About what?"

Kinchen rolled her eyes. "About how to save Pip. About a plan."

"About history," said Ren. "It might be good to remember certain things—to help us understand why the Raft King wants Pip in the first place. And to help you to stop him from making . . . a rash mistake. And to remember how Raftworld came to be, and why our countries are friends."

"We're friends because we have to be," Kinchen said. "Because there aren't any other people here."

"There's pirates," said Caesar. She was perking up again.

"There aren't any pirates," said Kinchen. She turned toward Old Ren. "Why do we need to remember the history of Raftworld? And why *rash mistake*?"

"I know the history," Caesar said proudly. "Our storyteller on Raftworld tells us about it all the time." She closed her eyes and recited. "We escaped from the first world because the English were trying to enslave us and send us to our deaths on plantations. Almost two hundred years ago. We stepped through to the second world when we escaped— by accident, in a storm—and we've been trying to find our way home ever since. For almost two hundred years. Looking for Africa, where we will settle and find our families back." She shrugged. "That's why we live on the rafts, because we haven't found our home."

"Is there actually an Africa?" asked Kinchen. "Maybe it's just a story."

"Just because it's a story doesn't mean it isn't real," said Ren.

"Of course it's real. That's where Venus came from," said

Caesar. "The one who lived in the caves nearby, with her puppy, like you told me."

Ren smiled as if he could picture the puppy. "Yes, her dog. She called him Tricky, because he could wiggle into any cozy spot no matter how small."

"I never heard that bit before," said Caesar. "About the puppy's name." Kinchen shook her head; she hadn't either.

Ren shrugged. "I'm not sure that's an important detail," he said. "Except to the dog. But come, let's sit outside in the breeze, and I'll tell you a story."

Caesar clapped her hands and jumped up.

Kinchen groaned. "A story? Shouldn't we be—I don't know—packing or something? So that we can take off as soon as we meet up with your friend?"

"A story," said Ren.

9

THIS IS THE STORY Old Ren told:

It is two hundred years ago, almost exactly: summer 1775, and we are in the Bight of Benin, on the west coast of Africa. We are standing on the shore—or near enough, in the brush right before the sand begins. We will call this tale "What Old Man Caesar Found There." Because to understand what came after, we have to start at the beginning, with what he found and how he found it.

This was the day he found his children, his twins.

He was gathering wood, Old Caesar was, on the shore. And he glanced up at the sea, as people do who live near water, just to check on it now and then. And when he glanced up, he saw them: two children, a boy and a girl, neck deep in the water, faces toward shore. As he watched, these two—just entering the lanky years between toddlerhood and puberty—walked up from the water. They were holding hands. They were naked. The waves did not jar them, nor did they shiver in the breeze. They moved upright as pillars and almost as slow. They were walking from the water, as if they'd been born there.

Old Caesar, the man who would become their uncle, watched them from the trees. He watched, slack-jawed, as they waded

shallower and shallower. No Guinea boat in sight; no slave ship on the horizon. But he knew somehow, immediately, what they were. What they meant. Caesar hadn't known there were any more people like him. He let fall his bundle of sticks and stared until the children reached the wet sand, where they both dropped, slow as leaves, to their knees. Their fingers still entwined, these two little pilgrims. Couldn't be more than six or seven, and no family left in this world. None free, anyway. Of that you could be sure.

Their faces thin and hungry. And they'd be half dead from their long walk.

Old Caesar decided the way he always decided things: quick and sharp. He strode out of the trees to them, took their free hands, pulled them to standing, and brought them home. He fed them and clothed them. They became his adopted children, and he called the girl (who would become Venus) Water-Drinker, and the boy he called Swimmer—to allude to their gifts without giving them away. The gifts were kept secret, as most strong gifts probably should be.

"More," said Caesar, leaning forward. Kinchen listened grudgingly. Both girls had heard this story before.

They were like newborns, *these two. Swimmer and Water-Drinker, boy and girl, brother and sister. They didn't talk, not for the whole first week. They didn't do anything of their own volition. Old Caesar fed them by hand, cut the meat small for them and mashed the pumpkin like they were babies. The boy slept whenever he wasn't eating. The girl stared. At the walls,* at the floor, at her new uncle Caesar's chin or hands or feet (but never his eyes), her face vacant and unfocused.

Old Caesar thought maybe they were addled. Maybe they'd always been addled (though clearly with gifts), or maybe their dip in the ocean had unfixed some crucial gears in their heads. When he'd worked on the slavers—before he'd stolen himself back, before he'd taken his own long walk to freedom—he'd once seen a broken sextant scatter itself on the deck, and he imagined the children's heads filled with little brass screws and fittings, and he not skilled enough to repair.

But after a week of eating and sleeping and staring, the children began to look around. The boy picked up his own spoon, and the girl scratched her nose, and the old man figured that was a good start. By the end of the month, they took care of their necessary business in the woods on their own, and they started helping to draw water and prepare dinner. The boy went with Caesar to gather wood.

Then the two children started to talk. They didn't speak Caesar's language, nor he theirs, so their attempts to communicate were halting, mostly overblown gestures.

Caesar decided to teach them his language, which would be useful here on the coast. (Their talk being unfamiliar to him, he guessed they'd lived far inland before they were kidnapped.) He'd also teach them English, the language of trade and of power on these shores. He began that evening, at supper, with the names of foods.

Within a year they were fluent in his language and as fluent as he (which is to say, pretty good) in English. But whatever life *they had before they came to him was lost—as if it had never happened. They had no memory of the slaver that must have taken them or where they had lived before the slaver. They had no memory of the ocean or how they appeared in the surf that day. They only knew that they were twins and they were special and they were loved by this man, their uncle, who had always taken care of them and always, always would.*

"WHAT IS YOUR POINT?" said Kinchen. "We know this story already, and it's getting late."

"Patience. These details are important to understanding what is to come." Old Ren paused in a long moment of silence while Kinchen glared and Caesar sat perfectly still with her face squished up, as if trying not to wiggle were a painful experience for her.

"All right," said Ren. "I'll skip ahead to 1778. Three years later. The twins are living with their uncle Caesar in the Bight of Benin in the west of Africa, and they are learning to swim." He cleared his throat.

WATER-DRINKER—THE GIRL *who would become Venus— sputtered and squinted as her head resurfaced. Uncle Caesar thought that she and her twin brother should learn to swim (especially given her brother's name, Swimmer), but despite three years of Uncle's periodic tutoring from shore, neither of them had yet acquired the skill.*

Water-Drinker (that is, Venus) disliked the lessons, as they made her uncle cross, but she loved her uncle so she kept trying. Still—

"Hopeless, isn't it?" said Swimmer, spitting out a mouthful of water as he climbed on the sandbar next to her. His rare fountain of words showed his disdain for swimming lessons.

Uncle Caesar yelled from shore, "Back to the deep water, and paddle!"

They sighed and stepped off the sandbar again, flailed—and sank like stones. This time they walked back up together, and when their heads were above water, their uncle waved in resignation. "Come on in."

At supper he shook his head, but his voice was kind. "We'll try again in a few months. Meanwhile, don't let anyone see you in the water. Your walking" (he gestured to Venus) "and your talking" (he gestured to Swimmer) "and how you twins share these gifts with each other—this is powerful magic—"

Swimmer grunted. "We know. Keep a secret."

Water-Drinker (that is, Venus-to-be) was tired of this conversation—and tired of trying to swim. She said, "Who would see us, anyway? And who would we tell?" Her brother glared at her to stop her talking, but she didn't stop. "Why must we live so far from everyone?"

Uncle put down his dish and cleared his throat. "You have me and your brother. Isn't that enough?"

She hung her head. Of course. Of course they were enough—they loved her.

Then he said, in a softer voice, "Is there something that's missing for you? Maybe you'd like to see another girl sometime? Talk with another girl?"

Venus nodded, still looking down at her calabash. She was

something close to eleven years old now; another girl would be nice. But what she wanted wasn't only another girl. She wanted people. She wanted to belong to a people. Not just a family, as good as that was. Something even larger.

"What else is wrong?" the uncle asked. Across the table she could see the concern in his deep brown eyes. "Tell me."

"It's just—I don't—" But she couldn't tell him exactly what she wanted. It would hurt his feelings, to know that he wasn't enough, and not simply because he was a man. So she asked a question instead. "Why do we study languages if we aren't ever going to live among other people?"

Uncle Caesar looked astonished, as if he were expecting a different question, and the boy stopped chewing to stare at her. The uncle said, "We speak my own language because it is mine, and you are my children."

She nodded, and so did her brother.

"And we learn English because the Englishmen are the traders who visit the coast. It's important to know how to speak to them."

"Reading and writing?" said the boy. (He struggled with writing.)

"Reading and writing, too. If you can speak and read and write in English, you will be able to keep from getting caught; or, if caught, you can free yourselves. Now why don't you open the book and study?" He grinned at their faces and took the dishes out to clean.

The children owned one book, an ancient primer, which Uncle Caesar had acquired on one of his trading trips. He kept watch for another book when he went trading, but so far he hadn't found any. Thus the children knew "Through Adam's fall / Sinned we all" as if it were engraved on their own hearts. But that wasn't enough, not nearly. So the uncle, a good writer with a strong, clear hand, had penciled a story for them in English in the margins of the book. It was the story of how he'd found them. They often studied the tale.

Water-Drinker (Venus) didn't like the story much, and Swimmer liked it even less. He thought it made him sound weak and babyish, and when he was asked to read the tale aloud, he'd often feign a sore throat. Water-Drinker read aloud when asked, but she disliked what she read. The story didn't make sense. Not knowing the facts, Old Caesar had embroidered. How had she and her brother saved themselves, exactly? What had they done to end up walking in the surf? What had happened to the slave ship, if there really was one? Why couldn't they remember the water, and the time before the water? The story leaked like a sieve.

Sometimes she would wake up at night with a jerk, recalling a piece of a dream. It was always the same dream. She was walking slowly, raising little clouds of sand with her feet, and the air was so thick and cool, it felt like a real living thing, like it was pressing on her, kissing her everywhere. Light drifted down from above, and everything around was green and deep. In her dream, she never had to draw a breath.

10

Ren stood, stretched, and said, "Now, we need to meet my friend."

Kinchen shook her head to clear the cobwebs of the story. "Where are we going?"

"What about Venus?" asked Caesar. "What happens next?"

Ren smiled. "I thought you knew the tale."

"Yes, but I want to hear it again. Anyway, where did you get the details from?"

"From someone who knew." Suddenly Ren was all business, packing a bag with dried food and handing them each a waterproof jacket (Caesar got Pip's—and it was just about the right size). "But we really must get going. To the beach," he added to Kinchen. "To the bay."

"Oooookay," said Kinchen. His answer didn't mean anything to her. No one lived at the bay.

"Will you tell more of the story after we meet your friend?" Caesar begged.

"If we get there early enough, I'll tell more as we wait for him to . . . show up."

"Let's hustle!" Caesar grabbed Kinchen's hand and tugged her to her feet.

Kinchen rolled her eyes but allowed herself to be tugged. She wanted to hear a bit more, too. And she wanted to meet this friend of Old Ren's.

As the girls walked to the water, Ren following at his own pace, Caesar said, "I have a question. Your brother. He's only a year younger than you, right? Eleven?"

Kinchen nodded.

"Then why did you say you need to take care of him? Can't he take care of himself?"

Kinchen pursed her lips, thinking. She never told anyone about Pip's strangeness with people; not wanting anyone to make fun of her brother, she covered up for him. But if Caesar was going to help rescue Pip, she needed to know. "He's not stupid."

"I didn't say he was!"

"He—has a problem. He can't see people. I mean, he can *see* them. He's not blind. But he can't recognize them. He doesn't know who they are."

"Not anyone?"

Kinchen shook her head.

"Is that why your hair?"

Kinchen stared at Caesar. No one had asked before—even Ren had never commented on her hair. She fingered the white stripe she'd bleached into it. "Yeah. So he'd always know me." She shrugged. "My skunk stripe."

"Well, I think it's *amazing*."

"My hair?"

"And Pip, recognizing your hair." She fingered her own

braids thoughtfully, then grinned up at Kinchen. "Amazing is a good thing, you know."

At the bay, they looked out at the blue expanse, calm today. "Where is he?" Kinchen asked Ren when he arrived, panting a little. "Your friend."

"We'll wait." Ren rested on a large rock that faced out to sea.

"And you'll tell more about Venus!" said Caesar. She threw herself onto her back next to him. Kinchen perched on the other side. The sun brushed lazy late-afternoon fingers across her face. She closed her eyes to it and listened.

11

OLD REN'S STORY, continued:

Now it's a few years later. The twins are about fourteen years old, adults in how they work but still children in how they day-dream. Swimmer is tall—he has all the height in the family—and deep voiced, someone one would instinctively listen to, though he rarely speaks. Venus, still lean and small, now has a woman's curves under her loose clothing. She wears her hair short and often dips her head, as if in doubt, before she talks. When she has a truly important idea, however, she lifts her chin high just like her uncle Caesar—and then her brother and uncle listen closely.

It's 1781. Mid-November and getting chilly, and the two no-longer-children and their uncle are on a slave ship. The Zong. They are somewhere between São Tomé Island, Africa, and the island of Jamaica in the Caribbean, trapped in the hold of the boat as it takes the Middle Passage. They are enslaved.

None of the three had ever learned to swim—and none ever knew how to free themselves from chains—and now they are caught. Bound in iron. And afloat on a rancid bit of wood in the middle of the ocean.

At first, Water-Drinker, the girl who was immediately re-named Venus, comforted herself with the knowledge that they'd all been captured and traded onto the ship together; that way she and her uncle and her brother, though enslaved, would at least live and work together, and have a home together as before. And someday they'd escape.

That comfort did not last. She understood the slavers' English—low-class as it was, spat out by the albino-skinned, hairy-faced sailors—and she quickly deduced that if she and her brother and her uncle survived the trip, they'd be sold separately. No respect for family ties.

She also discovered that she was the wrong age and sex to expect to be left alone for long. She could hear the sailors' comments, and even though her ears were innocent, she soon learned the meaning of the words. The slave ship was a new kind of primer.

She formed a quick, sharp plan: to play ill. No one would want to mess with a sick girl, she reasoned, one who could infect you. Her decision was powerful: immediately she began to run a fever.

Most of the nausea she felt wasn't acting, either. The hold of the slave ship was packed with bodies and even more packed with noxious fumes. Incarcerated in the main space, the men (including Swimmer) lay fettered to one another, left leg to their neighbor's right leg, left arm to their neighbor's right arm, like children in a handholding game. They each occupied tighter space than a man in a coffin, and to turn or scratch involved negotiations with the neighbors. No one sat upright, for the ceiling sloped too low and more men were bunked above.

The women and children huddled in a small room, just as

crowded and smelly as the men but with slightly more freedom of movement—and more liberty for the sailors to take them off on their own, if they desired. They stuck together as if fettered. The necessary tub, where they relieved themselves, spilled repeatedly—and stank even when it wasn't sloshing on the floor. The women and children were taken on deck only infrequently, and then they were forced to dance in the harsh sunlight or, worse, to witness someone being punished for refusing to eat or for acting rebellious. Venus saw a man—not her brother or uncle—lowered slowly into the water from a rope, as punishment for what crime she never heard. The sharks ate his legs before his chest was wet. His screams stayed in her ears for many days. There was no escape.

Not that she was afraid of the sharks. They circled the boat continuously, eating trash and the odd dead (or live) body that was heaved overboard. But she knew herself and her gifts, and the sharks didn't scare her much. No, it was the white-skinned men and their whips and guns and ropes and manacles; it was their iron and their love for blood. That was what scared her. She'd never before thought that she wasn't a person, but now she knew: to them, she wasn't anyone.

Her uncle had told her that she and her brother must have been aboard a slave ship when they were little, before he found them coming out of the sea—a slave ship that sank, maybe, and they with their luck and their gifts had walked and survived. She didn't remember. But now, on this ship, she felt as if certain moments were familiar, as if she'd had this nightmare before and even though she couldn't recall it, it might come back to her *waking memory at any moment. As if it were just barely out of reach.*

And she didn't want to have it back.

WHEN THE PRISONERS *on the men's side started to get sick (actually sick, not pretending like Venus was), the slavers worried. Then one of the white men died, and then another, followed by several African men. Soon the women were coming down ill, too, and a few of them died. The captain—until this voyage, a ship's surgeon—and his friend Mr. Stubbs walked through the hold and scrutinized the ailing who lay in the women's cabin (including Venus, still faking).*

"More than one kind of contagion here," said the captain. "Some have the bloody flux, some gaol fever, and this one"—he pointed at Venus—"this one is where it all started. I don't even know what she has."

They stood in front of her, the two white men, and peered through the stench as if she were a specimen. They didn't know she understood English, and she wasn't about to enlighten them. When Stubbs prodded her with his foot, she coughed and groaned obligingly.

"Number Eighty-Six," said the captain. He coughed, too.

"I remember her," said Stubbs. (She remembered him as well, with his groping hands and bad breath. She hacked again, and let the snot dribble out her nose.) "Venus. We all thought she was a pretty one till she took sick. That's why the name."

"I don't know how you can tell 'em apart. All their faces look the same to me." Swaying, the captain considered Venus. "Not

much of a looker now." His face glistened with a thick sheen of sweat.

Venus propped herself to almost sitting and threw up in the necessary tub stationed next to her. She had nothing in her stomach, so she heaved up drool.

Stubbs pulled a grimace. "Animals." He turned to his companion. "I have an idea for this disaster. You've already lost seven. You don't want to lose the whole lot."

"It's a financial tragedy," the captain agreed. "Once these diseases start, we can't stop them spreading—not without quarantining the sick property, and that's impossible to do on a ship this size." He spat. "What a way for my first captaining to end."

The men turned to walk out of the women's cabin. "I know a good bit about the law," Mr. Stubbs said. "Deaths from sickness aren't insured. But other losses are. Come have a drink and hear my idea. There may be a way to save this voyage."

They strolled out, trailing eddies of putrid air behind them.

THEY WERE on their way to the West Indies to be sold as slaves—but only provided they survived the Middle Passage. Venus paid attention to how time slid past, because things were bad all around her and she needed to think what to do and when. By the eightieth day, the captain staggered with fever, and seven crew and sixty slaves had died. Gaol fever, bloody flux, despair. Their bodies cracked open from beatings and malnutrition, and distempers slipped in and racked them quickly. When they expired, the crew were thrown overboard tied with weights to pull them to the bottom. The dead slaves were heaved without weights, whereat they served as shark food.

The ship stank like rotting meat.

There was more room in the slave quarters, but no one moved easier.

Her brother and uncle, she heard through passing of messages, were alive and still healthy. She sent intelligence to them: Act sick. Uncle Caesar complied and began to cough. Her brother refused. He would not pretend anything for the white men, not even when she told him to trust her, that she had the seed of a seed of a plan.

Then the captain—or the people acting for him in his illness—put a scheme in motion, a strategy to save his employers' investment even though the property were lost. A plot to collect the insurance money. A ghastly design.

VENUS WAS not the only captive woman who understood English, but two of the five others were dead, and the last three were too sick to comprehend anything when the captain and Mr. Stubbs came in and discussed throwing them overboard. She shifted her head to hear them and cracked her eyes open in the gloom.

The captain's clothes were drenched in sweat; yet as he swayed in the sweltering women's deck, he shivered.

Mr. Stubbs said, "We've overshot the land. We're short on water. A lot more will die. Your bosses can't collect on property that expires of disease or thirst. They can, however, collect on property that falls overboard."

The captain swore, frustration etched in the lines on his flushed face. "This mess'll be the death of me. To be ruined by a single voyage gone wrong—they'll never trust me to captain a ship again. I ain't going to let that happen." He pitched more than the ship's rocking required. "It's a bad business."

"But a lucrative one," said Stubbs. "If you play your cards right. Why, when I last captained a slaver—this was over twenty years ago now . . ."

They walked away. Venus crawled to the side of the room that overhung part of the men's quarters below. She knocked her message into the floor with her bare knuckles and her heels, carefully. It was time. Eventually her uncle's reply message echoed back to her, with added information. He was ready. Her brother still refused.

Venus crawled back to the women. She did, in fact, feel a touch of real illness, a little wobbly. Too much darkness and bad smells and anxiety. The water would wash that away. She sat and thought of her brother, and she tried not to vomit. People had to make their own choices. She would choose to save herself and as many others as she could. She only hoped it would work; she'd never in her memory tried such a trick before.

12

SUDDENLY THE water rippled, and Kinchen startled. It was as if someone had dropped a large stone into the middle of the bay—but someone hadn't; it was a still afternoon—and the waves echoed out from it, round and perfect.

"Ah," said Old Ren. "It's time." He waded out into the bay, the children following a few steps behind. When the water reached his knees, he stopped. The tide slapped gently; Kinchen's feet went immediately numb from the cold. His back to them, Ren swayed, perfectly silent. Kinchen waded next to him and looked up into his pale, wrinkled face questioningly. But he didn't seem to notice her, his features so focused on the bay that it was as though he were in a trance, communing with the water. She looked out again; now the sea had calmed completely and unnaturally, right in the center of the bay: a circle of quiet within the lightly dancing water.

Something was out there, just under the water's surface. Something big.

Caesar materialized at her side, and without meaning to, Kinchen took her hand. They watched the water.

"Odd Bay," murmured Kinchen. "That's what we call it."

Ren sighed deeply as if completing a long vigil, and he took Kinchen's free hand. "Here he comes. He's agreed to show himself."

"Himself?" said Kinchen. At that moment, Caesar squeezed her hand so hard, she gasped.

And then Kinchen saw, and she gasped again.

Out of the bay rose the domed head of the biggest—what was it, anyway? *Squid* didn't describe it correctly. More rounded, and more—well, more solid. *Octopus?* But by a hundred times the biggest she'd ever seen or heard tell of. As big as an island, and as craggy. Brown and covered in algae. One eye, large as a house, rose out of the water and aimed at them. It blinked.

"He says *Good day*," said Ren.

"Nice to meet you," called Caesar, her voice high with awe. She raised her free hand to wave.

Kinchen didn't speak. Her mouth had gone dry. Surely this wasn't real?

"He's going to get you started on your trip," said Ren. "He'll take you close to Raftworld—and Caesar will take you the rest of the way." Then, to the creature: "Thank you for coming up for an introduction."

The beast blinked its eye again, a moon eclipsing and reappearing.

This is what lives in the sea? The sea that Pip walks into every day? "What—What *is* that thing?"

Ren squeezed her hand gently. "Not polite to say *thing*."

Kinchen's mouth opened in a giant O, but no more

sound came out. She couldn't think what to say. How could she let Pip go into a sea that held such monsters?

The eye blinked again.

"I heard stories," said Caesar, her words round and clear in awe. "That's a Kraken."

Kinchen's voice returned. "A *sea monster*?"

She nodded, her bright eyes fixed on the creature.

Ren said, "A Kraken."

13

WHAT OLD REN did not say, because he did not know this part of the story:

What happened, as the abolitionist-backed court case of 1783 would make clear to all of England, is this: on the 29th of November, 1781, Captain Collingwood of the Zong slave ship—or passenger Mr. Stubbs, or First Mate James Kelsall, acting in place of the increasingly sick and sometimes delirious captain—ordered approximately fifty-four slaves who were exhibiting signs of illness to be thrown overboard, in the middle of the Atlantic. Two days later, the crew threw another group of approximately forty-two slaves, and shortly thereafter yet another group of slaves (including ten who jumped to join their brethren): about 133 souls in all. (Witnesses disagreed on the exact number.) The slaves' deaths allowed the ship's owners to collect from their English insurance company, because slave property, though not underwritten against natural demise, was worth some cash if it suffered expiration from falling—or jumping or being thrown—overboard.

In other words: if the slaves were murdered, the insurance would pay.

Why? Because if they were killed—if they were thrown

overboard, for example—it would surely be to stop a rebellion, to save the ship and crew and the rest of the cargo. So, yes, insurance paid up for murdered slaves. The logic was illogical only if you insisted on thinking of slaves as people.

Among the Zong captives flung overboard and drowned, though never mentioned by name in any of the court documents, was the girl who'd first come down with the illness—and presumably brought it on board with her. The used-to-be-pretty one with the too-old uncle and the intractable brother. The one called Venus. That one.

PART TWO

Pip

Raftworld, Summer 1978.

1

PROPPED ON a bench between two silent rowers, en route to Raftworld, Pip woke to moonlit darkness. He could see the Raft King sitting ahead of him, along with more rowers. Groggy but not terrified, he felt as if he *should* be scared—coming to consciousness on a rowboat, kidnapped and far from his sister and her protection. And on the surface of his person, in his skin and even deeper, in the layers under his skin, he *was* scared. Very. But deep under those strata of fear a little nerve of excitement sparked in his spine and heart and lungs. Here he was on an adventure, a trip to see the world, exactly what every Islander who joined Raftworld wanted. And—a still deeper, quieter voice inside him said—the fact that Pip was adventuring alone, without his sister, would make the trip even more exciting. No one to watch out for him, yes, but no one to remind him of his shortcomings and his oddness, either.

He felt immediately guilty for that thought. Of course Kinchen should remind him of the things he couldn't do: recognize people, keep track of them in groups, remember who they were; and the things he *shouldn't* do as a result: go to town, go to school. He felt himself rise back to the top layer of his being, the fearful layer.

Even so, he found it hard to be completely scared on the water. The ocean comforted him, and now was no exception. He could hear it murmuring, not in words but in feelings, right in his heart: *Don't worry, don't worry, don't worry. I'll take care of you, I'll take care of you, I'll take care of you.* Once when he was little, he had tried to explain ocean talk to Kinchen—how it didn't travel through ears or mouth, but rather, it felt as if the water in your own body was talking to the water in the sea—but he could tell his explanation didn't make sense to Kinchen and even troubled her, so he hadn't mentioned ocean talk since then.

That was one of the things that made him weird, he knew: that he could understand water and the things in it. He couldn't eat fish, even though it was one of the main dishes in the Islands. (How can you eat a creature you can have a conversation with?) And he could feel the water's moods—which Kinchen assured him was *not* normal. But people didn't even need to know this water-gifted part of him to know he was odd. They knew it the moment they saw him standing in a crowd, confused, the moment he looked at everyone—even his own sister, before she'd bleached her stripe of hair for him—as if he had no idea who they were.

Pip took a deep breath. He could do this. No vacant looks. Memorize every detail possible for each person he met. Try harder to navigate in a world crowded with people who all looked the same. He could do this, just like anyone else.

No, he couldn't.

But he would try.

Though the rowers he was seated between surely knew he was awake, neither they nor the Raft King spoke to him on the boat, which meant he was able to listen uninterrupted to the ocean and to his thoughts. The moon glowed in the sky, the vessel sliced through the water, the rowers paddled swiftly, the spray leapt in arcs; and occasionally the caped Raft King, seated at the prow, grunted something to one of the lead rowers. *Purple cape,* thought Pip, squinting through the moonlight and remembering the color. *Easy. I can do this.* But then he studied the rowers seated next to and in front of him, and each of them looked to him like a clone of the next: male, dark-skinned, muscular, with short curly hair. And if he put a cape on any of them, they'd all look like the Raft King. He sighed. This would be impossible.

They neared Raftworld as a glimmer of dawn began to glow at the horizon. The boat glided to a stop near what looked—in the half-light—like a small marina at the edge of the rafts, at which a rower leapt out and tied the boat to a post between two smaller vessels. The rowers stowed their oars, and one of them took Pip's arm—gently, firmly—and guided him off the boat.

Stepping onto the wooden dock, Pip saw immediately that *Raftworld* was the wrong name; it would be more accurate to say *Rafts-world*. The nation was composed of raft after raft—each one, including this square of dock, the right size to hold a small house and garden—stitched together with flexible cords, so well knit that he could not see the water through the seams, though he could see the way the rafts bent gently at their hinges to allow for the water's swells and waves.

From where they stood in the dock area (several rafts long), a path led away through houses and other small buildings, and everywhere Pip could see—and smell—thick gardens reaching for the sky. The air was rich with mint and lavender overlaid with something sharp and tangy he couldn't identify. Birds trilled.

On either side of them but far in the distance, engines started chugging.

The Raft King spoke to Pip for the first time since he had woken on the boat. "Tonight we'll have a party, welcome you in style. I can tell that you'll be an enormous boon to our great campaign." He turned to two of the rowers standing nearby. "This is Pippin."

"Pip." He looked up into the rowers' faces. They were both tall with strong shoulders for rowing. Their pleasant faces both exactly the same, though Pip imagined that Kinchen wouldn't think so.

The Raft King spoke to the two rowers. "Fancy dress tonight. Make sure he's presentable." Then he strode away, purple cape flapping in the breeze. The other rowers left, too, except the ones on Pip's right and left who said they'd escort him to a house where he could wash and change.

Pip watched the departing king. "Does he always wear that cape?"

The rower on his left answered, his voice flatter and with longer vowels than Pip was used to hearing: "He likes to switch colors."

Pip groaned inwardly. Nothing easy to identify the king with.

"He'll probably wear the blue cape tonight," said the rower on Pip's right, watching the Raft King's departing back. This rower spoke in a deep, scratchy voice, like he had a cold. "The sky-blue one. Fancy dress and all." He looked down at Pip. "I'm sorry we had to take you from your island. But the king will return you when your job is complete . . ." His voice trailed off. "He's been king for less than a year. He'll be a good one; he just needs to settle into the job."

"Hmm," said the left-hand rower.

"He's done great work with finding houses for everyone, and helping people expand their dwellings."

"That he has. But that doesn't make him a good king. It makes him a good housing advisor."

The right-hand rower ignored his companion and spoke to Pip. "The king says he needs your help to save Raftworld. I don't know what he means; we're doing fine."

The left-hand rower shook his head. "We're too crowded. New buildings won't solve that. And we can't add more rafts. Raftworld is already as large as it can get," he explained to Pip in his almost-monotone voice. "The hydraulics can't handle any more. So we either need to split ourselves into two rafts, or we need to find a place to settle."

"We've got time to decide," said the right-hand rower.

But the left-hand rower shook his head. "We don't. And

that's what worries him—the king, I mean. And that's why he had to get you to come on board to help us."

"Well," said Pip, hesitating. This was all new to him, the idea that he would be someone who could help. He was fine at math and reading: but with an overcrowded nation? How could he possibly help? "I wish"—he said, thinking of the governor and especially of Kinchen—"I wish the Raft King would've explained the whole problem on Tathenn. The governor could have gotten together some of the really smart grown-ups to help the king figure out a solution. They probably could have fixed it. I don't know what he thinks I can do. I'm just"—he almost said *nobody important*, but instead he finished—"a kid."

The two rowers shrugged. "He says you can help," said the left-hand rower. His voice flattened even more. "With your magicky stuff."

Talking to fish? How could that fix an overcrowded world?

"Let's get you cleaned up for dinner," said the right-hand one, and they led him off.

As they walked, Pip first paid most attention to his two escorts; Kinchen always told him to try to memorize something unique about people when he first saw them. He glanced sideways at each of these men and mentally groaned again: *they were exactly the same.* They were dressed just like the other rowers in white shirts, blue pants, and soft rope belts, their dark hair cropped similarly short to their head. No scars, no missing teeth, nothing unusual about either of them as far as he could see. Both of them the same dark, clear skin. There was no way he'd ever know them again. His heart sank. Even the Raft King was a mystery: when he changed his clothes, Pip would lose him. *Sky blue tonight,* he told himself, and hoped it would be true.

In the growing light of morning, Pip started looking around more, and he realized that his first impression of Raftworld's dense greenery wasn't quite accurate. It was a beautiful place, yes; but unmistakably it strained at its seams. As they left the dock and entered the interior of the raft, the path grew narrower and started zigzagging, jogging around homes that looked as if they'd been haphazardly added onto (or simply built from scratch) right into the roadway. While the houses near the dock had been neat cottages centered one per raft and surrounded by lush vegetable and fruit gardens, the houses farther in squished two or three to each square of raft. Some of these homes were pitiably small; others loomed over Pip and the rowers with second or even third stories. Around all these houses, the plants were thin and scraggly, shaded by the taller dwellings and squeezed into the small open spaces left on the rafts.

The left-hand rower seemed to know what Pip was thinking. "A lot of the gardens are on the roofs now." And sure enough, leaves and vines draped down from the flat-roofed taller homes.

Craning his neck to see, Pip stumbled; the ground had a funny way of moving under his feet. The men took his arms and kept him from falling. "Takes a while to get used to the rocking," said the left rower. "Watch for the seams." They stepped from one raft to another.

People were awake now, and a few early risers worked in the gardens and walked the paths, talking to each other in a language Pip didn't know, carrying baskets or nets or other things that suggested they were starting a busy day. People said hello in English, and most gave him funny looks—not unfriendly, but curious. Pip realized that his lighter coloring and straight hair gave him away immediately as an Islander, and though he saw a few other people who also looked like Islanders (probably, he realized, people who'd volunteered to trade themselves onto Raftworld the last time it came, or the time before that), he surely must stand out as a new person. *The* new person. The person the Raft King had gone to the Islands to find.

A couple of people said as much. To the rowers, after saying hello to Pip, they said, "This is the envoy?" or "So young?" and the left-hand rower answered, "Yes," in a way that did not invite further questions.

To Pip this all seemed like a strange way to greet a visitor, especially when your nation received so few. But the rowers didn't comment. The right rower pointed at the long pipe next to a house, as if he were giving a tour. "Irrigation," he said in his growly voice. "We grow a wide variety of food— everything we need."

Pip nodded. Several more Raftworlders passed by, staring.

"The Raft King told the people not to bother you," said the left. "He told everyone he'd be picking up an esteemed advisor at the Islands who would solve our overcrowding." His narrow voice sounded doubtful.

"If the Raft King says Pip will fix things, then Pip will fix things," said the right-hand man. "Not that things *need* fixing."

Pip tripped on another seam, this time righting himself before one of the men caught him. The left man made a "huh" sound under his breath. And Pip understood—and agreed. How could *he* solve any problem so huge? He carefully stepped over the next seam. Everything was foreign here, and suddenly nothing seemed like an adventure anymore. And he missed Kinchen and Old Ren.

ALMOST AS BAD as missing his family: Pip couldn't see the ocean, not even a glimpse, and this made him jittery. Although he could smell its fishy sharpness, hear occasional slaps against the rafts' bottoms, and feel the rhythmic rocking of the interconnected rafts, he couldn't actually *see* the water. Or touch it. Old Ren had said that Raftworld was huge, but Pip hadn't realized it was so big it would feel like a lurching island. The ocean was there, under Raftworld's skin, but he couldn't reach it and talk to it.

However, there was a lot here to grab his attention, especially now that the sun was fully risen. The gardens, even as crowded as they were, were impressive. Raftworld squeezed more out of each inch of space than the Islanders did, that was for sure. Stunted trees with tight green apples grew in giant pots, next to flats of beans and multicolored peppers, tomatoes of different shapes and sizes, leafy greens and flowering herbs, round melons and gourds. Small land birds hopped; butterflies fluttered; bees buzzed. The brightly painted and heavily carved wood houses—even crowded as they were—nested inside the gardens, their windows peeking out like eyes beneath the arching vegetative brows of their lintels. Small canoes and coiled ropes lined up tightly but neatly outside doorways and under trees.

Every now and then an otherwise empty raft held a red shack, undecorated and gardenless, water barrels and axes at each corner of the building. "What are the red buildings for?" Pip asked.

"Those are the cooking houses," the left-side rower said. "With ovens."

"Why all alone on the raft?"

"In case of fire."

Pip immediately understood. On a wooden world, any uncontrolled fire would be a terrible thing. To cut the risk of accidents, people cooked their food only in these red houses. But that would mean no fireplaces in their homes—and no heat, either. That sounded like a cold way to live.

"But how do you keep warm in winter?"

The rowers looked at each other and smiled at the question. The right-hand man answered. "We head north. We stay in the warm year-round, mate."

Of course. Raftworld could follow warm weather. Pip felt silly for asking, and he walked in silence for a few minutes. They passed more people who gave them curious looks but did not talk to them.

How large this world was! The air grew more still as they

walked farther and farther in, crossing raft seam after raft seam, until he thought they surely must have passed the middle and be headed out the other side. But just when the air was as flat as it could be, and the sun sat high in the sky, and Pip felt he couldn't possibly walk any farther—not even the length of one more garden plot—they arrived at a red cooking house somewhat larger than the others they'd passed. Up close, Pip could see that its paint was beginning to peel—but the building itself looked sturdy and well built. Its lower windows had been boarded over, and the door had a lock on the outside. The two rowers guided Pip to the house, where the right-hand man pulled out a key and unlocked the door. "Here you are."

"Um . . . why is there a lock?" asked Pip.

"Safety," said the right-hand man. "Don't worry about it."

The left-hand man frowned but didn't say anything.

Before he stepped in, Pip took one last look at Raftworld. The houses blazed with color around him, and the gardens pressed themselves around the buildings, green and buzzing. "Wash and change," said the right-hand man. "Rest. We'll be back for you in a few hours."

Pip went in, and the lock clicked behind him.

2

AFTER HE'D washed in the big kitchen sink and changed into the much-too-large Raftworld-style clothing set out for him, and sat for a long time listening to the water pat the bottom of the raft, two muscular, dark-skinned men came to take him to the dinner.

"We're back," said one: it was the right-hand man, his voice scratchy with his cold.

The other grinned at Pip. "We were expecting someone taller when we laid out those clothes." The left-hand man, with his flatter voice and longer vowels.

"I'm ready," said Pip.

THE DINNER was fancy, just as the Raft King had said. There were twenty or thirty people in a courtyard near the dock, seated on cushions at low tables in the dusky outdoors. Planters of small cherry trees surrounded them, providing dappled shade as the sun set. If he hadn't seen the crowded houses and gardens farther in, Pip would not have thought anything was wrong with Raftworld: this outdoor dining room was airy and open, scented with cherry blossoms.

As the rowers predicted, the Raft King wore a sky-blue

cape; and the two men had pointed him out when they entered the courtyard. Pip wasn't expected to know anyone else, which certainly eased the tension—though he realized that he would soon be expected to recognize people and remember their names. He stood to the side until a rower (one of his two? He didn't know, since the man didn't speak to him) motioned to him to sit at the central table, across from the Raft King himself.

Dinner was served immediately, and the food was good: fruits of all kinds, spicy greens and root vegetables, fish (which he did not eat), and warm, delicious bread with a green tint and a slightly vegetable taste. Someone must have been working in one of the red kitchen houses all day to prepare such a meal.

During dinner he focused on eating things in the right order—studying his neighbors and imitating them—and listening to the talk around him. The Raft King mostly ignored him, talking with other advisors about the hydraulics issue (as he called it) and then halting discussion when it became too heated, promising to resolve the issue soon. "Anyway," he said, "the boy is going to advise us tomorrow. So let's not worry about it tonight."

One of the important-looking grown-ups at the king's table said, "He's a child. How can he help us?" The others nodded as if they had the same question.

Pip sat up straight and tried very hard not to look stupid or babyish. But really, he had to agree with the advisors.

"With his magic," said the Raft King. "Now eat."

The advisors gave one another worried looks and small head shakes. The one who'd asked the question shrugged and murmured, "We'll discuss this again after the 'magic' doesn't work." Everyone began to eat, and the talk turned to music and tapestries and flowers and, finally, stories. Pip wasn't sure who was who—or what their roles were—but these seemed to be important people at this table. And they seemed to love their king—they weren't deferring to him out of fear or with resentment. They chatted, and agreed sometimes and disagreed other times; they occasionally interrupted one another (and their ruler); and there were even some shared jokes that seemed to have long histories behind them.

Finally, the Raft King called for the storyteller, who had been sitting several tables over. An old man rose and made his way over, leaning heavily on a cane as if his hip hurt. He had white hair, not as long as Old Ren's but much thicker and tightly curled, pulled back in one fat ponytail at the base of his head. His face wrinkled in all the places that suggested he smiled often. This man at least—with his shoulder-length white hair and his cane—would be easy to identify.

As the old man approached, the Raft King called out, "Jupiter, let's have a tale."

Jupiter, thought Pip. *Old man with white hair and cane. Storyteller.*

Jupiter nodded but did not speak. He seemed to be waiting for something.

The Raft King said, "Something to entertain our guest."

The old man nodded again, then turned to look at Pip

for the first time. And when he did, his face crinkled into a smile before falling back into calm. "A young man," he said, with a slight emphasis on *young*, "from the Islands. What kind of story would you like?"

Pip thought. On Tathenn, the storyteller would choose the story, because he or she knew best what was appropriate and right to tell. "Well," he said, "it's summer, so maybe . . . a summer story?"

Jupiter frowned slightly, and Pip felt he'd given the wrong answer, so he added quickly, "Something about magic gifts? Since that's why I'm here?"

At that the old man nodded crisply. "Magic it is. I'll tell the story of Venus and her gifts."

Pip forced his face into a smile. He'd heard the story of Venus many times from Old Ren—it was one of Old Ren's favorite stories, one that Ren knew well, almost as if he'd been there himself—and Pip was a little disappointed that here in this new country he'd have to hear the same tale again. Why not something new? But he hadn't specified, and it was clear that Jupiter wanted to tell this story.

The old man set his cane to the side, stood up tall, and raised his arms to encompass the whole courtyard. His voice filled every nook, deep and full. "This is the story of what happened to Venus after she was thrown from the slave ship."

3

THIS IS THE STORY that Jupiter told:

It was the 29th of November, 1781, and Venus was on the Zong slave ship. The ship was sailing for the Caribbean slave islands; but Venus was not. She was about to be thrown overboard. You know this part, right?

PIP NODDED. He knew this part. Old Ren had told him the story so often and so fully, he almost felt like he'd heard it straight from Venus herself.

DO NOT WORRY. *That was what she told her companions as they awaited their death. I do not worry about Venus, and you do not worry about yourselves. They crouched in the women and children's cabin, tied to one another and waiting while the crew ate supper before tossing them over.*

"Drowning!" the woman next to her had whimpered, shaking with fever.

A woman farther down the chain snorted. "We won't drown. We'll be eaten by sharks first." It was not a comforting thought. People who were well enough to produce tears were crying.

"Listen," said Venus urgently. Not everyone could understand her; only a handful of the fifty-five humans chained together spoke English more than a few words, and maybe another dozen spoke languages in which she could make herself plain. In all the tongues she could muster, she said, "Listen! They will throw us overboard; we know this. Here is what you must do. Hold hands. Ignore the ropes, and hold hands. Tight. I will help you. We will go to the bottom together. I think—I think it will work."

The woman next to her shook, her face glistening with fever. "I heard of people like you," she said in a voice round with awe. "Are you—are you what I think?"

"I can do it," replied Venus. "I think I've done it before, for myself. And I will try to do it for you, too. But we must stay connected, always connected."

Up and down the line, the women and children whispered to one another, translating where possible, gesturing when words failed.

The fifty-five were thrown overboard. They clasped hands as they hit the water.

THE FIRST THING *Venus did, upon plunging into the water with the other fifty-four women and children, was talk to the sharks. She didn't tell the hungry predators to go away; she simply told them to* Leave my people alone.

For that is what she suddenly knew: that these were her people. As soon as her face submerged, in the second before she talked to the sharks, the realization hit her. These people she'd

never met before the slave ship, these sick and maybe dying people who held her hands, these were her people. And she would do everything she could to save them.

She would have spoken to the sharks even if she hadn't understood that these were her people. But who knows if the sharks would have listened? It was always her brother who was best with sea creatures. As twins they shared their gifts, but hers was the walking and his was the talking. The sharks were the trickiest part of her plan; when her brother refused to play sick, she knew it was up to her to talk to them. Worried about the reach of her powers, she told the creatures something not too hard: she told them that they were already full. She didn't command them anything, like "Go away." Just suggested: "You don't want us"—which, sickly as the people were, was probably true.

The sharks circled idly, lazily.

The people sank.

Venus looked at the line following her into the deep. She couldn't see the end of the chain, only that it went on—it seemed—to eternity. All holding hands. She peered through the murky water, her vision gradually clearing as they drifted deeper, the light coming to her as it did in her dreams. She did not feel cold. She did not need to breathe. She watched as her companions filtered into focus, and then, finally, she knew what she had hoped. Her plan was working. No one struggled. No one flailed. Her gift flowed outward to all of them, as if they were one creature, as if her magic were blood and she the pumping heart. They moved as one.

When the people finally touched bottom, the light gifted

their skin a greenish cast and their rags flowed like fancy robes, cleansed already of vomit and snot and sweat. The water breezed through them. Hills rolled out in dunes. Venus dipped her toe in the sand and swirled it, puffing up a cloud at her ankles. The people spiraled around her like a snail shell. Everyone held hands.

One person bowed to her, and then another and another— everyone. She shook her head, but still they bowed.

Then they looked up at her with the same question on every face: What now?

What indeed. Venus had no idea; she felt fourteen and lost— not a leader. The woman next to her squeezed her hand, hard, and she gasped with the almost pain of it. A last bubble of air left her mouth and floated upward. All around, other bubbles followed hers as everyone released their last breath. A little girl five or six people down from Venus screwed up her face to puff out that last bit of Zong.

It was the little girl's face, so harsh with the effort of spitting out that bad air, that persuaded Venus to lead. The people needed someone. They were under the water where she had taken them. It would be okay. Venus pondered for a moment, listening with her gut to what the ocean was telling her to do. And she felt it: the pull to go forward, the pull she always felt underwater, the pull that led her every other time toward land and safety. Now it was tugging her toward—the slave ship.

Finally she understood. She knew what she needed to do.

Venus pointed up with her free hand, to where they could no longer see the boat, and then gestured forward. They needed to follow the ship. Her uncle was not among her fifty-five. And her brother, refusing to play along, was not here. And there were others, many others. They needed to follow.

She led them—away from Africa, toward the West Indies—and the people considered; and the people followed. They rippled along the bottom of the ocean in waves, one step for every ten or so they might have taken on land, as if gravity had little force in their lives anymore. Occasionally the sharks would drop down to point the way, then drift upward again. The people walked. Her people.

Venus was their leader.

AFTER VENUS *and her people had followed the Guinea boat for almost a day, leaping and drifting along the ocean's bottom in their elongated strides, they were joined by forty-two men, all of them fettered together in a line, and all holding hands. Forty-two more thrown overboard, forty-two more saved. Uncle Caesar, feigning deep illness aboard ship, had miraculously revived upon touching water, whereupon he led his fellows to the bottom, just as Venus had done the day before. The people numbered ninety-seven in all, nearly one quarter of the original number that had crammed onto the ship and rotted next to one*

another, now stretching their limbs and holding hands. They formed themselves into two long chains, Venus and Uncle Caesar walking next to each other and the others trailing them like a jellyfish tail, or the tentacles of a sea monster. Because Uncle Caesar's gift didn't extend to speaking with fish, and he didn't experience any urge telling him where or how to go, he deferred to Venus's lead. She could feel in her gut what they should do.

They followed the slaver. She didn't understand why they continued this course, for she and her uncle couldn't save any more people. If others were thrown overboard the next day or the next, they wouldn't reach the bottom alive. Surely no one was left up there to hold their hands and save them—except her brother, and he had made it clear that he wasn't going to play sick and get himself thrown over. He wanted no part of anything. No bowing to the slavers, none at all.

Yet the ninety-seven walked the bottom, following the ship like its deep, deep shadow. And the next day, the impossible happened—in a world of impossible. Thirty-six more arrived—alive—at the bottom. Venus's brother, the one called Swimmer, led them.

Some of the people were fettered, others not, but all held hands, pulled downward by Swimmer. Aboard the ship, twenty-seven ill men and women had been chained to one another and tossed. On deck with nine healthy men, seeing what was about to happen to these sick and knowing there was no Caesar or Venus to help them, Swimmer had taken action. He'd roused his companions, and they had swarmed over the rails and plunged, nine of the ten holding hands as he'd instructed, one turning back to the ship. The one was lost, of course, fished out of the sea and returned to the Zong. Swimmer led the rest, diving down after the bubbles rising from the twenty-seven drowning people, and sinking toward them like the stone he was.

When Swimmer grasped the hand of the first drowning man as he thrashed below the water, dragged down by the chains, that man felt life and peace infuse him. It was better than air and more filling. In turn he grasped the woman chained next to him, and she the woman next to her, and she the boy next

to her, and so on down the line of chains until all twenty-seven were sinking slowly, gazing around in wonder, and feeling for the first time since they'd been kidnapped—or stolen or sold or traded away—comfort. No one needed breath.

When these thirty-six reached Venus, she knew that this reunion was what she'd been following. All these people. Her brother, returned to her. Their gifts and their lives twined together again.

Uncle Caesar walked on one side of Venus, and Swimmer on the other. Swimmer rearranged his people into one long line, so that he and Venus could join their free hands. Once again they followed Venus's gut, now away from the Guinea ship. South. The people trailed behind like long braids.

All told, 133 souls walked the ocean's bottom. The water warm and full of light, the people no longer pained with hunger or thirst, none feeling sick, all quiet with the awe of a good dream. Venus led them. They walked.

4

"PERFECT!" CALLED the Raft King, clapping. Everyone joined in politely.

"I haven't finished," said Jupiter.

"It's the right stopping point," said the Raft King. "All about success. All about how you can rescue your people if you follow your gifts. All about how someone's gifts with the water will save the nation. And how magic solves everything."

"So many were left behind, too, on the slave ship—"

"That is all for tonight, Jupiter. Thank you." The Raft King patted the cushion next to him for the old man to sit down and raised his water tumbler in salute. "Praise for success stories!"

People echoed, "Praise for success stories!"

Pip mouthed along with the toast.

"Praise for the new envoy from Tathenn!"

"Praise for the new envoy from Tathenn!"

Pip didn't move his mouth this time, as he was pretty sure the toast was praising him, and he didn't think it would be good etiquette to join in. (Also, he thought it was wrong to call him an "envoy" and imply that he was going to do something special when he was, in fact, no one important.

And: he was tired.)

When Pip yawned for the third time, just after the cheering finished, the Raft King seemed to notice him for the first time as *him*—as an exhausted kid, not just as someone who was being toasted. "You need sleep," he said. "Kept you up too long. And you'll have a big day tomorrow." He motioned two rowers over—men who had been serving food all night. "Take our envoy to his bed. Mr. Pip needs sleep."

"It's just Pip." Tired as he was, he wasn't looking forward to the empty red house with the locked door. He slumped in his seat.

The old man, Jupiter, suddenly stood again, leaning heavily on his cane as he rose. "I would like to invite the envoy to stay with me." His voice carried almost as much as when he had been storytelling. People paused their post-dinner conversation and turned toward him.

In the sudden hush, the Raft King shifted and scratched his nose. "That's not—that's not possible. He's already settled in a perfectly good place. Nice and peaceful. Children need quiet."

Jupiter tilted his head. "He's staying—by himself?"

"Of course not. There'll be someone standing just outside the door all night, in case he needs anything."

Jupiter tilted his head to the other side. "Is this boy a . . . prisoner?"

The important adults at the table began to murmur to one another. So did the people at other tables.

The Raft King glared at Jupiter, who smiled mildly back

at him. "He is an esteemed visitor," said the king. "I just thought—he'd want some privacy. But if he *wants* to stay with you—"

"I do," said Pip. Kinchen would probably say that he'd be better off by himself—where he couldn't make a fool of himself and people wouldn't know that he had the problem with faces. He himself wasn't sure why he felt so strongly that he wanted to stay with this old man he didn't know at all. But he did. Something about this man promised adventure—more interesting, anyway, than staying in a locked kitchen house all by himself. And he wanted adventure. He did. Also, the storyteller had a kind face. So he said it more firmly. "I want to stay with Jupiter."

JUPITER LED Pip away from the dinner. Two rowers followed almost as if guarding them. Jupiter explained that he was one of the few Raftworlders to have a house to himself: his wife had recently died, and he had no children—and no apprentice. So he lived alone.

"I'm sorry about your wife."

"Thank you."

After a pause, Pip asked, "Why isn't there an apprentice? Is someone already trained to be the next storyteller?"

"I've never had an apprentice," the old man said. "There isn't anyone in Raftworld—there hasn't been in a long time, not since I was a boy—who has a gift for storytelling. There are a lot of people who tell tales," he said with a little bitterness, "but no one with a real gift."

"What will happen when—?" and then Pip realized his question could be considered rude.

"When I die? People will still tell stories. That won't stop. But there won't be a storyteller—one person with a special gift for it, one person who works to remember everything and to retell it just so. Maybe we'll be reduced to writing everything down." They walked a few paces in silence, Pip waiting to see if there was more. "So," the storyteller finally said, "it's lucky for you, because it means I have room for you to stay with me—for as long as you're here. Which might be a long time."

"He *is* going to send me back, right? After I help him?" *If I can help,* he thought but did not say.

"Well, that's the tricky thing," Jupiter said softly. "But we'll talk more of that later." He jerked his head back toward the rowers behind them.

"They're fine," said Pip. "They're nice. They walked me here earlier."

Jupiter gave him an odd look. "Not these two. Didn't you notice? These are the Twins."

Both Pip and Jupiter turned back to look. "He didn't notice that you were twins," explained Jupiter. "They're our only set of identicals right now," he said to Pip. "They look exactly alike." The Twins grinned.

Pip said slowly, "Yes, they do look exactly alike. I see that now." He considered telling Jupiter about his face problem, but Kinchen had forbidden it—though he wondered if it was really true, as she'd said, that people would make fun of him.

At the house the Twins said good-bye—and Pip noted their voices, so similar, fruity with a little sharpness at the back of each word. *The Twins.*

INSIDE THE TINY, one-room house, so small Pip suspected it had at one time been a gardening shack, Jupiter said, "You didn't recognize the Twins as twins." He quirked one eyebrow in a question.

Pip didn't answer.

"At dinner it looked like you were memorizing—me, the Raft King, maybe other people, too. I saw you say *long white hair* to yourself at one point." He leaned his cane in the corner and turned, one hand on the wall for balance. "Which is appropriate to describe me, of course, but not a usual thing for people to *say* to themselves."

Pip stared at the ground. The wooden floor had been covered with a soft round rug that looked like it would be comfortable to curl up on.

"You don't recognize people's faces."

Slowly, he shook his head. "I'm just—not smart."

"What's smart about recognizing faces?" Jupiter said in a sharp voice. "Surely you don't think *that's* what makes a person smart?"

"Well, no, but . . ."

After a pause, Jupiter said, "Thank you for telling me. I'll be sure to remind you who I am when you meet up with me, so that you won't have to worry about misrecognizing me." Pip looked up, finally, into his unremarkable face. "There are several old men with white hair on Raftworld—one even uses a cane almost exactly like mine. I'll tell you what—I'll wear this trinket"—he pulled a red beaded bracelet out of his pocket and slipped it over his wrist—"and then you'll know I'm me." He fluttered his hand and the bracelet rotated and sparkled. "It was my wife's. It's a good excuse to wear it."

Pip nodded. "My sister bleaches a stripe in her hair."

"Smart girl. Smart boy, too. Now for a tour of the house."

Jupiter showed him the partition behind which stood a bed and a little end table. "You'll sleep here. I'll sleep on the kitchen bench." Before Pip could protest, the old man said, "That's where I usually sleep, since my wife died." In addition to the cushion, the bench had a rumpled blanket on one end.

"And your clothes." Jupiter shook his head with a smile. "We'll find you something more your size tomorrow." He paused, leaning on the counter that formed his kitchen. "Is there anything you need?"

Pip thought. What he really needed was answers. And he didn't think it would hurt to ask. "What am I supposed to *do*? And what do you mean that it would be tricky for the Raft King to return me when I'm done with—whatever I'm supposed to do?"

Jupiter smiled. "That's a couple of hard questions, young man. I need to recline." He hitched over to his bench, plumped up the pillows, and leaned back, legs straight out before him on the long wide seat. Pip took a cushion from a stack by the door and sat on the floor in front of him.

"That's better," said Jupiter. "My hip bothers me by the end of the day. And today was a long day. For you, too," he added.

Pip waited.

"You want to know why you are here. It's because of your gift. With . . . ?"

"Water," said Pip. "I can talk to sea creatures. I put my face under the water, and the fish and I understand each other. I recognize *them*," he added.

The old man's face opened up in surprise. Then he nodded. "I see. Oh, I see."

"What?"

"Why he wanted you." He shifted his pillows around so that he could sit up straighter. "I have two stories for you, and I think they'll answer some of your questions."

Pip nodded. He liked stories. Kinchen always rolled her eyes when Ren told stories instead of answering questions, but she didn't understand that the story *was* the answer. Pip did, and he liked the task of figuring it out. But he was tired, too. He picked up another pillow, made a little bed on the floor, and lay back on it to listen.

5

"BUT FIRST, a question: you've heard the Venus story before today, right?"

Pip elbowed himself up to look at Jupiter. "Yes, from Old Ren, back at home. I've heard it dozens and dozens of times."

The storyteller nodded. "I'm going to tell some more, even though you already know it, because I think it will help you see what the Raft King is planning."

THEY WALKED *a long time, three lines of survivors, hand in hand in hand in hand, following Venus, Swimmer, and Uncle Caesar. How long? Time and distance disappeared down there, and there was just the walking. People grew weary but not exhausted, thirsty but not parched, peckish but not starving. So they walked, trusting Venus to take them all the way back home.*

But she knew something they did not: there was no safe place in the world to which they could return. They walked and walked, past sunken ships, under sharks and dolphins, through families of small black squid, over endless dunes; and she did not lead them home.

The fetters fell off along the way—disintegrated, really, the rust melting the metal and chewing away at it so quickly, they could almost see the chains and shackles crumble. One day the people wore thinning, flaking, eaten-away bracelets, and the next day everyone walked free. Still they held hands.

After a long time walking on the bottom, Venus had—what?— another feeling. She couldn't describe it exactly. Neither could Swimmer, but he felt it, too. He squeezed her hand; something was different. The sand slanted upward, and they began to climb. They walked uphill for hours, maybe—it was hard to tell how long, as there were no days and nights where they were, no sleep or eat, just peaceful walking and warm handholds and soft clouds of sand. Eventually, though, they left their light at the bottom and moved toward the daylight at the surface, until they were so close, Venus wondered whether she might touch the air if she jumped. The world above shimmered, a bright blue jewel.

Then, quickly, the light clapped away. Venus looked up again; the glittering sky above them flashed dark with storm. She and Swimmer glanced at each other and knew without discussing: they should head back down, away from the storm. Safer that way. They turned toward Uncle Caesar, and he nodded confirmation.

But when they folded back on their lines of handholding followers to retreat to the deep, that was when Venus felt it strongest. The urge to go up. This was the spot, right here. Right now. She couldn't explain—she just felt as if she must go up, up into the storm. As if there were a door standing open, and they could slip through, but only if they hurried. When she looked at Swimmer, she could tell he felt it, too, at least a little.

Uncle Caesar did not feel the same urge, but he'd felt very little since they'd entered the water. He was old, and his gift was weaker than the twins' gifts, as he had reminded them on many occasions. On top of that, he was sick. Here, in the water, he felt better—almost normal—but the truth was, he hadn't only been faking illness on the slave ship. He had, at the end, taken ill. He felt no urge for anything.

When Venus refolded her string of people and continued up the sand, Swimmer and his line accompanied her. Uncle Caesar shrugged, turned, and followed with his own line, up and into the storm. He trusted his adopted children. He trusted them completely. They couldn't swim, but by God they could walk.

VENUS, THE GIRL who traded slavery for death at sea and death at sea for walking, stood with her people beneath the raging storm, under the shallow water. The storm itself was an opening—she could feel it, in her gut—but to where she did not know. She only knew that once they went through, there would be no going back. This was their moment to decide.

With the water buffeting them, gaining force even as they paused, she turned to Swimmer and Uncle Caesar, the question on her face. What to do? Swimmer shrugged; although he spoke to sea creatures more fluently than she did, he did not feel the underwater land as deeply, and this doorway was dim to him. Uncle Caesar nodded, but it was a nod of acceptance, not a nod of direction: he would follow whatever Venus chose to do. It was up to her.

Venus turned to the person at her other hand, the fellow traveler whom she'd been gripping for so long, so many miles of

*walking through the bottom. For the first time, she really saw
the woman. This person grasping her hand in such a firm, warm
hold was substantially older than Venus, perhaps as old as Uncle
Caesar. Symmetrical scars decorated her cheeks, and double holes
dotted her heavy earlobes, the jewelry that had hung there long
gone. Her hair clouded around her head, black and gray like a
puff of pepper. The woman squeezed her hand, and Venus, realizing she was staring, lowered her head in embarrassment. The
woman squeezed again, and Venus looked up to see a wide gap-
toothed smile and a nod urging her to continue. Not acceptance,
not confusion, not apathy or any number of other possibilities:
pure joy. Both hands occupied, the woman pointed with her chin,
upward and forward. Go on, she mouthed, still smiling. Go on.*

*And Venus turned back and led her people through the
doorway she could feel but not see, up and into the storm. She
led them into the second world. They emerged to air, struggled
through the waves crashing to shore, fought to remain standing
in the pull of the sea. They supported one another: they'd held
hands for so long, they didn't remember how to let go. Everyone
would survive or no one.*

*When they finally gained ground in this new place, on the
far side of this doorway to who-knows-where, they were spent,
exhausted, used up. They crawled, still hand in hand in hand,
into the brush and as much out of the wind and rain as possible, and they waited, half asleep, for the storm to abate. When
it did, hours later, they slept the sleep of the dead.*

*In sleep, their hands slowly loosened and unfurled. Upon
waking, when the people asked her where she had brought them,*

she told them the truth. I don't know. I walked into an open-ing, and I led us through it to safety. I found where to slip through. It was—there was something sweeter on this side. *The explanation felt broken, but she couldn't find the words to describe the way the doorway had pulled her, how in the heart of the storm it seemed like the entrance to something safe and warm, almost like crawling back into the arms of the mother she could not remember. The doorway felt less like an exit and more like a return.*

Someone asked her name. The people nodded; they wanted the names of those who'd saved them. She swayed for a mo-ment, trying to remember. Before Venus, before Water-Drinker? Had she ever had a name of her own? The people looked to her brother, who answered without a pause: "Swimmer." Reclaiming the name their uncle had given him, he folded his arms over his chest and stood silent.

The people looked back to Venus, expecting an answer, but before she could open her mouth, Uncle Caesar coughed and said, "You have a choice, daughter. This is a new world. You can choose your own name. I know Water-Drinker never felt quite right to you." He coughed again, his body rocking forward.

She looked away, not wishing to offend him and not sure what to say. He said, "Before you choose, you should know that the first Venus was a powerful woman, a god, the only one of the gods to rise fully formed from the sea."

"She rose from the sea?"

"From the depths. Standing on a clamshell like a warrior. The slavers didn't know it, but they gave you a strong name.

Maybe even the right name. Up to you to decide." He hacked again.

She nodded, thinking. *Powerful might be nice. Goddess, too. But even more: rising from the ocean. Rising. It seemed fortuitous, hopeful.*

"My name is Venus," she said.

6

THE PEOPLE *found food, shelter. The island was tiny, just a circle of hilly ground around a deep cold lake, but it was big enough for them to find coconuts and fish and mangoes—and from a sunken ship and other storm detritus, wood for building whatever they might want. There were monkeys, and birds of all kinds, and not much else. Most of the people wanted to return to Africa, to their original homes.* There is no going back there, *said Venus.* It's done for us. *But people didn't want to believe that. And everyone felt this island was too small to keep them.*

They talked of where to go next.

Venus didn't. She slept deeply, for the first time in months; and she began to dream. Images drifted back to her, not just the walking underwater as a child, but also: the shock of waking to a rough hand pressed over her mouth, the gray outline of a ship even bigger than the Zong, *tiny hands grabbing at a mother's sleeve as it slipped away. And so much more.*

She couldn't. She didn't want to. She didn't want to remember. She was only fourteen. She wasn't ready. So she stopped sleeping, and she walked and walked and explored the island, forcing her mind to consider only what was here, in front of her, and dozing in uneasy snatches, until the dreams receded and she could sleep and live again in peace.

By then she knew there was something different about this place; she'd brought her people somewhere entirely novel. But it wasn't until the day she spotted—just off the coast—the giant sea monster, bigger even than the island, waving a tentacle at her and winking its enormous eye, that she knew: *they were in the second world. She didn't use those words then, of course; she just thought,* This is nothing like the same waters the slaver sailed. This is completely different. *And in her heart she pondered the sea monster and this new world, and considered how her people had finally arrived at their freedom because they had disappeared from the world that stole and sold them.*

Uncle Caesar, meanwhile, sickened. His lungs bloomed with phlegm and his skin raged with fever and sweat. Three days after they landed, the old man died, holding the hands of his two beloved children. Venus and Swimmer buried him deep in the sand near the spot where they had stumbled ashore.

Afterward they stood and looked outward, across the bluegreen waves, and Venus wondered what could possibly lie ahead.

AFTER UNCLE CAESAR'S *death and burial on the little island, Venus's mind spun with the need for something more to think about. She turned her back on the monkeys and multicolored birds and the deep central lake, and she fixed her worry on the ocean and the giant sea monster, which appeared whenever she walked alone on the beach. Its rolling eye contained a message she could not decipher.*

The day after Uncle Caesar's burial, she walked into the little bay to look for it, but when she plunged her head underwater she could see only a dim shadow far in the distance. It would not come near her. Finally, after days of seeing the eye blink at her from shore and losing sight of it when she entered the water to converse, she asked Swimmer, whose gifts were greater in this area, to try to commune with it.

Swimmer strode into the bay, submerged, and returned an hour later with a tale of his meeting—though owing to his clipped way of talking, it took a couple of days to ease the story out of him. The creature was called a Kraken, he was a male, and he had lost his mate. His wife had left after an argument—he'd wanted to settle down; she'd wanted to travel and see the world—and though the Kraken had stewed for many decades, finally his resentment over being left behind had dwindled. He wanted to find his wife again. He missed her desperately.

"Desperately?" said Venus, smiling when they finally reached that part of the story. How desperate could a Kraken be? He wasn't human, after all.

Swimmer glared at her. "He's looking for his wife. Asked if we'd ever seen her. I told him no. He was—disappointed."

Through prying at her brother like he was a clamshell, Venus found out a few more details about Swimmer's meeting with the Kraken. Swimmer had promised the Kraken he'd keep his eyes open for the wife. The Kraken had said he was sorry he'd fought with his wife, he missed her, he wanted her back. He asked: could they relay this message if they ever found her? Could they tell her to please come home? He was going to go there now and wait for her. Maybe she'd return.

"Where's home?" asked Venus, intrigued.

Swimmer shrugged. "A string of islands. Long way. With people. But no slavers. Maybe we'll visit."

Venus wasn't sure where she wanted to go from here, and a faraway group of islands sounded just as good as anywhere else. People kept looking to her for advice, her and Swimmer. They might have looked to Uncle Caesar instead, but he had died and left them alone to make all the decisions.

Walking in the deep, she had known what to do, where to go. Here on the surface, she felt like a child, alone and unsure of herself. She didn't want to make choices anymore. She was tired of choices. "Where do you think we should go—for good, I mean?" She wondered whether Swimmer felt as she did, unfettered and directionless. But even if he did feel that way, would he tell her? He'd always been short on speech, and now that Uncle Caesar was gone, his jaw seemed locked.

He answered without a pause. "Africa. We go back to Africa."

There was an of-course tone to his voice that made her ask. "Why?"

"It's where we're from. So we go back."

He walked away before she could ask all the questions that wanted to burble up: Go back even though that world isn't safe for us anymore? Even though you and I have already been stolen—twice, according to our uncle—and only escaped at great loss, at the loss of all else? *And the hardest questions:* How many times must we return before we look for elsewhere? And: can we even get back?

But they were questions she never voiced. He seemed so sure of himself.

THERE WERE OTHERS *besides Uncle Caesar who died in those first days. The people were sick when they were tossed overboard, after all; and though everything unpleasant had receded underwater, here in the second world, their ailments resurfaced. Of the 133 souls, a full thirty-three died during that first week on land. Burials everywhere. The woman who'd held Venus's hand all that time below—her with the facial scars and the wisdom lines and the pepper-gray hair—died the same day as Uncle Caesar, though Venus didn't find out until the next day. She never knew the woman's name, but she felt a sharp loss at the news of her death, as if at the passing of a dear aunt. She could still feel the woman's hand pulsing in her own, warm and strong.*

The remaining hundred, under Swimmer's leadership, constructed rafts. That is, he told them to build, and they found a man among them who knew something about raft-making and built with this man's direction. They fashioned small floats, enough for a family to make a shelter on, and linked them together so that they could walk from one to the other and yet ride the waves with flexibility. The center rafts they built strongest and with real wooden shelters where a hundred people might gather to ride out a storm. They built a floating island to take them home. To Africa, *Swimmer said.*

Venus watched as Swimmer, still silent about almost

everything, became a leader of the people. He was so tall and handsome! How had she not noticed her own brother becoming a man? His chest was wide; his voice was deep enough to stop a howling monkey in its path; when he said, "We go to Africa," people listened to him and asked, "When?" and "How?"—and then they heeded his compressed answers.

By the time they departed the little island, Venus had grown to like the place. The round shore and sandy beach and, like a gem in the center, the small deep lake. The trees around the lake. The bright birds and the iguanas and even the monkeys. The burial plots up the dune and the endless sunshine. The fish flashing like jewels. The shells glittering like fish. The openness, and the feeling that no slave ship could ever find them here, not ever. She liked it more than she could say.

And yet, memory always pressed on her. She could feel it threatening to return, the more time she spent alone and quiet. So when the day came to leave, she left. When everyone else climbed on the rafts, and her brother twitched his lips and said, "Come," she stepped on, too, away from the island, away from the graves of Uncle Caesar and the scar-faced woman and all the others she'd rescued only to lose, away from the comfort of sand and the endless coconut milk and mangoes, and headed out again, into the big blue sea. She could have stayed, of course, alone. But she didn't want to. And it wasn't just that she wanted to avoid her old dreams. These were her people. She'd saved them, she and Swimmer and Uncle Caesar, and she'd see them again to safety, even now that someone else was leading.

7

RIGHT AROUND the words, "now that someone else was leading," Pip fell asleep. Jupiter probably said more sentences after that, but Pip didn't hear them, and somewhere along the way the old man must have realized Pip wasn't listening and stopped talking. When Pip woke up in the middle of the night, he was lying on the floor cushions, a blanket tucked over him. Jupiter was snoring, half sitting, a few feet away on his bench. Pip staggered to his feet and dragged himself to his own bed.

When he woke for real, in the morning, the sun was streaming in the window above his pillow, and he could smell fresh bread. He peeked around the partition. The old man was humming, the steam from the bread rising around his hands as he tore it.

He turned to Pip. "Sleepyhead. This bread is so new it doesn't even have a name yet." He sat down and spread tomato jam on a hunk. "Hurry before it cools."

As Pip took a heel—his favorite part—he sat down across from Jupiter.

The old man pointed his knife at him. "You fell asleep midway."

"I'm sorry," said Pip.

"No matter." They chewed for a few minutes, Pip working to get through the thick crust. "There were two stories I meant to tell you, and you heard only one. *Part* of one."

"But I think I understand why you told it," said Pip. He'd been thinking about it since he woke up. "The Raft King wants someone to save his people—like Venus saved her people by taking them to this world."

The old man nodded, watching Pip.

"But what I don't understand—" Pip shook his head. He still felt groggy.

"Go on," said Jupiter.

"What I don't understand is how I could save Raftworld. I mean, Venus *walked underwater*. And she brought your people here, to the second world." Pip took another hunk of bread and studied it. It was good, higher rising than bread on the Islands—and with a green tinge.

"Seaweed," said Jupiter. "In the dough. My neighbor bakes many loaves and brings me one each morning."

Pip nodded his appreciation. "But the Raft King can't expect me to do the same as Venus. I mean, where would I take you? I couldn't take you to another world."

"Why not?" the old man asked mildly. Now his eyes were on his bread as he ladled jam onto it.

"Well, because—we're already here. There isn't a *third* world, is there?"

"Not that we know of."

"Then—I can't do what Venus did. There's nowhere for us to go."

"Unless," said the old man slowly, putting down his bread. "Unless we go back."

8

So THAT was what the Raft King wanted—to go back to the first world? Why?

Jupiter couldn't explain it all. He didn't know what the king wanted; the king hadn't told him. He was surmising, based on what the Raft King had said—and his own knowledge. "There's one more story I want to tell you. About Amelia." They sat outside the hut now, side by side on a wooden bench in the little garden, soaking up the sun and breeze and listening to the birds and the hum of the insects. Jupiter's garden dripped with tomatoes in every stage of growth; his neighbor, he said, gathered some when she dropped off the bread, and so did the man who brought Jupiter eggs.

"I know who Amelia was."

"Yes?"

Pip tried to pull together all the details he could remember. "She had pale skin, almost white, like my grandfather, and reddish hair. She was the Raft King's mother. Adopted mother, that is. The old Raft King rescued her when she came here, in a storm, from the first world. He picked her up from the island she crashed on, and she stayed with Raftworld and she adopted the Raft King and named him Putnam—he was a baby then—and she was his mother." Pip worked up to the most important detail of the story, in his opinion. "She could fly. One day she flew away, and she never came back. Some people say that she's going to come back someday," he confided. "But in other versions of the story, they say she turned into a bird or a butterfly and she doesn't know how to return to human."

"Well," said Jupiter. "I'm going to tell you a still-different version. I was there when she arrived and lived with us, and I was there when she left. I knew her."

"How old *are* you?" gasped Pip—before he realized how rude the question was. He hung his head, embarrassed. Kinchen would be furious with him for saying such a thing to an elder.

But Jupiter laughed. "It was thirty-odd years ago—which, as I get older, seems less and less in the past. However. You want the story?"

Pip nodded.

It was *1942—quite a while ago now, and a different world in many ways. We barely had hydraulics then, not nearly the capacity we have now. And we weren't quite so crowded. But that is a different story. This is about Amelia.*

She was Putnam's adopted mother—the only mother he ever knew, as his first mother had died giving birth to him—and she was funny and adventurous and wild and full of hugs; exactly the way a mother should be. And then one day, right out of the blue, she left him. She'd been tight-faced for weeks, twitchy. Unhappy. Even a little boy could see that something was wrong. That something she wanted wasn't there.

Five-year-old Putnam did everything he could to make Amelia happy. He called her "Darling Mama" and told her over and over that he loved her; he brushed her floppy hair with the little bristle brush she liked to feel against her scalp; he brought her orange juice in a bright yellow bowl she once said reminded her of the sun; he sang to her all the songs he could think of. Nothing worked. Her lips smiled at him as he carried the bowl, the brush, and the songs; but her smile wasn't alive. She loved him—but she wasn't happy.

One day, however, she woke up glowing. It was like a birthday, she said, and she could feel something coming. "Anything can happen today. I know it."

"An adventure?" said Putnam, hoping for good times again.

"I don't know what," she said, "but something."

The old Raft King, Putnam's father, said, "If you believe something will happen, it probably will." The boy Putnam made a wish right then that Amelia would be happy here forever, and that she would be his mother for always. And he believed it would come true.

But of course nothing happened as he wanted. Later that afternoon, the birds arrived, dozens of them, large ones, mostly albatrosses and terns—even an oversize eagle, so out of place.

They landed on the roofs of Raftworld, where they rested silent and almost motionless. The boy Putnam slipped his hand into Amelia's as they sat below the birds and gazed up. Amelia stared at the birds for a long, long time like she was asking them a question inside her head and listening to their answer. Then she dropped Putnam's hand and stood up to her full, lean height. "I'm going now, my love."

"What?" said Putnam. "Where?"

"With them." And she gestured to the birds.

"How?"

She bent and kissed the top of his head. "If I could stay for anyone, it would be you. Believe me, little man. But I can't stay— not even for you. I'm sorry. My gift is to fly, and if I can't fly I'm not really alive. You understand?" But he didn't understand. He didn't. What could be more important to Amelia than staying with her boy, her special boy? He was her son. How could she leave him? What did the sky have that he did not?

He wished then, more than anything, that he too had a gift: the gift to make her stay. Angry tears coursed down his cheeks.

Or—he thought in later years—if not the gift to make her stay, then the gift to make her return, and to hurt her exactly as much as she was hurting him. That's what he wanted.

She wiped his cheeks with her hand and sighed and kissed his forehead one last time while the birds rustled and shifted themselves into a clump on the raft behind her. She walked toward them, then turned and waved and called—not just to him, but to everyone—I'll come back as soon as I can! I'll come back for you, Putnam—and anyone else who wants to join me! I'll take you back to my world, I'll take you to Africa if that's what you still want! *And she leapt into the center of the birds and they lifted, a flurry of white wings, and he couldn't even see her anymore, her red hair flaming in their soft center somewhere, the whole mass rising and rising and then gliding away until they were merely a dusky blur and then a dot and then, finally, altogether gone.*

She never came back. He waited and waited and watched the sky, for days and months and even years. She never came back.

He hated her.

9

"HE HATED HER?" asked Pip. "Because she didn't come back? But maybe she couldn't. Maybe she tried and she couldn't."

"But he never knew whether she wanted to come back or not. Yes, it's possible she wanted to return and couldn't. But maybe, instead, she got to the first world and forgot about him. Maybe she never loved him at all. He never knew for sure," Jupiter said. "There is a little more to the story, a piece I've never told anyone, not since I saw it happen all these many years ago."

Pip waited.

Jupiter folded his hands and said, "The old Raft King, our king's father, went out to the edge of Raftworld the next day—the day after Amelia left." He was telling it like it wasn't a story at all, like it was just information. "He knelt down on the edge of the dock and stuck his head into the water and talked to the fish."

"He did *what*?"

"Didn't you know? The old Raft King had the gift of talking with sea creatures. Like you. He'd plunge his head into the water and find out what was going on in the finny deep. It was a grand skill for a Raft King, let me tell you."

"Can *our* Raft King . . . ?"

"He doesn't have any magical skills. None at all. Amelia did—with birds—and the old king did. But their child had nothing."

Pip nodded. The Raft King sounded a little like Kinchen, who had to put up with Pip and Old Ren both having gifts while she had none. For the first time it occurred to him that this might be a burden for her. That it might bother her.

"So the old king talked to the fish, and the dolphins told him that they'd seen Amelia fly into a storm, riding her flock of birds. That she'd soared into the storm and gone back to the first world through a doorway the storm had opened. They didn't know anything else, except that she had gone back to where she'd come from." He paused. "At any rate, that is what the old king told Putnam, who was standing behind him on the dock. He turned to his five-year-old son and told him that his mother was gone, that she was safely in the first world again, and that he shouldn't expect her back. And he gave the boy a hug and that was the end of it."

"The end of it?"

"The end of them talking about it, at least as far as I know. Neither Putnam nor the old king ever mentioned her again in my presence. Our Raft King, Amelia's own son, doesn't want to hear stories about her. I fear that when I die, she'll be forgotten."

"Not on Tathenn," said Pip. "We still talk about her. Of course," he said, "we say she turned into a flying creature . . ."

Jupiter nodded. "My point exactly. She was a real person.

And she hurt Putnam terribly when she left. I could see that in his face that day. It's never really gone away, that look."

The two sat in silence for a moment, the garden humming and trilling and rustling around them.

"So you told this story . . . ," said Pip.

"Yes."

". . . because you think the Raft King might want to go to the first world. He might think it's possible because Amelia did it. He might even want to find Amelia."

"You're a perceptive kid."

Pip could feel himself flushing.

Jupiter continued. "Amelia would be very old by now, if she were still alive. But he'd at least find out what happened to her, maybe, and why she never came back as she promised."

"The king thinks that I can help him find a way to the first world because Venus found a way here. But I don't have the same walking gift as Venus. All I can do is talk to fish."

Jupiter nodded. "Maybe he thinks the fish know something about how to find a doorway to the first world."

Pip thought about it. The Raft King wanted to go to the first world. Why not? Raftworld could name a new king, after all. The people would miss him—it was clear at the dinner that people liked him—but it wouldn't be the end of the world if he left. "So . . . I should help him? Maybe if he's so unhappy here, he should go. Right?"

Jupiter spread out his hands. "It's not just him. I have a suspicion."

Pip felt something drop in his stomach. But he wasn't sure why.

"Do you see it? How he might be thinking to solve our population problem?"

Pip shook his head slowly, puzzling through the stories he'd heard.

"How he might be thinking of the Venus story as a model for himself?"

And then Pip saw it. Venus leading her people. "He's going to bring everyone there? To the first world?" His chest tightened with panic. "But I don't want to go. I want to stay in this world. And see Kinchen and Old Ren again."

"Then perhaps—perhaps you don't want to rush to help the Raft King figure out how to leave, and how to take his people with him. Perhaps you want to stall, until—" He shrugged expressively and spread out his hands.

"Until what?"

"Until we can figure out a way to stop him."

Pip sagged. What could he do? He wouldn't even recognize the Raft King the next time the king changed his clothes. Anyway, how could he stop the king from doing whatever he wanted—especially with all those guards around? Pip put down the bread, stomach churning with worry.

"You don't need to stop him by force," said Jupiter, as if he could read Pip's thoughts. "It would be enough to change his mind."

10

ALL THE REST of the morning, Pip knew he *should* have been thinking about what to say to change the Raft King's mind: what argument to make, what logic to win the king over. Jupiter had seemed to think that he, Pip, could actually *do* something.

But instead, what kept intruding on his thoughts all morning, as Jupiter gave him a leisurely tour of the neighborhood—interrupted with rest breaks for elderly joints—was Pip's own life and how he'd lived it up to this point. And how he might live it differently in the future.

It was a fact that he didn't recognize faces. All his life, it had made him uncomfortable to be around crowds—in the market, on the docks, anywhere. So he'd stayed home; and Kinchen, eager to protect her little brother, had encouraged this choice. Old Ren thought hiding was a bad idea but, being somewhat hermetic himself, hadn't pushed Pip to meet people.

The thing was, Pip *liked* people. He liked talking to Jupiter and the other adults at the dinner, and the various rowers, and he'd like to meet kids, too, and he liked learning about how people on Raftworld lived their lives; and, he decided, he loved traveling. Especially by water. Other than missing Kinchen and Old Ren—and worrying that they were frantic—he was, in fact, having a wonderful time here.

Pip wondered whether it would really work—as it had worked with Jupiter—simply to tell people that he didn't recognize faces, and then he could ask them to introduce themselves each time he saw them. Would people think he was crazy? Or would it really be okay? He'd spent so much of his life trying to hide his face blindness and being ashamed of it that he didn't know how he could shout it out to everyone around him.

And if it *did* work, then what? He'd help the Raft King? He shook his head, and Jupiter, on one of his periodic bench breaks, glanced up inquiringly. "Nothing," said Pip.

But it *was* something. As he and Jupiter strolled, and the old man pointed out the various houses, listed the types of plants in the gardens, and named the birds that fluttered and stalked around them; as Pip stood on the slightly undulating Raft and felt the ocean breathe beneath him; as Jupiter nodded at and Pip waved at various people they passed on their meandering; as they sat together on benches along the way and lifted their faces to the sun and felt the breeze rustle their clothing—as all of these things happened, Pip thought about how much he was already coming to love this world, this nation where he was really just a visitor. It felt like—not like it *was* his home, because that was back on the Island with Ren and Kinchen—but like it *could be* a home, and a good one at that.

And then he thought, *I love this place, too. And I do have a special talent. Maybe I can make a difference.* He and Jupiter were seated once again on a bench, resting Jupiter's hip. Pip leaned back with his eyes closed, taking long deep breaths of the sea air.

Someone cleared his throat—someone with a deep rumble in his chest. Pip opened his eyes to see a man in a purple cape: the Raft King, probably. He nudged Jupiter, whose eyes were closed, and the old man opened them and said, "King." It was an address to the powerful ruler as much as it was a label for Pip's benefit.

And at that moment, he felt something—something powerful deep inside him, the small secret part of him that hadn't been scared when he was kidnapped—swell and burst into flower. This was his adventure: to be himself without fear, and to change the Raft King's mind. And he could do it.

"I've been looking for you," the king said, throwing his shoulders back. "People told me you were out wandering around, both of you." His features indistinguishable against the bright sky, he towered over them in an almost silhouette.

Jupiter shaded his eyes to look up. "We've had a busy morning," he said agreeably.

Squinting up at the king's dark outline, Pip felt small, like a toddler about to be scolded. It wasn't a good feeling. He stood up quickly, as tall as he could, and moved so that he wasn't looking at the king against the sun.

"I need to ask you something," he said. His voice was tiny and high, not the way he wanted to sound. He cleared his throat.

"Of course." The king stooped forward, hands on thighs, to speak to Pip. Their heads were almost the same height.

"About Raftworld. I think—I think you want to find a portal. What are you planning?"

At that question, the king jerked upward, sputtering, "What business is it of yours?"

Jupiter said, "Now then—"

But before he could say any more, Pip answered, as firmly as he could, "It's my business if you're asking me to help you. I need to know what I'm helping *with*."

"I make the decisions around here." The king puffed out his chest and stood tall.

"Don't be ridiculous," snapped Jupiter. Now he rose, too, though not nearly as smoothly as Pip had, and rested one hand heavily on his cane, the other on Pip's shoulder. "I've known you since you were born, Putnam, and you've never been one for megalomania. Don't start now."

(Pip didn't know what megalomania was, but it sounded bad.) "You don't get to decide *everything*," Pip said. "Your job is to lead—but to lead people who can see where they're going and agree to it."

The king glowered. "I want you to talk with the fish," he said to Pip, "and find out where a portal is."

"Okay," Pip said slowly. Out of the corner of his eye he could see Jupiter's head swivel rapidly toward him, and as Jupiter's grip tightened on his shoulder, he almost grinned at the old man's surprise. "I'll talk to the fish," he said again to the king, more deliberately. "I'll help you." And he meant it. "But I'm also helping Raftworld. So: I'll ask the fish if they know where a doorway is. But I won't ask them *where* it is. Not yet."

"What's that?" said the king, his unmemorable face suddenly displeased. He turned to Jupiter. "Did *you* put him up to this?"

His big hand relaxing its grip on Pip's shoulder, Jupiter shook his head, smiling.

In his best commanding tones, the king barked, "Young man. Ask the fish *where* the door is."

"No."

The Raft King's head jerked back in surprise. Pip had startled even himself. Jupiter patted his shoulder, a congratulatory tap. And Pip saw that he didn't have to change the king's mind all by himself; he just had to make it so that people could talk with the king—so that all their voices would be heard. He said to the king, "We need to talk first. You and me and all of us. Jupiter. The people of Raftworld. We need to know what you're planning to do—before I tell you how to get to a doorway." Pip waited. He'd said his piece. He would help the king, but he'd help Raftworld first.

The Raft King stood a long time, glowering, his cape rippling back from his broad shoulders. Finally he nodded. "Okay. Go ask the fish if they know. Ask if it's possible to get there. Then we talk."

Thus on a sunny summer morning, the Raft King, Jupiter, and two guards strolled to the edge of Raftworld, where Pip knelt, plunged his head into the water, and talked to the fish.

He was there a long time.

PART THREE

In Which We Take an Enormous Detour
That Will Eventually Lead Us to Our
Destination, I Promise.

The First World, Summer 1978. South Vietnam.
A Small Village in the Mekong River Delta.
Three Years After the Fall of Saigon.

1

THE IMPORTANT THINGS to know about Thanh[1] were that, although he was twelve and old enough to do an adult's work, he was so scatterbrained that he sometimes hitched the water buffalo incorrectly, and so daydreamy that he often forgot which rice field he was supposed to be working, and so incorrigible that even though he promised to do better next time, every new day was a new adventure in messing up. Now he was even failing at running away.

Next to him in the muddy reeds near the river—one of the many that ran through the Mekong Delta—his sister, Sang, was fuming. "If we get out of this alive, I will kill you. Stupidhead." Her voice was barely a whisper, but he could hear the frustration in it. She'd been gone all evening, bringing a mended dress to an important customer, and while she was gone, Thanh was supposed to gather their things and wait for her in their agreed-upon spot.

He'd remembered to hide and wait for her, but he'd forgotten everything else: the cooking pot, their good knife, the bag of rice, the *xoi vo* they planned to eat before they boarded the boat, their extra clothes. They had their parents'

1 Pronounced "Tahn."

rings in their shirts, and Sang was wearing their mother's necklace. But the knife and pot and clothes and food—he'd left them all behind.

"I guess you forgot the pomelos, too?" He could barely make out her words.

"I'm sorry."

She shook her head and did not answer.

Around them in the dusk the air held the aroma of rice, and water buffalos made quiet night noises somewhere behind them. The river gently tapped the shore—it was a still evening, with only a light breeze—and somewhere far upriver, paddles slapped the water lightly as a fisherman pulled a late net home. Voices, homey and indistinct, carried across the water. If you sat here, Thanh thought, in the dark under the coconut—if you sat here all night long and it was a night just like this, and the quiet lasted, unbroken by gunshots—then you might be able to fool yourself into thinking that the terrible long war in Vietnam had never happened, that the Americans had never arrived (and left), that North Vietnam had never invaded the South, that South Vietnam had never lost the war, that the southern capital city of Saigon had never fallen, that your parents had never died, and that you lived with them and your sister in a little house in a sleepy village in a peaceful delta where rice flowers scented the air and fruit trees bloomed and fish jumped to your net and fighting never came.

That was a story he'd like to tell.

But before he could completely lose himself in the fantasy,

the reeds rustled. Next to his sister Sang, Uncle Truc materialized, with his youngest child—nicknamed Rùa, The Turtle—
on his hip. Uncle Truc was immediately recognizable even in
the dark, because he was tall and lean; and his right shoulder,
which had been badly broken during the war, slanted lower
than the left. Dodging police monitors, he'd spent the day in
hiding in order to meet them now, and Thanh felt a rush of
relief that he was here, and that he'd somehow managed to
bring The Turtle, too.

The baby was asleep—she'd been given drops of medicine
to make sure—and her head lolled to one side, her chubby
face slack, her fuzzy hair damp against her head with sweat.
At two years old, The Turtle was really a toddler, not a baby,
but she didn't speak beyond a few words yet, and because
of her twisted foot she didn't walk, though she was good
at scooting across the floor. Sang reached out and took her,
tying The Turtle onto her hip with a long cloth Uncle Truc
handed her.

Uncle Truc was not their real uncle; he was their neighbor and their parents' close friend—and the nearest thing
they had to a father since their own father had died.

He nodded at Thanh. The moon was a sliver, and Thanh
could barely see him even now that he was so close.

In the darkness Sang sighed, and Thanh knew she wasn't
going to stay mad at him. After all, as she said almost every
day, he was the only little brother she had, and she was his
only big sister. They had to take care of each other. She'd
forgive him. She always did.

But Thanh knew he'd disappointed her, and the sour taste of it stayed in his mouth. If only he could stop himself from daydreaming all the time! All day long, the story had lived in his head so vividly. Out in the rice field that morning, Thanh had thought about the tale he'd someday—maybe years from now—tell of how they'd escaped from their village, how they'd rowed down the giant river, how they'd left behind the house and Sang's sewing business, how they'd arrived somewhere—America, he hoped—where they'd gotten an education and made something of themselves.

And that was where the daydream petered out, for how could he get an education? He was no good at anything except telling stories to himself—which was not a job one could make a living at.

Next to him, on the other side from Sang, the bushes swished. The quiet snapped momentarily: a low grown-up cough and a lighter sniff. Uncle Truc's older brother and the other kid—the brother's orphan neighbor—must have arrived. Uncle Truc's brother, though the elder, was shorter than Uncle Truc and stockier. The neighbor boy was taller than Thanh by several centimeters and had an almost-shaved head, his hair just a little longer and fuzzier-looking than a crew cut. In the darkness they nodded in greeting.

Everyone was there. It was time to go.

UNCLE TRUC'S BROTHER led them away from the village and to a secluded inlet where he had stored his boat. When they reached it, though, Sang stopped short. Thanh, directly behind her, stumbled into her before righting himself. The line of people froze.

"In *this*?" Sang murmured. "A rowboat?"

Larger than a typical rowboat, and with a motor attached to the back end, but yes: basically, a rowboat, flat-bottomed, wide—big enough from side to side even for Uncle Truc to stretch out on his back and sleep with room to spare—maybe eight meters in length. The sides were tall enough that if people sat in the bottom, next to the food and the barrels of water and fuel, they would be (just barely) hidden from view on shore. The craft was big for its type—but for an ocean-going boat it was pathetic.

It was not what Thanh had imagined, and he could tell from Sang's rigid back that it wasn't what she'd expected, either. A boat for escaping should be much larger, a *real* boat with a big motor and a cabin to protect them from the weather. Navigational equipment. A radio. Not something almost level with the water. This thing was hardly worthy to float on the bigger rivers of the Delta, much less on the ocean.

Uncle Truc cleared his throat. "The engine is almost brand-new. And powerful. My brother installed it for this trip. He was lucky to get it. And we have a good tarp and poles and ties to make a tent and keep out the weather."

"Also," said the crew-cut boy, "Uncle Hung and I packed a lot of extra fuel and water and food this morning. This ship will do fine." His matter-of-fact voice sounded proud of the feeble boat.

"I see," said Sang. She didn't move forward.

"She's like me." Uncle Truc's brother spoke in his gruff voice. "Small and ugly but very, very strong." He flexed in an exaggerated imitation of a bodybuilder, then straightened, stone-faced except for one quick wink at Thanh.

And how much choice did they have? Without the money for the huge transport fees, this was their only chance to escape—maybe ever—and they knew it. Sang took a deep breath and climbed aboard. Thanh followed.

Thanh and Sang's father and Uncle Truc grew up in the same village, good friends; but when Uncle Truc had married and moved away to join his wife's family, they'd lost contact. During the war, Thanh's father had been an officer and a pilot for the Vietnamese air force, while Truc had been a soldier in the army. When the war ended—with both men on the losing side, and the American allies leaving them to their fates—their lives had slowly come together again. Uncle Truc had been briefly arrested. He returned to his home, facing a lifetime of surveillance, no good-paying work, and little hope for his children to do better—but at least he was alive.

Thanh and Sang's father, meanwhile, had frantically forged new identity papers for himself and moved his family to his wife's village to disappear—or try to. Wonderfully, when they arrived at the village, there was Uncle Truc, just returned from prison camp. Still a true friend, Truc invited them to live in a little house behind his family.

Soon after the move, Thanh and Sang's mom had sickened and died. Their father had been found and arrested less than a year later, sent away to a prison camp from which he never returned.

When Uncle Truc had finally, earlier this year, tracked down someone from their father's prison camp and confirmed that he had died there, he talked to Sang for a long time, trying (as he did periodically) to persuade her to move in with his family. "I respected your father greatly. And I promised him that if he got arrested, I would take care of his family. I mean to keep my word."

"I'm sixteen," said Sang, looking up from her sewing. "I take care of us." Her face was tired, circles under her eyes.

"But I'll help," said Uncle Truc. "And I'll help you get out of here."

Uncle Truc's plan was that he'd save up money and eventually he'd buy passage for them all on a boat, one big enough to make it down through the Mekong Delta and out into the ocean and, with luck, transport them all the way to a refugee camp in Malaysia or Thailand. It would take time, but they would escape someday, when they'd carefully planned it all out and bought all the correct supplies and found a good safe boat and a skilled captain.

But there was never any money, and day after day, no work. Because he'd fought against the government, he had to keep checking in with the local police—the guerillas, as they were called—to report his activities, especially after a pilot was discovered hiding in a house practically in his backyard. (They'd had a lot of questions about that.) He looked more desperate with each passing week.

So when Uncle Truc came to them early that morning and told them they'd leave today—even without money to pay their way—Thanh wasn't wholly surprised. Long before breakfast, long before daylight, Uncle Truc entered their house, closing the door carefully behind him and not saying hello. "My older brother—the one who sells fruit up and down the Mekong? He says he can get us out. Tonight." His lean face twisted a little. "I can't take it here even one more day."

Sang nodded, glancing at the window. No one was there. Thanh sat down.

"We're taking his riverboat. We figure there's just room for five." He held up his fingers to count off the people. "Me and my brother Hung. And Hung's neighbor kid—an orphan like you two, who won't get out any other way—is coming as Hung's adopted nephew. And The Turtle." His face creased as he thought of his little daughter. "When she was born, the doctor said if she had surgery she might be able to walk someday. Wherever we end up, maybe she can get her foot fixed. And if not, she'll get better treatment than here."

Sang crushed mung beans into a powder, making *xoi vo*—she'd had the idea that Thanh could sell the food in the village later in the day. Another small business to add to her income. "That's smart to bring the baby."

"Your wife and the other kids?" Thanh said.

"They'll stay here, and I'll send for them when I'm settled somewhere. My new country will surely let me bring my family over." He paused. "It's a really dangerous trip."

Sang checked the steaming rice. And still Uncle Truc didn't say all of what he'd come to say.

"That makes four," said Thanh. His stomach felt all twisted up. "That's four people on the boat. Out of five."

"Yes," said Uncle Truc slowly. "There's room for Sang. Then when she's settled, she can send for you. Safer now for you to stay with my wife and our other kids and wait." No one spoke for a moment; Thanh watched Sang to see what she would say, but she only picked up the pestle again, her hand hovering over the beans.

Finally Uncle Truc cleared his throat. "We *could* take both of you, since The Turtle's small. But it'll be extremely crowded. And risky. What do you think?"

"Both," said Sang, once again mashing mung beans. "I'm in charge of him. We stay together." And Thanh's stomach untwisted.

AFTER UNCLE TRUC left, Sang said, "You know we can't take the books." Her voice was flat. She didn't want Thanh to argue.

He nodded, but as he ate leftover rice for breakfast, his eyes strayed to the small stack—the little hardcovers about planes and flying, the paperback English-Vietnamese dictionary—that their father had brought back from his brief pilot's training in America. Anxious to learn English, Thanh read in these books every day and thumbed through the dictionary each night before bed. He loved the books more than anything else they owned. And they were all Thanh and Sang had left of their father. But Sang was right. They weren't practical to bring on a voyage.

Sang sat next to Thanh as he ate, and she sewed their father's wedding ring—which he'd given her for safekeeping long ago—into the hem of Thanh's shirt. Then she sewed their mother's ring into her own hem, and pulled their mother's silver Buddha necklace over her head, tucking it inside her shirt. She told Thanh to work in the neighbor's rice field as usual and to try to act as normal as possible. No one could know they were escaping. "Don't daydream. And don't go telling people any stories about what we're going to do."

"I wouldn't," he said, stung. Still, to make sure he kept quiet, he decided not to talk to anyone today. "Am I going to sell the *xoi vo*?"

She shook her head. "We'll eat it before we go."

Which was exciting—he hadn't had such a treat in a long time—and somehow made the idea of going to sea less scary and more like a good story. At least for the moment.

As Thanh left that morning, Sang was beginning her sewing. Her plan was to finish the dress, bring it to her client, buy a bag of rice, and maybe even have a little money left over. His job, she told him, was to return home when he finished work, collect the cooking pot with their extra clothes, the good knife, and the *xoi vo*, fill the pot the rest of the way with some pomelos from their backyard tree, and at dusk, bring the pot and its contents to the reeds where she would meet him.

All day, he worked in the rice field, trying to act normal.

But what was normal? The ring made a lump in the hem near his hip that he could feel every time his hand brushed against it. By lunchtime he'd irrigated the wrong fields twice, and even he couldn't think of a story to explain where his brain had been—except the truth, which he bit his tongue back from telling. The farmer he worked for sent him home in disgust.

But he couldn't go home—he couldn't tell Sang that on his last day in Vietnam he'd gotten fired from his job. So he took his lunch and walked slowly off. His feet decided where to go without his thinking about it, and soon he arrived in the cemetery outside the village. By then he had a thrilling story running through his head, not about his failure as a buffalo boy, but about what their trip and their new life might be like. He sat near his mother's grave and told the story, knowing she would have loved it.

He hadn't fallen asleep—he hadn't—but he had lost track of time, and when he looked around him, it was late and the sun was rapidly declining in the sky. He'd run all the way to the meeting spot, staying carefully out of sight of the road and the villagers and the village guerillas.

But of course he'd forgotten the clothing, pot, food, and knife. And of course, Sang had gotten mad—and then forgiven him.

Now they all hunched on the floor of the flat-bottomed boat, except Uncle Truc and his brother, who rowed. They didn't have permission to leave the country, and if caught they faced harsh consequences—prison at best. The boat slipped silently down the river. Too dangerous to use the noisy engine until they were closer to sea.

The other boy, the adopted nephew, tied everything securely to the boat before he stretched out to rest. The Turtle, groggily waking, sucked her thumb, leaning against Sang. Sang put her arm around Thanh's shoulder. "I'm sorry I snapped at you, *Cu Ty*," she whispered, calling him by the nickname their mom had given him when he was a baby. "Uncle Truc has a pot and a knife we can use. And even without today's sewing money, I was still able to buy some rice. I should have taken care of the clothes myself, not asked you to do it. I'm four years older, after all. I'm in charge." She echoed what their mother had said to them just before she died: *If anything happens to me or your father, Sang is in charge.*

Sang's words were kind, but a thread of unhappiness wove through her voice. Thanh knew what she was thinking: that she should be able to trust her brother with simple jobs. He was already twelve. There were a lot of kids his age living on their own, taking care of their little brothers and sisters, earning a living. He was glad she wasn't mad, but he cringed at what she must think of him. "No sewing money?"

"It was so frustrating," she whispered. "The woman said she didn't have the money to pay me today, and I should stop by tomorrow for it. She even said she'd give me extra *dong* for the hassle." Thanh could hear her voice smile into the darkness. "Well, what could I do? Say 'No, that isn't convenient for me, since I'm running away tonight'? So we'll never see that money, and I might as well have saved my time on the last-minute sewing. What did you do today after you finished working?"

"I said good-bye. At the graveyard. I brought wildflowers there." He'd left them on their grandparents' graves. He'd had that long talk, too, with their mother's gravestone. Thanh had made up a story about how happy they were going to be when they got to America. But he didn't mention that to Sang. It had made him late. And it sounded weird.

Sang was silent for a moment. Then she sighed. "Well, I guess I'm glad. Mom would want us to go, you know that."

Thanh nodded. *Mom.* Hidden on the bottom of the flat boat while the two men steered silently down the river, he wondered if their mother, somewhere, was worried about them. But before he could drift into a daydream, Uncle Truc's brother grunted. "Quiet. Someone on shore."

"They'll think we're just fishermen," said Uncle Truc, but he, too, froze.

The baby, who'd been silent as a ghost up to that point, whined. Sang patted her back and whispered to her. Uncle Truc opened a small bottle and handed it to Sang, who gave The Turtle a couple of drops.

"Everyone quiet," said Uncle Truc's brother again. "Not a sound." His own words were barely audible. Their boat, unlit and silent, slid down the dark river. Thanh was glad the moon was only a sliver.

Voices mingled on shore, overlapping and impossible to decipher, and then, suddenly, a shout: "Hey there! Stop or we shoot! Stop!"

The Turtle whined again. Sang covered her mouth and hugged her close.

Uncle Truc whispered, "Are we in range?"

Uncle Truc's brother swung an oar. "Let's go," he said. "This is it." He started paddling, strong fast strokes. Uncle Truc reached back to start the motor.

But before Uncle Truc could pull the engine's start, the night was punctured with popping, dozens and dozens of *pop-pop-pop-pops*. Then moaning. Several voices at the same time.

Thanh had heard that noise—both the *pop* and the moaning—many times. He knew exactly what it meant. People had been shot. He looked around. Not him, not Sang, not anyone in the bottom of the boat. Above him sat the lop-sided silhouette of Uncle Truc, hand on the not-yet-pulled engine cord. Uncle Truc wasn't shot either. Thanh lifted his head a few centimeters, just enough to see Uncle Truc's shadowed brother. Not shot. He sat as still as the small statue of some unknown hero that stood in the corner of Thanh's old schoolroom. But somewhere nearby, people were crying.

Thanh looked up at Uncle Truc again, motionless at the engine. Uncle Truc unthawed and drew his hand slowly away from the engine cord as if it were a coiled snake. Thanh peeked over the edge of the boat even as Sang reached up to pull him back down. Behind them on the river, about a quarter mile back, another boat, much larger than theirs, an actually seaworthy vessel with a real cabin, floated white against the black water. The boat groaned.

On shore a big engine growled to life. Uncle Truc nodded to his brother, and they dipped their oars quietly and paddled toward a brushy island—really a sandbar and a downed tree and all the brush that had come to rest on it—away from the spotlight that the police boat was sure to bring. They left the white boat behind, still moaning, and they hid in the brush while the police arrived, towed the other boat to shore, and arrested the people on board, the officers crowing about how many they'd managed to snag at one time—forty of them still alive, and a nice stash of gold, too.

As they held their breaths at the island, Uncle Truc and his brother crouched with everyone else in the bottom of the boat, so that no one's eyes or clothes would catch the police boat's searchlight as it flicked around the river.

Thanh peeked over the side again, anxious for a glimpse of what was going on, and Sang and Uncle Truc both reached up and yanked him back into the bottom of the boat. The pull on his shirt made him choke, and he fought to keep his cough from making noise.

The other boy, the adopted nephew, watched, his crew-cut hair dark and fuzzy against the lighter wood of the boat. Suddenly his teeth flashed in the dark as he grinned. "Kind of a knucklehead, aren't you?" he asked in a soft voice. "Try not to get us killed."

GETTING OUT of the Mekong Delta was hard work and took more fuel than Uncle Truc's brother had calculated for; the tide washing into the delta was much stronger than he'd realized it would be. But they reached the big waters of the South China Sea the next afternoon, without getting caught or overturned by waves, and they still had just enough fuel to make it to Malaysia, as long as they weren't delayed by anything.

Maybe three more days, said Uncle Truc, shoulder slumping more than usual, as he studied his hand-drawn map. He didn't sound too sure.

The waves on the South China Sea were bigger than any Thanh had ever seen; they reminded him of a Japanese print that had hung on a wall at the village school he'd attended before his father's arrest. (The picture lurked behind the statue—and was much better than the nameless hero at provoking daydreams.) The print showed a little boat rowing up a giant wave, Mount Fuji in the background. As he sat in school day after day, failing test after test, Thanh gazed at the little boat, wondering why it was out in the storm, and if the tiny men inside were terrified—or maybe they were tough and not afraid of anything? He'd daydreamed until one day, he was asked to read aloud and had to admit he didn't know what book they were reading. "But I can tell you about the men on that boat, lost at sea. They're having a pretty bad day, and it's about to get worse." His classmates giggled and, before he could launch into a full-fledged story, the teacher told him to pay attention—and took the picture down, facing it toward the wall.

That same afternoon, the teacher told Thanh he was probably not cut out for school and handed him a note to take home to his father. Thanh didn't read the note because he could guess what it said: he was too daydreamy and cloudheaded for school. He wished his mother were alive, knowing she'd understand. Dawdling on the road home, he wished too that he could make the words on the paper rearrange themselves into something full of praise: *Thanh is a great storyteller! So imaginative!* Something that maybe his father could be proud of. The afternoon sun slanted onto the path as he skirted the rice fields. Water buffalo communed in the river, drinking and digesting with one another. Swallows swished across the fields. Close to home, Thanh cut through an orchard. In the light breeze, grapefruit flowers dropped petals on him. As he walked, he crushed the white petals with his fingers, breathing in the tangy promise of fruit yet to come.

In the darkness of their house, Thanh's father read the teacher's note slowly and looked Thanh long in the face. He didn't say anything, but Thanh could see his own failure reflected in his father's eyes. His dad folded the note in half, then in half again and again, until it was a small thick square he held between finger and thumb.

"What did the teacher say?" asked Thanh. He knew. But he wanted his father to say it was nothing, the teacher was stupid and wrong, and he, Thanh, was smart and just needed to be left alone to make up stories.

His father turned the square over in his fingers, as if it were a coin and he was wondering what to spend it on. "I'm disappointed, son. I thought you would try harder."

His father—once a respected pilot and officer in the South Vietnam air force, now in hiding and unable to find a job except of the lowest kind—sat at the table, his hands grimy from fieldwork. Sang's cooking permeated the house, and Thanh could pick out the smells of home: cabbage, sweet potato, onion. She brought the soup out, stopped when she saw them sitting in silence, then placed the bowls of watery broth on the table. "Supper's ready." And the evening proceeded.

That was all Thanh's father said. *I'm disappointed, son. I thought you would try harder.* He didn't speak in anger—anger might have been easier to hear. As Sang put the soup on the table, Thanh's father looked away, shook his head, and slid the many-times-folded note in his shirt pocket. They ate in silence.

The village school had been closed shortly afterward, in the chaos that followed the war. But Thanh always knew he'd been kicked out.

That same night as the letter, Thanh's father was arrested and taken to a prison camp. He never returned. He still had the note in his pocket when he was taken away, and his last words to Thanh had been of disappointment.

As Thanh slouched in the bottom of the boat, lost in his memory, an enormous wave washed over the boat, drenching everyone and shocking him back to the present. The sun was low in the sky. Sang and The Turtle and the other kid crouched next to him, tense and sodden messes. The two grown-ups, Uncle Truc and his brother, had been working the engine together, one guiding the tiller and the other adding fuel when necessary. Now Uncle Truc (in charge of fuel) half stood and stretched his bad shoulder, rolling it as if trying to get it to slide into place.

"I know you're all scared," Uncle Truc said, stooping to pick up The Turtle. He patted her back but looked at Thanh as he talked. "Everyone should try to rest as much as possible. Drink some water and then try to sleep. Three days from now we'll be at the refugee camp." His voice rose in confidence as he spoke, and his daughter planted a wet kiss on his chin and babbled. He rested one hand gently on her twisted bare foot.

The adopted nephew scrambled up to help his uncle Hung. In the daylight he looked even more capable than he had in the dark: tall and strong and focused on the job. As the older man directed, the boy took the tiller and steered, gazing determinedly into the distance and flexing his muscled arms casually, as if he guided boats across the ocean every day. Uncle Truc's stocky brother, meanwhile, tottering with weariness, unfolded a large oilcloth and, with wooden poles and ties, tented it over Sang, Thanh, The Turtle, and himself to shelter them from the waves as much as possible. They lay in the boat's bottom, in a puddle of warm water, under the tarp and away from the hot afternoon sun. Uncle Truc's brother dozed off immediately, despite the rocking boat. After Uncle Truc sang a good-night song to his daughter, Sang took The Turtle and whispered her to sleep and then shut her own eyes, exhausted. Much later, after helping around the boat, the adopted nephew joined them.

When the boy closed his eyes, Thanh studied his face. Even in the tarp's shadows and with that fuzzy, uneven crew cut, the boy was handsome. Thanh knew this kind of boy— popular at school and liked by all adults, full of common sense and matter-of-fact about the many, many things he did well. He knew this kind of boy; he just didn't know how to *be* this kind of boy. This kind of boy usually didn't like Thanh.

The boy's crudely cut hair accented his small neat face, now at rest. He wore baggy, too-large pants held up with a rope for a belt, and an even more oversize red T-shirt, probably made for an adult. He looked cool and unworried and sure of himself, even in sleep. Why couldn't Thanh be like this kind of boy?

The boat bobbed more and more gently as the waves began to calm, almost rocking him. Thanh slept, dreaming of his mother.

2

THANH DOZED and woke through the night and into the next day. There wasn't much to do other than worry and try not to be sick. *Only two more days,* he told himself. Outside the triangle opening of the tent, the adopted nephew and his uncle Hung sat at the engine—the adopted nephew with a fuel can at hand. Uncle Truc was asleep just outside the tent. The boat rose and fell with the choppy water.

Thanh's clothes were still damp, but he was warm under the oilcloth. He slid out, careful not to wake Sang, who lay next to him, or The Turtle, who was curled on the other side of Sang, stepping with extra care over Uncle Truc as he stooped out of the tent. He lurched over to the engine— the boat jerked under his feet—to sit near the two who were awake and to sun-dry his clothes. The engine growled ceaselessly; they could talk without waking the others. Uncle Truc's wide-shouldered brother looked at ease, like he was simply on a job trawling up the river to deliver goods, and his adopted nephew sat next to him. The man and boy did seem like they could be related—not so much in looks, but something about their personality Thanh couldn't yet put his finger on.

The man nodded hello. "Thanh, is that right?" He was from a village up the Mekong, and although Thanh had heard about him, they'd never met. "Call me Uncle Hung," the stocky man said. "And this is Mai."

Thanh blinked. *Mai* was a girl's name.

Mai laughed, one short low *ha*. "Fooled you, didn't we?" Her voice was low and measured, with a little bitterness underneath, like the caramel sauce his mom used to make.

"Why do you have a girl's name?"

"Knucklehead. Because I'm a girl."

Thanh almost said *Why are you a girl?* but he managed to stop himself in time. And slowly the boy's compact, neat features rearranged into a girl's face, and he wondered how he hadn't seen it. She was not what people would call pretty—especially with that almost-crew-cut hair—but she looked like a girl, now that he knew she was one. "You sure fooled me."

Uncle Hung said, "I think you two are the same age, maybe? Twelve?" They both nodded, Thanh surprised again, for he would have guessed she was older from her height. Hung said, "We heard that girls can sometimes come to harm on these trips. So we decided that until we reach a refugee camp, she would be my nephew. Then my nephew magically turns into my niece."

At that, Mai's face transformed. Her smile was slow and deliberate, like a bonfire taking its time to light. She held out her hand.

Unsure what to do, Thanh took it. She shook,

Western-style, with such a strong grip that his fingers tingled afterward. She might be a girl, but she was stronger than he was. She was probably better at everything than Thanh was. Inside his head he sighed.

"Now you: off to bed," said Uncle Hung to the girl.

Mai frowned, but Uncle Hung said, "No arguing." To Thanh he said, "She's been awake since Truc dozed off. A great helper." Then to Mai: "You can be first mate again after you get some sleep."

Mai slid under the tarp.

Thanh was not unhappy to see her go. He said to Uncle Hung, "If there's anything you want me to do . . ."

Uncle Hung shook his head. "Mai already did everything that needs doing. She's a natural sailor, that kid."

More silence. The sea stilled and the boat stopped bumping, now skimming across the flat smooth water.

Uncle Hung said, "Your sister, how old is she?"

"Sang," Thanh supplied. "Sixteen." Sang was small with delicate features, smooth clear skin, and thick hair that cascaded down her back, straight and glossy. Men would turn to look at her when she walked down the street, and she would ignore them but sometimes smile to herself. She liked being pretty; she'd even insisted on bringing her tortoiseshell combs along on this trip (though Thanh had forgotten them). In addition to being pretty, she was realistic, so she had in recent months slept with a knife under her pillow. But none of the men in their village had ever bothered her.

Uncle Hung said, "Sang should become a boy, too. If she can." He sounded doubtful. "She should've cut her hair before we left. Tell her to cut it now. Remove the necklace. Wear my extra shirt. Her pants are okay. You talk to her about it."

Thanh nodded. He'd heard things could happen to girls on these trips, too. But not in this boat. Not anyone here. Still, they might meet up with other people in their travels. He'd talk to Sang about her becoming a boy.

As soon as he worked up the courage, he'd talk to her.

She wouldn't like it.

Uncle Hung said, "I know something you can do. There's a package of cooked rice I brought. I thought we'd share that today. Why don't you find it and give everyone some food? And we'll finish that first container of water. We're making good time."

Thanh got out the rice and, using the leaf wrapping for plates, divided it into little piles, spilling a few grains. Maybe trying to make plates was a bad idea, but he wanted to feel more like home. He finished his task just as The Turtle crawled out from under the tarp, so he fed her rice until her pile was gone. Uncle Truc jerked awake and relieved his brother so that Uncle Hung could eat. And then Sang woke and ate. Lastly and finally, Mai poked her head out of the tarp. "Are we there yet?" Her face was blank, but her mouth twitched as she spoke, absentmindedly ruffling her smooshed hair to make it stand up again.

Sang smiled. "Almost."

As Mai joined them, the sky darkened and the waves

started to build again. She grimaced. "I was hoping my clothes would dry."

"You missed the best part of the day," said Thanh. "It was sunny and calm for hours while you were sleeping."

At the engine Uncle Truc shrugged lopsided, stretching his bad shoulder, and studied the sky. "Let's make sure we're ready for a storm," he said. "Tie down anything that's loose, put the tarp over." His voice softened. "Turtle. Sweetie." His daughter replied, saying *Daddy! Ba!* "Go to Sang," Truc said.

The toddler scooted toward Sang, pushing her twisted foot in front of her. Sang picked her up and tied her onto her hip, where The Turtle played with Sang's long dark hair.

"Sang and Thanh," said Uncle Truc, "find the ropes and fasten yourself to the boat. I don't want to have to dive in after you."

"What about Mai?" Thanh was appalled that he had to tie himself in if Mai did not.

She snorted like he'd said something ludicrous, then spoke in her caramel sauce voice. "Not only do I swim like a fish, but I can help steer if Uncle Truc needs a break. You can't." She glided across the boat—loose and graceful, moving with the waves—carrying a water jug to Uncle Truc, who took a small drink.

Thanh frowned at her back. *Show-off.*

Sang obeyed Uncle Truc, tying a rope from her waist to a metal loop on the boat's side. She handed Thanh the other rope, and he tied himself in, grumpy.

But the storm was coming quickly and there wasn't much

time to sulk. When it hit them, it slapped with such precision that Thanh first thought they'd struck a giant rock. It was only a wave—and then wave after wave after wave, slamming the boat again and again, as the rain poured down and the lightning zigzagged across the sky.

Huddled in the bottom of the boat, he felt his food bounce around in his stomach and, several times, reach the back of his throat, though he was never quite sick. The baby, meanwhile, threw up on Sang's shoulder and hair. Uncle Hung, who'd been resting, went to help Uncle Truc; and soon Mai was sent below with Thanh, Sang, and The Turtle. There wasn't any rope left, so she wedged herself between Thanh and Sang and held on to the end of Sang's rope as the boat jangled them around like they were a handful of jacks tossed out over a concrete floor. Thanh thought again of the picture of the rowers at sea, Mount Fuji behind them, and he wondered if those rowers had arrived at wherever they were heading. And if any of them had lost their breakfast on the way.

3

THE STORM did not ease up as the night went on. Thanh worried less about throwing up and more about capsizing and drowning.

Mai ducked out, then returned to join them in the growing puddle. "Uncle Hung says this isn't a bad storm," she said as she wedged herself next to Thanh.

"Lovely," said Sang, on Thanh's other side. The Turtle's vomit still stained her shoulder. Like everyone else, Sang was bedraggled and soaked. Thanh wondered if she felt bone weary, too, as he did.

"It's just that the boat is small, so we feel the waves more." Mai's voice sounded unconcerned.

No one answered. Thanh wondered if Mai ever felt scared.

After a while, Sang shifted The Turtle, who hovered between asleep and awake, to her chest. The toddler's feet stuck out on either side of her, one twisted and one whole and healthy.

"Why is she called Turtle?" Mai asked.

"*The* Turtle," Thanh said.

"Okay, but why?"

Thanh didn't answer. But Sang nudged him and said, "You tell it," and leaned back to listen, rubbing the baby's back.

"When she was born," Thanh said, "it was a long labor and a hard birth, and the midwife worried that the baby would never come." As he spoke, he could feel his mood improving. This was a good story. "When the baby finally arrived, the midwife didn't say anything about her little dimple in her left cheek or her thick fuzzy hair or her perfect first breath. The first thing the midwife said was, *That's too bad. That leg.*"

Mai shook her head at such rudeness.

"But the baby's mother, resting against her pillows, held her arms out for her child. And she looked the baby over— every fingernail, the soft insides of her ears, her round little belly (still with the cord attached), her feet and toes, every bit of her. And she said, *No, this baby is perfect. Her foot is curled just like a turtle pulling its leg into its shell.*"

"Ah," said Mai.

"And then, too," said Thanh, who enjoyed telling stories as much as his sister liked to sew fancy cloth, "this baby is loved by everyone, which means that, like the turtle, she carries her home with her wherever she goes."

"You made that part up," murmured Sang, almost asleep. But her tone was approving.

Mai nodded. "That makes sense." She closed her eyes.

The storm continued, but Thanh felt better.

He woke from a doze hours later to find the storm had

passed. Sang was gone, but Mai was snoring, curled around The Turtle, who flopped, arms out, in her embrace. Mai's sturdy face looked younger and more delicate in sleep than it did awake. Thanh could almost imagine her making a mistake. He decided not to wake her.

If Mai slept, he wouldn't have to watch her being better than him at everything.

Outside, Sang was awake, as was Uncle Truc, who was running the engine. Uncle Hung slouched next to him, asleep and swaying back and forth like a rice plant in a breeze. Both brothers looked years older than they'd looked only yesterday, Uncle Truc's long face sagging with weariness and his bad shoulder tight and low, and Uncle Hung's forehead deep with wrinkles, his wide cheeks smudged with grime. Sang had deep circles under her eyes. The engine, too, ran sluggishly, as if tired.

The sea, once again, shone smooth as glass. Thanh was used to the big river and its constant small movements and seasonal floods. This enormous sea, yo-yoing so quickly between peace and violence, made no sense.

"Morning?" asked Thanh, looking at the sky. It was certainly morning, but he couldn't believe he'd slept that long. Or that the stormy night had ever ended. *One more day. Maybe even tonight?*

Uncle Truc nodded. "I didn't think we'd make it through that storm. You should have seen the waves at their worst."

"It's probably good you didn't," Uncle Hung said, opening his eyes. "You wouldn't've slept well." He waited for

Thanh's smile, then continued. "Mai and Truc and I thought we'd be boating at the bottom of the ocean by morning." Yawning, he closed his eyes again and swayed with sleep.

"Mai?" said Sang. But immediately she *oh*ed with understanding.

"My nephew's a girl," said Uncle Hung, eyes still closed. "And a great little sailor, it turns out."

"How can I help?" asked Thanh. Mai had outshone him again.

"Eat something," said Uncle Truc. "Sang, maybe you can take the engine for a few minutes for me."

As Thanh ate, he marveled again at how the sea could have quieted so thoroughly while he'd slept. The water lay tranquil—a person could almost walk on it.

"Mai's going to sleep right through all this calm," Uncle Truc said.

Just then, Mai's head rose from under the tarp, followed by The Turtle's. But by then the water chopped lightly, and the little boat bobbed on the waves.

"She *did* miss it," said Sang. "Mai, come have some breakfast."

As Uncle Truc picked his daughter up, The Turtle crowed.

"HOW MUCH did that storm set us back?" Sang asked later that morning. Uncle Truc steered, gray with weariness, while The Turtle played near his feet with a spoon Thanh had given her.

"Well," said Mai, who sat halfway in the tent, "the short

version is that we're lost. The storm really blasted us. But we'll figure something out."

She spoke as if she were part of the team of grown-ups who were in charge. It was irritating. "*We?*" Thanh asked.

She frowned at him. "Not a *we* that includes *you*, if that's what you're asking. *We* meaning me and Uncle Hung and Uncle Truc." She muttered something under her breath that sounded, again, like *knucklehead*.

Thanh decided there was nothing about this girl that he liked.

Sang didn't seem to hear Mai. She turned to Uncle Truc. "We're lost?"

He nodded. "The storm threw us off course, it's true. But no worries. We're still heading south. Even if we miss Malaysia we'll hit something. Eventually."

"Before we run out of gas?"

"We have some cooking oil, and if we run out of fuel we can power the engine on that for a little while."

As Uncle Truc spoke, Uncle Hung emerged from the tent, stepping carefully over Mai's legs in the doorway. "That's right," he said. "Also we'll keep an eye out for any big foreign ships, flag them down. They might be able to give us some fuel. I've heard of that happening." He paused, glancing at Uncle Truc as if wondering if he should say more. When Uncle Truc nodded, he said, "The fuel *is* a problem. And the drinking water, too. But we're okay." They weren't okay. They were miles from okay, but Uncle Hung seemed determined to put things in a good light. He stretched and took the engine seat from Uncle Truc, patting him on his good shoulder. "Take a nap, baby brother." Uncle Truc rolled himself under the tent.

As he checked over the engine, Uncle Hung said, "Sang. You haven't gone to the salon yet."

"What?" Sang grabbed The Turtle as she scooted past, stopping her from following her father under the tarp, and plopped the baby into her lap. The Turtle yelped, then laid her head against Sang's shoulder.

But Thanh knew what Uncle Hung meant. "I didn't talk to her yet. About cutting her hair."

In her slow voice Mai said, "Are you stupid? We need to get this taken care of."

Hung cleared his throat. "Mai."

Mai snapped her mouth closed and flushed. She walked, graceful despite the rocking, to the other end of the boat— only about six meters from where they sat near the engine—and pretended to be looking out to sea.

"Cutting my hair?" said Sang. A dangerous thread ran through her voice. The Turtle lifted her head and gazed at Sang's face.

Thanh glanced at Uncle Hung, hoping he'd take care of the conversation, but he just stared pointedly at Thanh, an I'm-not-joking-this-time look on his face.

Thanh sighed. "You should cut your hair. Short."

"Why?" Her eyes narrowed even further and the dangerous thread wove itself through the entire *why*. The Turtle reached up and patted her cheek.

"Borrow my knife," Uncle Hung said, "and cut your hair like a boy's. And take my extra shirt to wear. If we're found at sea, better that you are a boy than a girl. You know what I mean." Then he grinned. "You'll make a good boy. Scrawny and tough."

"I love having short hair," said Mai, from the front of the boat, running her hand over her fuzz.

Sang did not speak. The Turtle continued to pat her cheek.

"Yours doesn't have to be as short as Mai's. And you can be a girl again when we get to the camp," said Uncle Hung. "Just as beautiful. And safe."

"But my hair . . ." Sang fingered it. It was filthy with seawater and the Turtle's vomit. But Thanh could imagine it clean, thick and glossy with hints of blue deep inside like a jewel, framing her round, clear face. Artistic at heart, Sang was always finding pretty rocks and flowers to decorate their home, and embroidering everything she could with intricate designs. Her hair was, Thanh thought, yet another beautiful thing that made her happy.

Even with it cut, Thanh doubted she'd look much like a boy. But she *had* lost weight in the past months. He squinted, studying her. She was downright skinny. And dirty. Maybe with a man's shirt on, she'd look convincing. Maybe.

"Better your hair than something else," said Uncle Hung meaningfully.

"I'll borrow your shirt. Thank you." She bowed her head to him politely. "But I'll wait to cut my hair. We haven't even seen any ships yet. What are the chances that we will?" Then she froze, a stricken look on her face. For that was exactly what they were hoping for now—that someone would see them and help with directions and fuel and water.

"Well," said Uncle Hung after a pause, "keep thinking about the hair, hmm?"

THEY MADE IT only one more day before the fuel ran out, and the next morning—the third morning, Thanh thought, the morning they would have reached land if only they hadn't gotten lost—Uncle Truc and Uncle Hung decided to use the cooking oil as fuel. The engine coughed and sputtered, and the boat smelled like a kitchen fire.

Everyone was weary. They were running out of fresh water, so they only drank a little bit, and only when Uncle Hung said it was time to drink. The Turtle cried; she was thirsty and scared of the waves. They huddled in the tent to get out of the sun, and the tent grew clammy and too warm. No one spoke. No one slept. The waves made the little boat stutter and jump, and through the tent's triangle, Thanh saw only endless sea.

By evening of that miserable, nothing-happening day— still the third day? It was getting hard to tell—they ran out of cooking fuel.

Later that night, Uncle Truc sat on watch, quietly steering a boat that was no longer moving. Everyone else lay in the tent except Thanh, who curled on his side in the doorway.

He listened to the soft breathing behind him and the salt water lightly flicking the sides of the boat around him, and he licked his dry lips and fantasized about rain: in his mind he was lying on a soft, grassy hill with his mouth open to the dripping sky.

All night long it did not rain. And to hear the water around them—constantly tapping the boat—was maddening. But Thanh knew that salt water would kill much faster than simple dehydration would.

The next day, they spotted a ship—a transport that looked possibly Malaysian. (Uncle Hung hoped so, anyway, as that would suggest they were maybe near land.) But it didn't stop to help, even though Thanh and everyone else waved frantically and Hung swung his extra shirt—wet but still somewhat clean—high above his head like a flag. The ship passed them without any sign.

They drank even less water that day.

Near evening, when the two siblings were momentarily together at the front of the boat, Sang cried. She crouched next to Thanh, her hand on top of his as he gripped the edge of the boat for balance, and her face broke and her shoulders heaved. Thanh didn't know what to do; his big sister never cried, not since the night Uncle Truc had told them their father had died. Finally she cleared her throat and patted his hand. "I'm sorry. I promised Mom I'd be in charge. And I messed up, bringing us here."

She sounded defeated. Thanh knew why: they might die

here in the middle of the South China Sea. And they might die soon. They had no way to reach land, and no one to help them. Water was almost gone.

"I thought we should stay together." Her face collapsed again, but only for a moment before she took a deep breath and calmed herself. "I should have left you behind—you would have been safe in Vietnam."

Thanh shook his head. "You know that's not true." He didn't know what else to say, but the idea that he would have been safe in the country where both their parents had died was almost funny, even now. "We're going to reach land. I know it." But he didn't know it. And Sang knew he didn't, of course.

Her chin wobbled dangerously. "I hate being in charge. I hate it."

She did? Thanh always thought of Sang as the big sister: the one who cooked his meals after their mother died; the one who kept house for them after their father's arrest; the one who made all the decisions now that they were orphaned. She didn't *like* being that person? Then who did she want to be?

"I wanted to go to art school," she said, almost as if he'd asked the question out loud. Her voice had returned to normal. "I know it's silly, but I'm good at fancy needlework and at drawing on paper, and I thought maybe I'd be good at painting, too, if I ever studied it. One time Dad even told me—" She stopped as if she'd been cut off.

Thanh waited, but Sang didn't say more.

"It's not silly," he said. And it wasn't. "When we get to the refugee camp, I'll find you some paper and a pencil. And some thread and fabric. You made everything beautiful in Vietnam. And you'll make everything beautiful again."

Sang reached for her brother and drew him in. He could feel her sigh against him, and he knew she was trying not to cry again. "When we get to the camp," she said, her voice hitching just a little. "Sure."

THE NEXT MORNING began the fifth or maybe sixth day at sea. *We arrived two days ago to a refugee camp in . . . Malaysia,* thought Thanh. But his imagination felt blunted, and he couldn't take the fantasy any further. He couldn't stop himself, though, from picturing the mythical camp: barrels and barrels of water.

Mid-morning, they saw another transport vessel. Everyone waved as they had before. Uncle Hung snatched up his shirt and whipped it around like a small hurricane.

Uncle Truc had been dozing. "What country is it?" he asked groggily. His long face was deeply lined, as if he'd aged by years in the past days.

Uncle Hung shook his head. He was a riverboatman; he didn't know how to identify foreign ships. He kept waving. Uncle Truc lifted the baby in the air in hopes that they'd see her, and she kicked her good foot and cried for water.

The vessel let down a smaller boat, which ran a motor and sped toward them. When it reached them, a bearded white man introduced himself in English: the captain of a

Norwegian ship. He told them he'd heard all about boat people.

"Who?" Mai said quietly to Thanh. Her English was not strong, and "boat people" sounded wrong to her ears. Thanh's English was good, and it sounded strange to him, too.

The captain brought them jugs and jugs of water. And he brought them food—raisins, dried meat, tins of vegetables; even two loaves of American bread in plastic bags with a word on the side that the captain said, wrinkling his nose a bit, was WONDER—and several containers of fuel. He told them they were probably only a day or two from the Philippines, if that was where they wanted to go. They'd missed Malaysia.

Uncle Truc nodded, gray with weariness. He looked as if he no longer cared where they went so long as they got to land.

"I can't take you on board," the captain said regretfully. He didn't know what his rights and duties were as far as boat people were concerned. He could get into a lot of trouble if he brought refugees into an Asian port aboard his boat. But he could give them supplies and advice, and he hoped it would help.

Uncle Hung and Uncle Truc thanked him.

The captain glanced around, nodded at Thanh and Mai. "Fine young men you have to help you," he said. Mai snorted a little; everything they wore was dirty and torn, and they all swayed with fatigue. Then the captain saw Sang, half hidden behind Uncle Truc, and he saluted. "And a young lady. She'll be a heartbreaker, I can tell." He slowed his speech down here, as people sometimes do when they talk to a small child or someone not very bright or someone who doesn't speak their language, and opened his mouth carefully around each word. "Pretty little girl." Mai snorted again; Sang's hair was almost white in places from The Turtle's frequent spitting up.

Sang lowered her head; Thanh could see that she was rolling her eyes. "Sixteen," she muttered in Vietnamese, "is not a *little girl*."

"My *sister*," said Thanh in English. "Sir," he added, to be polite. He didn't like the captain's look.

The captain tossed his head back and laughed. "That's right, son. Watch out for your sister. Look after her." Then he tipped his head at Thanh. "You have good English." It was a question.

"My father taught us when we were little. Me and my sister. We lived at a base for a while, with some American soldiers, and I always talked with them. Later, I studied my dad's books." He thought of the small story collection and the dictionary left behind.

"Very good English," said the captain again. "You must be a smart boy." Though he grinned at the compliment, Thanh shook his head—he was good only at learning English and telling stories, not at anything else.

But the captain patted Thanh on the head, pulled an American quarter out of his pocket, and pressed it into his hand, explaining that he'd been to New York recently. "You get to the USA someday, you buy yourself a Coca-Cola and think kindly on the man who helped you out at sea." He gave a quarter to Mai, too, then motioned to his pilot to start the boat's engine and take him back to his ship. "Safe journeys," he said. "Good luck." And left.

Before the captain was even aboard his big ship again, everyone drank some of the fresh water he'd brought. Sang started to feed The Turtle bread slices, carefully opening the WONDER plastic so that she could reseal it afterward. Mai pried at a vegetable can with her knife and they drank that water, too, and ate the mushy peas while the transport ship chugged toward the horizon and away from them.

The little flat-bottomed boat was alone on the ocean once again.

4

ENGINE GROWLING on real fuel, they headed south, flush with food and water. Though they were still on rations, Thanh wasn't parched, just thirsty; and he wasn't starved, just hungry. Not like he hadn't been hungry before—almost every day since his father had been taken to the prison camp. Some days he'd worked for the rice farmer down the road, but the farmer didn't always need him. And since Sang didn't make a lot of money from her sewing, their bellies had often gnawed at night, especially if Uncle Truc and his wife, Aunt Duyen, had had a hard day, too—then there would be nothing to share among them. Today was certainly not worse than those days. *There are harder things than being on a boat,* Thanh thought. *We're almost there, we braved a storm, and we have enough food and water and fuel to make it to a port. And what a story it will make!* He could already hear it in his head: *The ocean reached over the vessel and struck our faces with her icy fingers—*

"Hey, spacey," said Mai. There was no malice in her tone, just matter-of-fact truth. "Do you see something?" She shaded her eyes and stared in the direction he was looking, then shook her head when she realized nothing was out there. "What're you thinking about?"

"Nothing." Then, when she turned her intense dark

eyes to him, he added, "Just . . . daydreaming." He waited for her to say something teasing or blunt. But she didn't.

She said, "I wish I could daydream more, like you. Instead, I just worry. And plan." She shook her head.

He was surprised at the almost compliment she'd paid him. "You shouldn't worry. We're going to be okay." He reached out, almost touched her shoulder like they were friends, and then pulled his hand back.

"Promise?" Her mouth twisted wryly.

"Promise." He crossed and re-crossed his pinkies.

Mai smiled—that slow, bonfire-lighting smile—and walked away to take the engine for Uncle Hung. At Uncle Hung's suggestion, Thanh scooted over to the rice pot to open food with Mai's knife, thinking they'd eat canned carrots (which The Turtle loved).

But just as Sang sat next to him with The Turtle, Mai called out, "Boat!"

Everyone froze for a moment. Sang looked up at Mai, who was peering at the horizon intently, hand still on the tiller. Squinting, Uncle Hung stood and shaded his eyes and frowned deeply; Uncle Truc staggered to his feet. Everyone looked. The boat was far off, hard to see. A fishing boat? It seemed to be moving toward them. Quickly.

Suddenly Uncle Hung took the tiller and swung the engine around. "Let's go." They began to head back north.

"What—?" asked Thanh.

No one answered, but Sang said to Uncle Truc, who half stood in the boat, "Is it—?"

Uncle Truc said, "Maybe just fishermen. Maybe not." He turned to them. "All of you get down." He gestured at the young people. His glance rested on Sang and his face softened. "Now is a good time to cut your hair."

Sang's mouth opened in a small O. Her face looked as if a stone had been tossed in the middle and sent ripples outward. Then she nodded just once and dropped to the bottom of the boat with the others. "Knife," Sang said, setting The Turtle down, and Thanh realized he still had Mai's in his hand. He gave it to Sang.

From above them, Uncle Hung said, "They're following. We can't outrun them."

"We can buy a little time," Uncle Truc said. "Sang's cutting her hair."

"Right," said Uncle Hung. "Here we go." And the boat sped up, engine groaning and straining.

As Sang hacked her hair, sawing it off in big wads, Mai snaked her hand up over the lip of the boat and threw the

clumps of hair overboard. When Sang's hair was chopped, Mai took the knife and hastily trimmed it closer, into a shaggy boyish cut that looked even worse for having been done in a rush by two people with a knife. Sang slipped Uncle Hung's extra shirt over her head.

"Will I pass?" asked Sang.

Mai looked at her, considering, her face suddenly serious. No one answered.

Sang pursed her lips. She took the knife and sliced her forehead in a quick gash near the hairline.

It wasn't a deep or long cut—barely a scratch—but it bled. "Bandage," she said. Mai took the knife, cut a strip from the bottom of Sang's shirt, and wrapped it around Sang's head. The blood still oozed on her face, and her hair stuck up, matted with it. But she looked much less like a girl.

They all crawled into the tent. Sang tucked the necklace into Uncle Hung's shirt just as shots peppered over the boat.

They all froze. Uncle Hung immediately cut the engine. "That's it," he said quietly. "I hope you're all ready."

"We are," said Mai. Her face was calm. But her body was tense, all her muscles flexed.

And they waited in the bottom of the boat for the pirates.

FIVE THAI PIRATES stepped into a dinghy and headed for Uncle Hung's boat. When Mai peeked over the edge, she reported that at least two more were standing on the deck of their own boat, machetes in hand.

A drip of blood slid down Sang's face. She swiped at it, her hand shaking violently. She looked like she was going to be sick. Thanh felt the same way; though he'd heard gunfire all his life, he'd never actually been shot at before.

"You look good," Mai whispered. "Manly." Sang glared at her but looked less sick. "I'm serious," said Mai.

"It's true," said Thanh. "You look great. I mean, you look really bad. Like a boy, I mean."

Mai nodded at him as if he'd said something clever.

The Turtle, who'd been quiet through all the hair-cutting and hiding, had crawled out of the tent and began to cry, banging her curled-up foot on the floor. Uncle Truc shrugged and picked her up. "Tuyet. It's okay." He rubbed her back, calling her by her real name. Thanh wasn't sure he'd ever heard Uncle Truc do that before. "Tuyet, honey. Shhh."

The pirates yelled something from their boat and laughed. Thanh couldn't tell what they said, since he didn't speak Thai, but he guessed that they'd seen the baby and now knew what they'd only suspected until then—that Uncle Truc and Uncle Hung weren't lost fishermen but refugees—and the pirates got excited, hoping for loot on board.

"Stay sitting," said Uncle Hung from above, "unless we tell you to move. Stay where you are. We'll get through this." Uncle Truc handed the quieted baby back down to Thanh, just inside the tent, and stood tall and lean next to his shorter elder brother, their shoulders—one lopsided and one broad—dark shadows against the blue sky.

• • •

THE PIRATES TOOK almost everything. They took the food and the water and the fuel that the transport captain had given them. They took most of the engine. They took the little money that Uncle Truc and Uncle Hung had saved up for their arrival at the refugee camp and had stored in a jar. They took Thanh's and Mai's shiny American quarters, also stored in that jar. They took Uncle Truc's extra shirt, which had two gold rings sewn into it—though they didn't know that when they took it. They took the tent poles. The tarp ripped when they tore it off the poles, and they dropped that in the bottom of the boat, laughing. They laughed even harder when they saw Sang, Mai, and Thanh huddled beneath with The Turtle, who started wailing again.

Then one of the pirates gestured at the three men—the two men and Sang, that is, who was thinner but as tall as Uncle Hung. The pirate pointed with his long knife, *one, two, three,* and motioned taking off a shirt. He wanted their shirts. Sang stood up slowly, her eyes darting to Uncle Truc, her head bent.

Hunched in the bottom of the boat with Mai and the baby, Thanh felt as if he could not breathe. The Turtle, now on his lap, finally fell silent, as if even she understood how serious it all was.

Mai spread her hands out on the floor, crouching as if she were going to spring. Or maybe—was she scared? Her face was clear as always, but her eyes sharpened as she watched.

The pirate gestured once more.

Uncle Hung stepped forward, a true big brother. "You've taken everything we have," he said loudly and slowly, hands held out in front of him. "Leave us now." Uncle Truc stepped to his side, so that they both stood in front of Sang, and nodded. Sang stood tall behind them, her head now raised to see the pirates, the blood still oozing from her forehead. Her face, in profile to Thanh, looked so strong and beautiful—even grimy and bloody, even exhausted and starved—he wondered how the pirates could not see that she was a woman.

Uncle Hung said again, louder, "Go."

The pirates may not have understood his words, but they knew what he meant. The one who'd demanded the shirts narrowed his eyes to slits. Quick as quick his hand shot out, a knife flashed.

And he stabbed Uncle Hung in the stomach.

Uncle Hung stood very still, gasped, and slowly brought his hand to his side.

Mai leapt up with a wordless yell. But before she could attack, Sang pushed her down, hard, and she landed with a thump next to Thanh.

The pirate with the knife turned toward Sang—who raised her hands slowly, as if he were arresting her. Even more slowly she brought her hands to her neck and fished out the Buddha necklace, showing the man, then pressed her hands together and sank to her knees. She was praying—or pretending to. Thanh didn't know which.

The pirate who'd stabbed Uncle Hung wiped his knife

off on his pants for several minutes before putting it away, his eyes flicking to Sang and the necklace. The other pirates turned away and spit uneasily out to sea. They didn't demand the shirts again; it was as if the Buddha made them change their minds. Maybe they weren't as bad as some. They got back in their dinghy with their loot.

But the pirate who'd demanded the shirts was still angry. He stopped before he got into the dinghy, pulled a pistol out of his belt, and shot once into Uncle Hung's boat. Not at the people. Just at the boat, near where Thanh and Mai and The Turtle huddled, where the tent had been. Screaming, The Turtle covered her ears and hid her face. The pirates left, their dinghy motoring back to their fishing boat, laughing and talking as they went.

Uncle Hung's boat, a hole in its bottom, slowly began to fill with water.

Uncle Hung himself swayed, his hand pressed to his side, his shirt blooming red like an opening flower.

5

EVERYONE AROUND Thanh moved in jerky slow motion, like a movie caught in a film projector at the wrong speed. Thanh could hear nothing but a roaring in his head, as if his ears were filled with water. He shook his head, back and forth, to empty the water out. But he still couldn't hear.

Wordlessly, Mai stuttered over to Uncle Hung, her adopted uncle, and took his free hand, the one that wasn't pressed into his side. He wrapped his arm around her and leaned, but she couldn't hold him up. Slowly they sank to the bench beside the gutted motor.

Churning away on the gray water, the pirates' dinghy reached their boat.

Sang's mouth moved. She pulled off Uncle Hung's extra shirt, and Uncle Truc tore it into strips and bound some of the strips around Uncle Hung's side where the blood came out.

The pirate ship pulled its dinghy aboard.

While Uncle Truc and Mai helped Uncle Hung, Sang ran to the middle of the boat. With her hands as scoops, she bailed the water that streamed in through the bullet hole. Her mouth moved again, and her face turned toward Thanh. But he couldn't hear her. There was no sound.

The pirate ship began to move away. It grew smaller and smaller, sliding toward the horizon.

Then, screaming: The Turtle. Thanh was still holding her. She screamed and screamed, right in his ear, and all the sound came rushing back.

Uncle Hung moaned, clutching his side. Mai murmured something to him. The baby screamed again. Thanh put her down, and she scooted to the middle of the boat, where she paddled her hands in the incoming water.

Sang spoke. "Help me." She looked angry more than anything else. "*Thanh.* Help me." Her eyes were fierce with unshed tears.

Thanh's head swung back and forth, back and forth, between Uncle Hung (with Mai and Uncle Truc still bandaging him) and Sang. Nothing made sense. Sang said again, louder, "*Thanh.*"

He threw himself to the bottom of the boat and scooped handfuls of water as fast as he could, flailing. One handful hit Sang in the face. Most others didn't make it over the lip of the boat. The Turtle shrieked. The water came in faster than they could scoop it out.

"I'm okay," Uncle Hung said. "Take care of the boat."

Uncle Truc brought Sang the empty rice pot, which had been kicked under the tarp and missed by the pirates. While Sang bailed with the pot—now with more to show for her work—Uncle Truc inspected the hole and clicked his tongue in disgust. "Well, we'll have to patch it." He rocked back on his heels and looked around the ship pensively. "But with what?" He glanced at Thanh, then away.

Thanh stopped bailing. His handfuls weren't doing any good.

"I still have my knife," Mai said. She slid it out from her waistband, where it had been hidden. "Saved a bit of the food, too." She pointed at The Turtle. Uncle Truc reached into the baby's clothing and pulled out a little sack that contained a few handfuls of dry rice. He gave his daughter a hug and lifted her out of the incoming water, then put her back down, as there was nowhere else for her to go.

"The rice was all I could grab," Mai said.

"Good girl," said Uncle Truc. "You always have your wits with you."

Mai shrugged, as if what she'd done was obvious and expected. "Too bad they took the water jugs."

"Thanh," Uncle Truc said.

Thanh hadn't saved anything from the pirates. He hadn't even thought of it.

"Plug this hole for a few minutes," Uncle Truc said, gesturing to the bottom of the boat, "while Mai and I figure out a more permanent fix."

He turned away, Mai following, and walked toward the front of the boat—as if there might be something there.

Thanh didn't move. Plug the hole—with *what*? And how would that help, anyway? They had nothing left—no motor, no food, no water. Uncle Hung had been stabbed. What did the hole in the boat matter? They were going to die. He stared at it, watched the water pour in.

"With your hand," Sang said, bailing. "Or foot. Or *sit* on

it. Just keep out the water. *Try.*" Her words were impatient, as if she thought Thanh didn't want to help.

And that idea—that he didn't want to help—suddenly made something inside him burst open. He *wanted* to help; he always wanted to help. But his help never helped anything. "*Try?* Why should I?"

Uncle Truc and Mai turned and stared at him, Mai's face confused, Uncle Truc's stern. Then their expressions folded, like sheets of paper, smaller and smaller, until finally they closed into an emotion that Thanh could put in his pocket and carry around: disappointment. Again.

No. Thanh grabbed the rice pot from Sang. It was undamaged, and somehow that made him furious. What right did the rice pot have to be whole and unharmed? There was a hole in the boat, a hole in Uncle Hung. A chasm in himself that he could feel growing and growing. His arm, of its own volition, whipped the rice pot away, and his voice yelled. "*Try?* What is the point?"

The rice pot flew through the air in a high arc and landed on the water nearby, floating like a little boat.

As soon as the pot hit the water, Mai dove out of the boat after it, retrieved it, and returned to the boat, where Uncle Truc hauled her and the pot back in, dripping. Neither said anything to him.

"Thanh." Sang spoke through gritted teeth. "Plug the hole."

"*Why?*" Thanh said. He wasn't inside his own body. Someone else was talking, making his mouth move. What that someone else was saying, though, made a lot of sense. "We're all going to die. Why should we fix the hole?"

"We're not going to die," Uncle Truc said loudly. "Not today."

Thanh whipped to face Uncle Truc, his own adopted uncle, his neighbor, his father's good friend. "Why did you bring us on this boat? We'd be better off back home! Why'd you take us out here to kill us?"

"THANH!" screamed Sang.

Startled, The Turtle wailed. Sang hugged her.

Ignoring Thanh and Sang, Mai studied the hole in the bottom of the boat. She pressed her sturdy knee into the bullet hole, peered down at it, and then raised her thumb to Uncle Truc. Around her knee, water seeped. But she'd slowed down the influx.

The hole wasn't fixed, though. Nothing was fixed. Thanh's hateful words floated in the air.

Uncle Truc flushed. His hands formed fists and his knuckles whitened.

Thanh knew that the person in his body spoke wrongly. It wasn't fair to blame Uncle Truc for what had happened. Uncle Truc had never promised a safe journey. In fact, he'd wanted to leave Thanh at home, unharmed, with his own wife and children. Sang had only brought him along because she thought he needed taking care of.

But as much as he wanted to, Thanh couldn't take his words back. The person inside him who'd yelled wouldn't apologize. Thanh saw Sang's anguished face, and he tried to get back in his body and say the words. But everything in his face felt stiff, and instead of *I'm sorry*, the words that came out were, "I wish I was home." He said it as much to Sang as to Uncle Truc.

And then he was—suddenly—back inside his body, wet and cold, and everything was all wrong, and he wished he was a little boy again with his parents, not a twelve-year-old who was supposed to be nearly grown-up and capable of doing things and instead messed everything up. He wished his mother were here, or his father.

He wished he weren't a disappointment.

Sang turned away from him and bailed. The Turtle, silent again, shivered in the water.

Uncle Truc had been breathing deeply. The redness in his face faded. When he spoke, his voice was tight with all the things he wasn't saying.

"Mai, help me. Thanh, plug the hole. Sang, keep scooping."

Mai stood up, glancing quickly at Thanh and then away. As Mai and Uncle Truc started scouring the boat, Thanh bent and squeezed his fingers into the bullet hole. The water shot out to the sides, the way a faucet shoots water when you block the opening with your thumb. Sang, soaked with the sudden shower, paused and glared. Thanh couldn't push hard enough with his hand to cut off the water. He knelt; his knee, knobbier than Mai's, didn't stop the water, which pooled into the boat. "It's not working," Sang said.

"I *know*," Thanh said. This world, this entire world and everything in it, was awful. He turned and sat, as hard as he could, on the hole. He sat in the puddle his sister was draining; if he shifted he could feel a trickle of seawater, but mostly her work lowered the water level, which meant that his butt was keeping the ocean out.

The boat wasn't going to sink, not yet, anyway.

Thanh looked across the boat to Uncle Hung, who slouched next to the gutted engine, ashen, hand on his wounded side, watching Thanh with a thoughtful look on his face. They stared into each other's eyes, and Uncle Hung nodded once but did not smile.

The others moved with purpose. Sang bailed methodically. Mai and Uncle Truc catalogued what little they had left, looking for a fix for the boat, shaking their heads and murmuring to each other about the stripped engine, the rice pot, and one empty dented water container they'd found, like the rice pot hidden under the ripped tarp. The Turtle silently slapped at the shrinking puddle at the bottom of the boat.

Slowly, Uncle Hung slid off the bench and eased himself to the floor, holding his side, breathing carefully.

"Uncle Hung?" Thanh said.

Mai ran over to her uncle, face grim, but he waved her away. "I'm not dying yet. I'll let you know if I do."

She turned back, taking only a fraction of a moment to narrow her eyes at Thanh before starting a low conversation with Uncle Truc while gesturing at his sandaled feet.

Thanh, sitting on the hole in the boat, thought, *This is not the story I want to tell. This is a terrible story.*

I am a terrible person.

6

IN THE END, they used one of Uncle Truc's sandals to fix the hole. It was better than nothing. The sandal's sole was rubber and easily cut to fit the hole, into which it was wedged as tightly as possible. On top of that patch they placed the rest of the sandal and the (empty and dented, but not broken) water container, filled with ocean water to weight it. The leak still seeped, but with occasional draining with the rice pot, they could get by. Now that no one had to run the engine or refill the fuel tank, it was easy to take turns at bailing duty.

When The Turtle wasn't in her father's arms, she was back in a sling on Sang's hip—Uncle Truc contributed his shirt for that purpose. She cried the first night from hunger and thirst, but now, late in the second day after the pirates, she'd stopped crying and just hiccupped and buried her face in her father's or Sang's shoulder. Her lips cracked from the sun and heat.

Uncle Hung was weak. There was no denying how serious his injury was. The morning after the pirates, Uncle Truc removed his elder brother's shirt-bandage and replaced it with a new one. The wound was still oozing blood—more if Uncle Hung tried to move—and there was no way to clean it.

So Uncle Truc bound it back up, hoping that the firmness of the bandage would help. They just had to believe that Uncle Hung's body could heal itself—without food or water. Mai made a shade for him by draping the biggest piece of ripped tarp over the broken engine he sat beside; everyone took turns sitting with him to take a break from the relentless sun. Every now and then the tarp would flop onto their heads and someone would readjust it to keep the sun off Uncle Hung as much as possible.

No one said anything about Thanh's outburst, for which he was both grateful and ashamed. It was like when a toddler peed on the floor in front of important visitors: he'd done something babyish and rude and embarrassing, and for his sake they were trying to ignore it. He wished he could apologize, but he didn't know how to talk about something that everyone was pretending hadn't happened.

And it wasn't as if people were talking about other topics; they saved their words for necessary things. There was not much to do but empty salt water out of the boat. And wait.

As the afternoon wore on, Thanh found it hard to think of anything but his thirst, so much that his brain felt blunt with it. He wanted desperately to drink the water that surrounded and taunted them; but he knew he couldn't. People died from drinking ocean water. At his turn bailing, he made and remade a mental list of all the things he wanted. First, fresh water for everyone to drink. Second, bandages and antiseptic for Uncle Hung. Third, fuel and a working engine. Fourth, food. Fifth, land. Sixth, a way to erase the terrible things he'd said. Then he shook his head and rearranged: the last thing on the list wasn't possible. And as for the rest: land alone would do, if they could reach it soon enough. Land would contain everything else.

UNCLE TRUC slept deeply that night, as did Sang and The Turtle, all at one end of the boat, away from the slow leak. Thanh, knowing that Uncle Truc wouldn't want to be near him, slept on the other side of the boat, near Uncle Hung and Mai.

Mai stayed up late that night with Uncle Hung, holding his hand and talking softly. Thanh could see them every time he woke, sitting against the night sky, and he could hear their soft murmurs. He thought of the awful things he'd said to Uncle Truc. Mai hadn't said or done anything to make her adopted uncle hate her. She'd tried her best to help—and to save Uncle Hung.

In the morning, Mai slept. As she woke, the weather turned choppy: a storm was coming. They could see it slowly fill the sky to the east of them, darker and darker.

"You need to sleep more," croaked Uncle Hung to Mai. "It's only when you're sleeping that we get good weather." She grimaced and nodded; her throat was dry, but she appreciated the joke.

Uncle Truc frowned. "We're sitting ducks." His voice scratched like gravel on paint.

"Sitting ducks in a sitting boat," Uncle Hung said. They would certainly not outrun this storm.

"If it storms," said Mai, in a froggy imitation of her usual slow, sure voice, "we'll at least have fresh water. We should cover Uncle Hung with one of the tarp pieces, but the other we can use to collect water."

"No," said Uncle Hung in a sharp voice cracked with thirst. "Use both tarps for water. I'll survive a little rain. And a washing will be good for me. I stink."

Mai grinned her slow grin, waving her hand in front of her face as if to fan away a bad smell. When her smile started, it was aimed at Uncle Hung, but after it built to a flame, it moved on to Thanh. Startled, Thanh grinned back.

Suddenly he understood why Mai and Uncle Hung seemed like they were related even though they weren't. They had the same dry sense of humor, even at a time like this, when joking didn't seem possible.

"Let's get the tarps set up to collect water," Uncle Truc said. "It'll rain any minute."

When they were ready, everyone was wedged at least partly under a piece of tarp. Around the smaller tarp sat Uncle Truc, Sang, and The Turtle; and around the larger tarp sat Uncle Hung, Mai, and Thanh—all of them (except The Turtle, who sucked her thumb and buried her head in her father's shoulder) propping up the edges of the tarp with their bodies to collect fresh rain in the oilcloth's center.

And then the rain came. Hard.

• • •

THE WIND and waves weren't as bad as the first storm they'd gone through a few days ago, but the rain was worse, pouring for about a day—as far as they could tell. The darkness made it hard to know how much time passed. But Uncle Truc said, *about a day*. Thanh had lost track of time by this point: was it day six since they left home? Or seven? Seven, he thought. But it didn't matter anymore what day it was. The journey was endless.

They had to shift the tarps periodically to bail with the rice pot. First, though, they'd drink whatever water had collected in the pot, and they'd reach the pot into the low middle of the two tarps to scoop out more drinking water.

The rainwater was life-giving, and each person took several large gulps. But lying back in the rain, mouth open—so wonderful at the start of the storm—got old really fast. For the first few moments, the rain felt wonderful on Thanh's parched face and lips and tongue, but within an hour, everyone was soaked and shivering. They rearranged, trying to keep warm: on one side of the boat, Uncle Hung lay carefully wedged between Mai and Uncle Truc. Across from them, propping up their tarp as much as they could, Thanh and Sang huddled around The Turtle.

No one slept, not even the baby.

7

FINALLY, JUST AS Mai dozed off and rolled away from Uncle Hung to lay curled by herself in a sodden puddle, the rain pittered away to nothing. In the slowly growing light, Thanh watched the storm die, amazed at how moody the ocean was, how it changed so quickly. The rivers in the Mekong Delta were never quite this impulsive except in spring floods—even those, however, were something one expected. And now this post-storm stillness didn't seem normal. But what did he know?

As the sea quieted, Sang and the baby fell asleep, too. Uncle Hung drifted into fitful rest. He seemed to be in less pain now that the squall had ended, but his calm worried Uncle Truc, who peered at him and shook his head.

Uncle Truc nodded good morning to Thanh—the only two awake—and gathered the tarps into two sacks to temporarily hold the water they'd collected while Thanh cleared the ocean water out from the bottom of the boat. When he was done, Uncle Truc filled the rice pot with rainwater from the tarps. The rice pot was full almost to the brim, but after that the fresh water would be gone. They would wait to drink it, Uncle Truc said, until they had to bail the boat again—which would be later that day.

Thanh nodded and slumped against the side of the boat, his clothes wet and clammy and the sun warm on his face. He felt tired, like he could sleep forever, and sluggish. But not hungry—as if he'd moved through hunger into something else.

"I'm sorry," he said. Finally the words came out. "For what I said before."

"Forget it." Uncle Truc folded the tarp in half and half and half again, squeezing a few more drops of fresh water into the rice pot.

"I didn't mean any of it."

Uncle Truc nodded but did not look up from his work. "Already forgotten."

"But—"

"Not something we need to discuss further. We all say things we don't mean sometimes. You had your day yesterday. It's done." Uncle Truc unfolded the tarp, apparently deciding he'd gotten all the water out of it he could, and draped it over Uncle Hung to keep the sun off his face. Then he sat near his brother, groaning a little as he slid to the floor. "My wife is a smart lady."

Thanh nodded.

"She always says, we'll let the past be the past, and forgive each other for words spoken in anger." He closed his eyes. "We're good, you and I. Now let me rest a bit."

WHEN THE TURTLE WOKE, Thanh gave her a little water. She didn't want to play or babble; she just wanted to be held.

Thanh picked her up before she could crawl back to Sang and disturb her sleep. Sang's hair flopped all over her head in a scraggly mess, and the gash on her forehead had scabbed in her hairline, but The Turtle still knew who she was and wanted her.

Before the baby could complain or cry, Thanh snuggled her onto his lap and whispered, "I'll tell you a story, okay?" She half smiled; she'd heard a lot of his stories in her short life, and even though she couldn't possibly understand all the words, she always seemed to be listening. Before they'd left Vietnam, he had told her a story almost every night while her mother made supper. "You want one about a turtle?" She usually liked those, and there were turtles in a lot of stories.

The baby flicked her hands open and shut and pointed at the sky. She wanted a star story, or maybe a sky story. Thanh was never sure about her hand motions, so he usually just picked something. She never complained.

"Should I tell you about an airplane?" he said, thinking of something his father had told him. His mouth was dry—but not as bad as before the rainwater. He could tell a story. "My dad was a pilot for the Vietnamese air force before the communists defeated them. He was a hero, just like your dad." She smiled and flicked her hands open and closed. "Your dad wasn't a pilot; he was a soldier. But still a hero." She nodded almost as if she understood.

Across from them, Uncle Truc's eyes were closed, but his face twitched. Maybe he was listening, too.

"That's right," Thanh continued. "My dad flew planes.

He told me about the men who invented the first successful planes, and that's the story I'll tell you today.

"Once there were two brothers, named Orville and Wilbur." His mouth twisted around the strange American names. "They were bicyclists and bike repairmen. And they wanted to fly. The plane they built was light and open—like a bike. It was—almost a kite, and one man could pilot it, lying on his stomach."

The baby flicked her hands again. Thanh always had to keep stories short for her, or she lost interest.

"They took the glider plane to a place called Kitty Hawk." Thanh loved names, and this name was one of the best. His dad had told him that it meant "cat" and "falcon"—which in Vietnamese would sound very odd together, but apparently in English sounded correct. And when he'd finally read the story in one of his dad's books, sure enough: Kitty Hawk was the name.

"Orville and Wilbur's dad said *fine*; they could invent planes and fly them, but only if they didn't fly together. One of the brothers had to be on the ground all the time—that way if the plane crashed, old Mr. Wright wouldn't lose both his sons at once. And that's good thinking," he added to the baby.

"Kind of like us," Mai said, and Thanh looked over his shoulder to see her awake and sitting directly behind him. She slid down next to him. "Like us on this boat. Like how only part of each family went, so that if people died, it wouldn't be the whole family at once. There would be some survivors." Then, seeing his face, she said, "We'll survive. Don't worry." But her scratchy dry voice sounded—for once—unsure. "Why did you and your sister both come?" she asked. "Why not just one of you?"

He glanced at Uncle Truc, but the exhausted man now appeared to be sleeping for real. "Uncle Truc wanted Sang to come, to take care of this one"—he held The Turtle's hands up and clapped them, and she smiled—"and to help him. Sang wouldn't go without me."

"She really loves you." Mai sounded almost sad.

He shook his head no. "I mean, Sang does love me. But the reason she didn't leave me behind is that she didn't trust me to stay alive without her. I'm . . ." He paused, thinking about his words. "I'm not very trustworthy. I daydream, and I'm not good at anything."

"You're good at telling stories. The baby likes it, and so do I."

"That's not anything special."

"It is. You just need to find a job someday that will let you tell stories."

Thanh sighed. "Right."

The Turtle hit Thanh's chest and grunted for more.

He clapped her hands together again. "Want to hear what the little brother, Orville, did after they got the plane working? He took his daddy up in the air. His dad was ancient by then, the age of a great-grandfather." The Turtle giggled. "He was eighty-two," he added to Mai, who nodded. "Orville helped his dad climb into the plane, and they took off. They flew for seven whole minutes."

"That's all?" said Mai.

"Seven minutes must have seemed like forever when you'd never gone up in a plane. When no one had gone up. When planes were still something miraculous and unbelievable. If you could be a bird for seven minutes, wouldn't it seem like—like magic?"

Mai nodded, eyes wide. The Turtle flapped her hands in her own private bird sign.

"So he took his ancient father into the air, and they flew under the puffy clouds and through the blue sky and past the birds, who were shocked to see this monstrous machine. And do you know what the old man said?"

Thanh paused, but Mai and the baby didn't answer. They just stared at him, spellbound. This was the best part of storytelling—bringing the listener in to the specialness of whatever the story was, getting them to live it.

"Orville's father said only one thing while he was up in the sky, being flown by his son on a plane not much better than a kite. He said, *Higher, Orville, higher!* And Orville knew then that his dad was impressed, that his dad thought what he'd done was something wonderful."

He patted the baby's back. "That's the end of the story."

After a pause, Mai said softly, "Your dad died in the war, didn't he?"

"After. In a camp."

"He would be proud of you, too. Just like the brothers' dad was. I'm sure of it."

Thanh shook his head. Mai didn't know his dad; she was

just trying to be nice. His dad hadn't been proud of him. The notepaper folded and refolded in Thanh's mind.

"We don't all have to be good at the same things." Mai paused. "I'm sorry I called you *knucklehead*."

"When?"

"Every time. Even the times I didn't say it out loud." She took his hand, and he realized it was the first time she'd touched him since her bone-cracking handshake when they'd met. This time, her hand was soft. And warm. And he thought about how she was all alone, without even a sister or brother for company. And he thought that here, at the end of their world, maybe he could be something for Mai—something like a brother. He held her hand.

Sang's voice rose from the bottom of the boat. "Why'd you let me sleep?" She rubbed her eyes and then her head, her face opening in surprise at the feel of the short shaggy hair. It would take some getting used to.

"We were letting you take a vacation," said Mai, sliding her hand, grimy and battered, off Thanh's. "On a cruise ship."

Sang grimaced. "It was really calm there for a few hours."

But it was bumpy now. Thanh hadn't noticed, but the change must have happened recently. Before Mai had started talking to him, the ocean was serene and still. When she was still sleeping.

"It's true. Every time you sleep, the water calms down," Thanh said.

"Me?" said Sang, startled.

"No—Mai. When she sleeps, it's calm, and when she wakes up, it's choppy. Uncle Hung said it earlier."

"Well, he was *kidding*." Sang reached for The Turtle, who scooted toward her and crawled into her lap. She bent her head over the baby and cooed to her.

Mai poked Thanh's side. "What? You think I have some kind of . . . magical power over the waves? A superpower, but only when I'm asleep?" There was a smile in her voice.

She made it sound crazy. And maybe it was.

He poked her in return. "I'm just . . . seeing a connection."

"Makes a great story," said Mai. Then, maybe realizing she sounded rude, she added, "How about this: next time it gets bad, I'll try to fall asleep and we'll see if it helps. Okay? An experiment. Prove your theory right or wrong."

Thanh nodded and grinned at her. She wasn't a bad person at all. In fact, she was pretty great sometimes. "It's a deal."

Uncle Hung woke, groaning a little across the boat. "Choppy water all of a sudden."

Thanh raised his eyebrows at Mai. Her face lit into a slow smile.

"I hate to say it," said Uncle Truc, yawning—how long had he been awake?—"but we need to bail again, so . . ." He frowned pensively at the rice pot. "We might as well drink it now as later."

They drank the fresh water, even Uncle Hung, who could barely sit tall enough to drink. As they drank, the sea grew rockier. Thanh didn't say anything. But when he glanced at Mai, she gestured to the waves and then to herself and shrugged, one eyebrow cocked. Thanh grimaced. Sure, it was crazy to suggest that Mai's sleeping calmed the waves, and on her waking the harsher weather returned. But there were facts: every time the water stilled, Mai had been sleeping. Every time.

And there was no doubt that the water had become suddenly choppy, and the little boat now bobbed in a way that made Uncle Hung hold his side and groan.

Well, at least it wasn't storming.

WHEN ALL the fresh water was drunk and the boat emptied of seawater, they rested. There was nothing else to do. People dozed in and out of sleep.

At one point, Thanh woke up to find Uncle Truc watching him, his lined face gentle. "With your hair all rumpled like that, and the dirt—you look the spitting image of your dad at twelve."

"I do?" He couldn't picture his dad any other age than grown-up.

"He was a handful. I think he almost drove his parents crazy, the number of times he did dangerous things without thinking about consequences. Wildness was his *big flaw*, your grandfather once said." Uncle Truc grinned. "But it wasn't really a flaw. Probably it's what made him a great pilot."

"I can see that," yawned Mai, curled nearby. "Guts."

Thanh nodded, deep in thought.

8

THE LITTLE boat drifted through a day of nothing: no rain, boats, or land, nothing to save the six passengers. Part of the time, Mai sat with Uncle Hung, and part of the time, she sat beside Thanh, holding his hand. Sang often sat beside him, too. No one spoke.

Thanh thought about how the world would keep going after they died, and death didn't sound as bad anymore now that he was so, *so* tired and thirsty, and the sun was beating down so hard, and the undrinkable water flashed and winked around them. His father had been Christian and his mother Buddhist; he himself wasn't sure what would happen to him after he died, but he thought there was a good possibility that it would be better than what was happening to him right now.

And maybe in the afterlife he'd get another hug from his mother. And he'd see his father again, somehow. His father, who'd also messed up as a kid. And maybe Thanh would have a chance to forgive his father—"*Forgotten*," he'd say, just as Uncle Truc had—for the hard words his father had spoken. His own regrets still fresh, Thanh understood that his father must have felt terrible about leaving him with *I'm disappointed in you* hanging between them.

Maybe, Thanh realized, he didn't need to wait until after he died to forgive his father. Maybe it was enough to think *Forgotten* now. Maybe it was important that he forgive his father in this world—so that in the next, they could meet with nothing standing between them.

THAT NIGHT the sea settled to a deep calm, and all the young people slept, exhausted. Uncle Truc periodically scooped water; but mostly he sat with his brother, holding his hand and watching the stars. Thanh, waking up off and on through the night, saw Uncle Truc's lean body folded next to his stocky older brother, head tipped back against the boat's side; and then Thanh would watch the stars, too, until he fell asleep again.

In the early morning, Sang woke up and bailed while Uncle Truc dozed. Thanh got up then, too, careful to let Mai and The Turtle keep sleeping. The water was calm as calm could be. Maybe Mai should sleep a long time.

"We're on some kind of current. It's moving us," Uncle Truc said.

"How can you tell?" Sang asked.

"Hung saw it. He said either we're moving or the stars are out of alignment. I think it's us."

"You think the current will bring us to land?" Thanh asked. He could barely get out the words, his mouth was so dry.

Uncle Truc shook his head. "I don't know anything about ocean currents, and neither does Hung. But he can read stars a bit. And he thinks we're going in a great big circle."

As IT turned out, they weren't drifting in a circle. Not exactly.

After Mai and The Turtle woke up (and the water grew choppier again, though no one mentioned it), Uncle Truc took a nap. By the time he woke up again, the day had turned warm and sunny—a perfect day if you weren't aboard a little boat with no food and water and very little shade. They did feel a breeze, however: the boat skimmed over the water, the wind blowing on their faces as they cut through the waves.

Uncle Hung, who'd been napping off and on all morning, waved his brother over. "I don't have proof," he said, "but I feel like our circle is getting smaller."

Uncle Truc stood tall in the boat and looked all around, shading his eyes and weaving a little with the waves. "You're right," he said. "We're spiraling inward."

"How can you tell?" Sang asked, cuddling The Turtle, who wanted her father.

Uncle Truc picked up his daughter, kissing her forehead and murmuring to her. "Tuyet, my sweet turtle." He looked at Sang, but spoke loud enough for all to hear. "I can see the center." His long face had never looked so grim.

UNCLE HUNG had heard of such a thing: it was called a maelstrom, and it pulled things into it. He didn't sound hopeful. There was no joke in his voice.

Now, when Thanh stood up, he too could see the center. They were spiraling in, steadily drawing closer, like soap bubbles swirling around a sink drain.

"What happens when—when we get to the middle?" Mai asked. Her face was calm, but her body coiled ready to spring, just as when the pirates came. Thanh knew this meant she was scared.

He took her hand and squeezed it. She squeezed back.

"I don't know what happens," said Uncle Hung. "I've never heard about maelstroms from anyone who survived one—never firsthand." He paused and placed his hand on his injured side. "I think we go down." Then he reached up and tousled his adopted niece's fuzzy head with his free hand. "It's a bit discouraging to go down now—I was just starting to feel better."

Mai smiled at Uncle Hung, that slow burning of light across her face. She squeezed Thanh's hand again. Thanh decided not to let go, ever, for as long as she needed him.

"Well," Uncle Truc said. "If nothing else, it will be an adventure."

"And I could not think of better people to have such an adventure with," said Uncle Hung.

Thanh hoped that Sang would say something brave, too, to represent their family. He knew that he could not come up with anything.

"When we—reach the center . . . ," she said. And she couldn't speak. Sang, who always said and did the right thing, couldn't speak.

"It'll be an adventure, like Uncle Truc said." Thanh realized he could be in charge this once, for Sang. "It'll be a great story," he added. With his free hand he reached for his sister's and took it, gently.

"A great story." She smiled at Thanh, her chin wobbling.

Mai stood up, suddenly, as if she'd made a decision. She held her hands out to Uncle Truc. "Give me The Turtle." Said in her slow, caramel voice, the words were nonetheless an order.

Uncle Truc frowned a question at her.

"I can't explain." Her face, calm as always, but her hands outstretched, shaking. "I need to hold Tuyet. *It's important.*"

Uncle Truc gaped at Mai. She sounded like herself, still the slow, low-voiced drawl, but more commanding than usual.

The Turtle batted at her father's chest and reached for the spiky-haired girl. "Mai-Mai!"

Though two years old, The Turtle spoke only rarely, only a few words. It was the first time she'd said Mai's name. Slowly Uncle Truc handed his daughter to Mai, Sang handed her the wrap, and Mai tied the baby securely to her own hip. The Turtle took a fistful of Mai's oversize red T-shirt and sighed as if she were exactly where she wanted to be.

"Now," Mai said, taking Thanh's hand again. "We should all hold hands."

It wasn't a suggestion.

"Right away, people," she said. "Make a circle."

"Okay. But why?" Sang asked. She took her brother's hand on one side and Uncle Hung's on the other.

"I just know," Mai said. "In my gut. That we should hold hands. Whatever happens to us—live or die—we live or die together."

"That's a good plan," Uncle Hung said, reaching for his brother.

Uncle Truc slowly nodded.

Mai reached out her free hand for Uncle Truc. "Circle up."

And they did, all of them.

WHEN THEY arrived at the heart of the maelstrom, the center of the draining sink, the boat was sucked downward and immediately cracked to pieces. To scraps: the force of the maelstrom broke it into shards that arrowed down into the depths of the ocean and disappeared. The six people—all holding hands except the baby, who was tied to Mai's hip—might also have flown into shards, but the handholding was so strong, so fierce, that it was as if they'd fused together, as if they moved and thought as one.

However.

No one could breathe.

The water sucked them down and pressed them together, yanking them under. *No air.* Tiny chips of wood splintered against them, leaving trails of scratches on their legs, as if they'd run through brambles.

Thanh closed his eyes when he was sucked under, so his first seconds were pure sensation: cold water, a crushing need to breathe, slivers and scrapes, a powerful tugging downward, strong hands holding hands.

He opened his eyes. If he were drowning, he might as well see it as not.

He peered downward, through all their flailing legs toward the bottom, to see what was pulling at the water and at them.

The vortex seemed to head straight down to nothing, to empty sand. What was causing it wasn't clear.

But on either side of the vortex, just outside the swirling water and debris, two . . . things. He must be already dead—or on the way to dead and hallucinating. Because these weren't things from this world.

One was a monster. Enormous.

He could see it through the water, murky but real, almost glowing in the green light that filtered down toward them. It sat on a sandbar on the bottom of the ocean, not far below them, near the swirling maelstrom that had no beginning point. The monster was something like a squid, but flatter on top. And so, so much larger than a squid, with massive tentacles and one visible eye, closed as if sleeping. It was a squid the way a skyscraper was a shack. The way Saigon was a village. The way the North Vietnamese army was a little boy with a toy gun.

It was not a squid, in other words. It was a sea monster.

The other thing—across the vortex—was . . . a portal? A

doorway? A lighted strip of sea that opened to somewhere else, like a gate into a garden. Thanh could tell that the water through it was different somehow. A shade bluer than their own ocean.

A doorway couldn't exist under the water. But neither could a sea monster.

And neither could they. *No air.* The need to breathe was crushing him. His head was going to explode.

All these thoughts flashed through Thanh's mind as he was sinking, as he was holding hands with Mai on one side and Sang on the other, part of the circle of six dying souls, as they all were sucked down into the maelstrom. There was no air. There was no air.

And then the monster shifted. A giant eye flicked open, big as a house, and stared at them. Thanh gasped like a fish thrown into the sky, and the very last of his breath left his body. He wanted to scream, but there was nothing left for screaming. His lungs burned. And all he could think was *help help help help.* As if the monster could or would.

The monster blinked.

Then it turned away from them, rotating quickly for such a mountain-like creature. One minute it was blinking at the humans, and the next minute it was spinning away. Through the burning of not breathing, Thanh tasted a bitter disappointment to know that he'd perish without looking the monster in the face again. It was turning its back on them as they died.

And then.

Then the monster shot a powerful jet of water in their direction. The pulse blasted the people out of the vortex, away from the monster, toward the doorway, and up. *Through* the doorway. They catapulted into the sky. One minute they were drowning and the next they were the high arc of a fountain. All still holding hands.

9

THE SIX whipped through the air as if cannon-shot. It was like flying except for the gravity part. Soon they were arcing down toward the ocean, very fast.

But when they came down again—that was the strangest part of all, more astonishing even than being shot into the air by a sea monster.

When they came down again, they landed on their feet, on the water.

Not *in* the water, *on* the water. The water caught them, and it held them, and they stood on it.

The five survivors (plus The Turtle) alighted on the surface. And then: they walked. They walked on the water.

THE WATER was wet; it was soft to their feet; it was sun-warmed; it flapped gently under them as if it were breathing. It was water. There was nothing magical about it, as far as they could tell.

Except that they were walking on it.

The Turtle vomited up salty ocean and cried and then snuggled into Mai's chest for a nap, overwhelmed by thirst and hunger and almost dying. The others coughed and hacked, looking around them. Uncle Hung let go of his brother's hand to grip his wounded side, and now instead of a circle they made an arc, still holding hands.

"Well," said Uncle Truc. "Any theories about this?"

"Are we dead?" asked Mai. She didn't sound worried. "I don't feel dead."

"I think if I were dead my side wouldn't hurt so darned much," Uncle Hung wheezed, and the two of them smiled.

"I don't think I'm dead, either," said Sang. "I feel very alive." She lifted her thin, exhausted face to the breeze.

"I vote for alive, too," said Uncle Truc.

"Me, too. What do you think?" asked Mai, squeezing Thanh's hand.

"I don't think we're dead," said Thanh slowly. "I think—I think we're in another world."

THE OTHERS had seen the monster, too, but they hadn't understood it as a monster. They hadn't put together the giant eye and the tentacles and the mountainous body and come up with *sea monster,* as Thanh had. And no one except Thanh had seen the not-exactly-a-doorway across from the creature or the monster's blink or its turning and shooting them back through the doorway and into life. They had all been too busy dying. So when he told them that story, they were in awe.

"You're an observant kid," Uncle Truc said.

"So you think we ended up . . ." Mai trailed off.

"I think the maelstrom opened up a doorway—or maybe

the maelstrom appeared *with* the doorway or maybe they're not related at all—but the doorway was there, and the monster shot us through it. I don't think we're in our own world anymore."

"That would explain the walking on water," Uncle Hung said dryly. "It is too bad, though, that we couldn't have been spit into a world that had some land."

"Or a boat full of water and food," said Mai.

It was true. The new world (if that's what it was) looked just like their old world: a seemingly endless ocean, a wide blue sky. Nothing to eat or drink.

"I don't think we need to hold hands anymore," said Uncle Hung, one hand on his wounded side, the other still holding Sang's hand. "It was a good idea, though, Mai. We all ended up together, just like you said. Live or die together— though I'm somewhat glad it ended up to be *live*. Now we should pick a direction and start walking." He shaded his eyes with his free hand, looking around for a likely direction. And he hunched with pain.

"Let me help you," said Sang. And she released Thanh's hand to turn to him.

At the same moment, Uncle Truc, on the other end of the line, said, "I'll help you," and he let go of Mai's hand.

And—and—

And all three of them, disconnected, sank. Sang, Uncle Hung, and Uncle Truc.

Thanh and Mai (with The Turtle) stood on the water, holding hands.

Everyone else slipped into the sea and disappeared.

And then came up, kicking and sputtering.

Thanh, in surprise, reached to grab his sister's hand as she treaded water next to him. In doing so, he let go of Mai's—and he also sank.

When he surfaced, kicking to stay up in the water, Sang was helping Uncle Hung to float. Uncle Truc was paddling toward Uncle Hung. Mai alone stood on the water, frozen as if in thought. Then she shook herself, walked over to Uncle Hung, squatted, and reached for his hand. As she rose, she pulled him out of the water. She drew him up gently.

When Uncle Hung, holding Mai's hand, stood again on the water, Mai reached her other hand down for Sang, who emerged and in turn reached for Uncle Truc.

Mai's face unfolded into that slow smile. "Want to come up, too, Thanh?" The line of people walked back to him. Uncle Truc reached down, and when Thanh took his hand he immediately felt the water gel around his feet—or rather, though the water didn't change at all, his feet were suddenly able to climb in it. He ascended.

Mai whooped. "You were right, Thanh! It's a new world!"

Thanh shook his dripping head, laughing, and the water flew into Mai's face. Mai whooped again. As the drops ran down her face, she licked her cracked lips and broke into a giant grin.

All on the surface again, they formed a circle long enough to rearrange without letting go of hands: Uncle Truc on one end, then Uncle Hung, Sang, Mai (with The Turtle), and, lastly, Thanh. Uncle Truc experimented with slinging his brother's arm over his shoulder, and this kept everyone afloat as well as handholding did. They faced inward, almost a circle again.

Uncle Hung said weakly, "That was . . . interesting. I didn't know my niece had magical powers." His voice was smiling as he looked at Mai.

"Walking on top of the water," Uncle Truc said.

"But I can't!" Mai said. "I mean, I never did in Vietnam. I've been in the rivers a million times, and I never walked on the water. I always swam, just like everyone else." Drips of water slid down her face, and she licked her lips again.

"When you slept on the boat, the storms got quiet. Every time." Thanh didn't understand *why* Mai could walk on water; but that didn't make her walking less true. And it was a great story. "Maybe that was your magic back then, and this is your magic now."

Deep in thought, Mai licked her lips a third time.

"But calming the water isn't the same as being able to walk on it," Sang said.

"Oh! Maybe—" Thanh said, an idea crystallizing in his head, "maybe Mai had a tiny piece of a magical gift when we were in Vietnam, and now in this new world, her gift has grown. Multiplied." Even as he said them, his words themselves sounded magical. A fairy tale. And yet they also made sense, like here was an explanation that was—in this world, anyway—real.

"Mai?" Uncle Hung said. "What do you think of all this?"

Mai did not answer. Her face glowed, the smile she'd lit up with a few minutes ago now burning bright. Like she had the best secret in the world and she couldn't hold it in for a second longer. More drips ran down her face from her hair, and she licked at them.

"Mai?" Uncle Hung said gently. "Don't drink salt water, honey."

"The water," Mai said. "THE WATER!" She slapped her foot through it in an arc that sprayed them all.

"Mai. Are you okay?" Thanh asked.

Mai laughed suddenly, and her voice pealed out as if she weren't at all tired or thirsty or hungry, as if she hadn't just been shot out of her world, as if she weren't lost, maybe forever. "Didn't you taste it when you went under? The water. We can drink it. It's fresh water!"

It was indeed. Everyone let go of hands, this time on purpose, and immersed themselves and floated and drank their fill. Mai, who did not sink, squatted and scooped water for herself and the baby.

The water was good. It was very good.

Then they joined hands again, and they climbed out of the water and stood, and they chose a direction, and they walked.

PART FOUR

Kinchen and Caesar, on the Island of
Tathenn in the Second World.

The Present (Summer 1978).

1

STANDING WITH Old Ren and Caesar in the surf of the Odd Bay, Kinchen faced the sea monster, and she trembled even as she stared into its enormous eye. The Kraken—Kinchen tasted the word on her tongue several times before even attempting to say it—did not charge them or shake its fists (or fronds or whatever it might shake), did not do anything remotely threatening; in fact, it didn't do anything at all. Its size and potential power, though, were enough to render it terrifying. The Odd Bay appeared too small to contain it. "How did the— How does it *fit*?" she finally asked. It wasn't the most pertinent question, but it was the only one that came out.

"Not *it*," said Ren softly, eyes on the Kraken. "*He*. The water here is deeper than it looks. Lots of unusual things under the surface." They talked in muted tones, as if not to disturb a sleeping baby.

"That how the Odd Bay got its name? Because of him?" asked Caesar. Neither Ren nor Kinchen replied; an answer wasn't necessary. All three of them stared at the Kraken, who stared back with his giant eye.

The eye blinked again, and the Kraken descended, slowly submerging and disappearing.

"He's ready to go now," Ren said.

• • •

EACH GIRL carried a waterproof backpack containing a jacket and some dried food as well as a little packet of matches. There hadn't been time to scrounge for more supplies—and if the Kraken took them all the way to Raftworld, they were unlikely to need much.

When she hugged her adopted grandfather good-bye, Kinchen couldn't help but ask about the Kraken. "How do you talk to—to him?"

Ren laughed, then coughed. "Don't be too impressed. Pip has had far more profound conversations with him than I ever did."

"Pip?" He'd never told her.

"The boy has more adventure to him than people realize. Especially you, child." Ren coughed, phlegmy spasms that made him prop his hands on his thighs and lean forward. When the coughs passed, he braced his lower back and slowly straightened up. The early moonlight made the wrinkles on his brow look like etchings. "You two need to get going," he said, pointing with his free hand, which shook slightly.

Out in the bay, the Kraken began to re-emerge closer to shore, the mound of his head cresting the water. Soon a half orb of eye glimmered above the rippled surface, the iris black; in its depths Kinchen could see the reflection of the moon. She turned to Ren to hear what the Kraken had to say, and she saw the old man's pale eyes reflecting the monster, his face gray in the dusk.

"How old are you?" she said. It slipped out—she hadn't

meant to ask. She knew it was a rude question, one she'd never asked before. Ren did not invite such personal questions.

But Ren answered. "*Too* old. I won't be around much longer."

"Are you sick? Should I stay . . . ?" Kinchen couldn't leave the old man if he was ill. But she had to find Pip—who was also in danger.

"I'll still be here when you get back. Not to worry. I'm just saying that I think this is my last big thing." He smiled, but she could see sadness in his eyes. Sadness and the Kraken.

"Your last big thing?"

"The last thing I need to do. What I came back for. To help you two, and him." The Kraken disappeared, then bobbed up closer to shore.

And Kinchen realized that when Ren said "you two," he meant her and Caesar; and when Ren said "him," he meant not Pip but the Kraken. "How are you helping *him*?" She looked back into the bay.

The Kraken submerged again.

Ren said, "I had a choice to make once, long ago. It took me an eon to make that choice and to return here. Now he has a decision to make, too. All I can do is listen, and help him think things through."

"What's his problem?"

Ren didn't answer. "He'll take you most of the way, and then he needs to hurry back here. He's waiting. And he's old—he'll be ready to turn into an island soon."

"Is that what happens?" said Caesar, still staring out to sea. "When they die?"

Again Ren didn't answer. "Time to go. Tide's turning."

Kinchen said good-bye to Ren. Prickly as he could sometimes be, she loved him more than she could say. "I'll bring Pip back," she said to the side of his neck as she hugged him.

He cleared his throat. "Come back yourself, safe and sound. I'll be here. Safe travels."

Kinchen and Caesar walked out into the bay, toward where they had last seen the Kraken. Before they were chest-deep in the water, Caesar took Kinchen's hand and pulled her onto a bumpy log—which was not a log after all, but a tentacle. They traversed the long limb until they reached the mantle of the creature, the top of which now rose above the water's surface, and they climbed aboard.

The Kraken began to move away from the Island. In the bright moonlight, Ren shrank to a waving dot and then disappeared.

Finally the Island disappeared, too, and they were truly at sea. Riding the back of a Kraken.

2

As CAESAR pointed out, they weren't actually riding the Kraken's back—since Krakens don't have backs. "At least, not according to the stories. It's more like we're sitting on top of his head." But to Kinchen it felt like riding the back of an enormous horse—an animal she'd heard of but never seen, as none lived on Tathenn anymore.

The Kraken's back (Kinchen decided to keep calling it that) was craggy and gray, like a mountain. It was not particularly comfortable to sit on, but it was large and it wasn't slippery—they didn't need to fear falling off. They seemed to be moving quickly; the wind whipped at their faces and the Kraken left a trail of white bubbles in its wake, like a long tail. Seaweed drifted past them at a respectable clip.

The Kraken carried them through the night. Both girls wrapped themselves in their coats and curled up uncomfortably on the rocky surface of his mantle. But once asleep they slept deeply, and it was not until bright morning that Kinchen awoke, stiff and a little damp from the spray.

"Where are we?"

Caesar looked up from her food scraps. "Close, I think."

"How can you tell?"

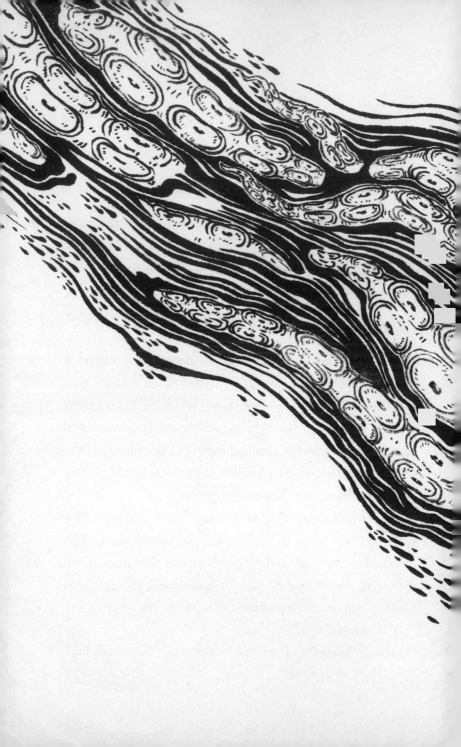

"Birds." She swallowed a bite. "There are a lot of birds on Raftworld. So when I start to see them out here, I think we must be near home. Or other land. But since we're looking for Raftworld, I'm hoping that's what it is. Did you sleep good? This food is amazing." She had devoured everything in her pack.

Kinchen opened her own pack and took enough for her breakfast, handing Caesar the rest.

"Thanks. Traveling is hungry work."

A short hour later, they could see Raftworld, a long line on the horizon fluttering with birds. Kinchen and Caesar repacked their coats into their waterproof backpacks (there was no food to repack), and Kinchen sat back to wait.

But they didn't draw closer. Raftworld stayed maddeningly on the horizon, and they drifted along behind it, not closing the distance. After a few minutes' silence, Caesar said, "Well, this must be the drop-off spot. Maybe Kraken don't like big crowds, and as your grandpa said, he wants to get back home. So we'll go from here."

"That's an awful long swim," said Kinchen. She was a strong swimmer, but this distance was ridiculous—especially if Raftworld was moving away from them. "Can you—can you swim that far?"

"Can't swim at all," said Caesar cheerfully, her braids swinging as she shook her head. "No, sir. I sink like a stone."

"What?"

"That's my gift, you see."

Kinchen shook her head.

"I sink to the bottom. And then I walk." She grinned. "And I can take you with me. At least, I'm pretty sure I can. I used to take my mom with me on walks, a long time ago when I was little. Before she died. And that was fine."

"I'm sorry about your mom."

"It was a long time ago. And my dad died when I was a baby. I'm an orphan—like you."

But without Pip and Old Ren, Kinchen thought. Without even an adopted family.

Something must have showed on her face, because Caesar said, bouncing a little as she spoke, "I'm fine. Totally and completely okay. No worries. Now: let's walk under the water."

"Oh . . . I'll swim." The distance was long, but swimming still seemed safer than sinking to the bottom of the ocean and trying to walk. *That* was not going to happen.

Caesar scrunched up her face and squinted at Raftworld. "That's crazy-far to paddle. You sure you don't want to walk on the bottom with me?"

"I'll swim." She'd never poked her head underwater with Pip—never wanted to be part of something that was obviously not her gift. She wasn't going to start now.

While Caesar put on both backpacks ("Since you're swimming, I'll carry"), Kinchen walked down the slope of the Kraken's back into the water. It was like hiking down a rocky beach. When Kinchen had descended deep enough, she pushed off and treaded water. Caesar waded down until she was up to her chest, then paused, bobbing gently up and down with the Kraken. "I'll thank him on my way down," she said. "I don't have gifts of talking to sea creatures, but I think he'll understand."

"Sounds good." Warmed up from treading water, Kinchen was ready to swim.

"And I'll be under you. The whole time. I'll be there. If you get too tired, just sink, and I'll catch you."

Kinchen held up her thumb in an "okay" sign. But really: *Sink if you get tired, and I'll catch you? I don't think so.* She would just have to swim for it.

Caesar slid down into the water, her waving hand the last thing to disappear.

Kinchen waited, treading water for a moment, to see if Caesar would come up again. But she didn't.

The Kraken, however, rose, its head growing until it resembled nothing so much as a mountain erupting from the sea. Finally, one great eye emerged, focused like a lamp upon her. Kinchen gasped; close up she could see that the eye was bigger than she was, even if she were to reach her legs and arms out like a starfish. She was barely bigger than the pupil.

The eye stared at her. It seemed to be waiting.

"Um," she said. "I mean, thank you. Very much."

The great eye blinked. The Kraken descended again until just the top of the head was visible. And then the top of the head submerged, and he was gone.

Kinchen was alone in the ocean.

She kicked out toward Raftworld and began to swim.

IT'S POSSIBLE that Kinchen might have made it all the way to Raftworld—maybe—if Raftworld hadn't been retreating as she swam. Every time she looked up, it was sitting on the horizon. She swam for what seemed like hours, stopping only to drink water—so sweet and cool—and, every once in a while, to flip onto her back and catch her breath.

Raftworld never got closer. Never. The sun got higher and higher in the sky—and then lower. And Raftworld stayed on the horizon.

Finally Kinchen was so tired she could not lift her arms to paddle. Gasping, she treaded water and wondered if a kind dolphin might come along and give her a ride. But that only happened in stories. No, she'd have to figure out how to swim faster.

Or she'd sink.

And if she did . . . would Caesar really catch her?

She lay on her back, utterly exhausted, thinking about her options.

After a few more minutes, she flipped to her stomach, eyes open, and looked down. The water was clear and green, and as with much of the ocean in the second world, the bottom was close enough to see. Brightly colored fish flitted through coral that rose from the sand.

There was something—a dark shape—just on the edge

of the sandbar—but she couldn't hold her breath any longer.

She flipped to her back again.

When she'd caught her breath, she turned over and looked down. There: Caesar, standing on the ocean's sandy bottom near the coral, waving up at her.

No: not waving. Motioning her to come down.

3

THERE REALLY weren't any options left, unless Kinchen counted drowning as an option. And she didn't. So the choices were to swim—which she'd proven impossible—or to sink down to where Caesar was and trust her to take them to Raftworld.

Caesar certainly looked fine under the water. She'd been down there for hours and hadn't died yet. She whirled her arms in giant come-here motions.

Kinchen was so exhausted, she wasn't even sure she could make it down—and back up again if this experiment didn't work. But she needed to try. She took as large a breath as she could, her lungs aching and cramped, and plunged downward.

She couldn't make it to the bottom. She couldn't. She could feel her arms giving out. She could see them, floating in front of her, and she thought, *Pull. Pull.* But her arms wouldn't work anymore. They weren't part of her body. They were just these things floating in front of her.

Her legs kept kicking, but weakly. She told them to kick harder, and they didn't obey. Her lungs were about to burst.

Caesar jumped and jumped, little clouds of sand rising

around her feet. But she was still too far away, and she was growing fuzzy, as if seen through a fog.

Then, as Kinchen drifted down, her last bit of breath leaving her body, Caesar gathered herself into a ball, leapt up higher than ever, and grabbed her hand, dragging her the rest of the way down.

AS SOON as Caesar grabbed her hand, they both dropped like stones to the bottom of the ocean—which wasn't far. And Kinchen immediately felt better.

Not just better: good. She couldn't breathe—but she didn't need to. With Caesar's hand in hers, Kinchen's lungs stopped burning, and they no longer felt like they were going to burst. Her arms and legs were still tired—her arms felt far worse than the day she'd challenged herself to do a thousand push-ups (and hadn't made it). But her body was now light, and her weary legs could support her. Next to her stood Caesar, shaking her head and grinning, braids swirling around her head like tentacles.

Amazing, isn't it?

What? Somehow Kinchen could hear Caesar's voice, as if Caesar was inside her head—even though Caesar's mouth didn't move. Caesar hadn't actually spoken, not in the usual way.

That's right! Caesar danced a bit, sparking the sand up around her feet. *Just think at me, and I'll hear you, as long as we're holding hands.*

Think at you?

Good job! Just like that. And isn't this amazing?

Kinchen looked around. The light filtered down to them at the bottom of the shallow ocean. Bright fish darted in and out of the coral. When Kinchen looked up, she could see a blue sky waving and sparkling overhead through the window of water. She had to admit, Caesar's favorite word seemed finally appropriate. *Yes, amazing.*

Now let's hike ourselves to Raftworld. Caesar tugged at Kinchen's hand. *Let's run!*

And they did, in slow motion. They ran the way swallows fly, looping away from and toward the earth in long waves. Each step was a leap, and each landing took them a graceful vault closer to Raftworld.

Until, finally, they slowed to a walk.

They walked in the shadow of Raftworld.

4

WE SHOULD GO UP. Caesar pointed, as if Kinchen might not know what she meant. In the cool green shadow of Raftworld, her eyes flashed bright.

Yes, but right now? Maybe we want to sneak up. After dark. As the goal was to rescue Pip, and there were only two of them to accomplish the task—and those two not exactly warriors—Kinchen saw no sense in moving *too* quickly. But she didn't think that part at Caesar—it was her own private thought.

Caesar knew, though. *We don't need only to rescue your brother. We also need to talk the Raft King out of it—out of a rash mistake, like your grandfather said. Remember?*

Of course she remembered. *Why do we need to talk the king out of leaving? Why not just let him go to the first world, if that's what he wants?*

If it was a good choice, yes. But your grandfather said rash. *And* mistake. *We need to at least talk to him.*

Kinchen glowered at the bright coral, the bright fish. *The Raft King kidnapped my brother. I say we let him leave. I say we don't help him.*

But. Caesar tugged on Kinchen's arm until Kinchen turned to look at her. Her eyes were dark and serious. *Before*

*he became king, he was always nice to us kids on Raftworld—
even someone like me who didn't have parents and wasn't anyone important. He was a kind person. And he's trying to fix our
problems with not enough hydraulics, and too many people. He
hasn't figured out a solution yet, but he faces up to problems and
tries to fix them. He could be a good king someday. And even if
he never becomes good—*

Yes?

We should still help him.

Kinchen sighed. She suspected Ren would agree with
Caesar. But Ren wasn't here. They walked again, keeping
pace with the raft, and she thought to herself as they walked.
If you could change someone's mind—keep him from making a rash mistake, whatever that meant—*should* you? She
wasn't sure. Especially if that person had done something
terrible, like drugging you and kidnapping your brother, then
did you really have to help him find a home?

And if you did help, would it be like you were saying the
terrible thing he did was *okay*? And even if Kinchen should
help this man—even if all the answers to her questions lined
up and spelled *Help him*—did she *want* to?

I can't go up without you. Caesar's thoughts contained a
slight tinge of pleading. *I'd just sink. I need you to swim me up.*

Kinchen sighed, then realized something that made her
decision a little easier. She could help *Caesar*, who could help
the Raft King—which didn't feel the same as she herself doing it. And she'd get her brother back. *Okay. I'll swim you up
now.*

• • •

AFTER A SHORT DISCUSSION, they decided that the best way would be for Caesar to climb on Kinchen's back and ride her to the surface like a shell rides on a turtle. It was not an easy swim for Kinchen—especially since her arms, though no longer exhausted reeds, were still tired from her earlier swim. But she made it to the surface and pulled up at a middle edge of the raft, away from the hydraulics at each corner. Both girls grabbed on and heaved themselves aboard.

They lay on the dock, dripping and (in Kinchen's case) panting, near a quiet garden outside a small house. Two children sat nearby, one on a folding chair and one on the ground, holding instruments: a small guitar-like harp that looked like its body was made from a bottle gourd, and a full-size xylophone. The first sounds that Kinchen and Caesar had heard when their heads popped out of the water were the sounds of children practicing scales in the plodding way people do when they would rather be elsewhere. The two young musicians—a girl wearing a brightly beaded necklace, and a boy with short twists of hair that ended just past his ears—froze when the girls rose from the water, dripping, the guitar-harp player with her thumbs and forefingers poised around the still-vibrating strings, the xylophonist with his mallets hovering above the wooden keys. The kids looked about eight years old.

Caesar waved. "I'm back," she said. "To rescue someone and to persuade the Raft King not to be stupid."

"Stupid and mean," Kinchen added, thinking of what he'd done to Pip.

Slack-jawed, the children nodded.

"This is my friend Kinchen. From the Islands. Kinchen, this is Ije"—she gestured to the girl with the stringed instrument—"and Okoro"—she gestured to the boy, who lowered one mallet in a wave, still staring. "They're learning music to accompany storytelling. Eventually, I mean. That's a beginner's kora."

The girl held out her harp-guitar, while the boy said, "Her kora only has seven strings. My balafon is a real one like grown-ups use." He banged a chord on his xylophone.

"That's because the balafon is easier to play than the kora," the girl said, rolling her eyes. "All you have to do is hit things with sticks. I have to prop the instrument up and play with my thumbs and fingers all at the same time. And I have to tune it myself." It sounded like an argument they'd had before.

Before they could continue, Caesar said, "Can you tell us where the king is?"

The kora player said, "Probably sleeping. There was a big party last night."

The balafon player added, "Mama went. But she came back early to put us to bed." He banged his xylophone again to punctuate.

"Where's the boy from the Islands?"

"Living with Jupiter," said the balafon boy, putting his mallets down. "They were at the party, too."

"I bet the new boy doesn't have to practice instruments," said the kora girl gloomily, resting the guitar-harp against her knee. "I bet Jupiter just tells him stories all day long."

A woman's voice called from within the hut. "I don't hear music. What will Miss Anna think? She might not let you study music with her anymore."

The girl with the kora rolled her eyes, then readjusted her hands and picked out a seven-note scale quickly and badly. The boy echoed her on his balafon slightly less badly.

"Concentrate or come inside," the woman's voice said. But not angrily. The scales continued.

Caesar waved at the reluctant musicians and pulled Kinchen down a path that passed behind the house. As they left, a brief tune emerged from the scales and followed them.

THEY WALKED toward Jupiter's house. The afternoon was warm and sunny, the light slanting into the gardens. Most people were eating supper—usually in their gardens—and didn't see the girls walking past.

Caesar certainly didn't attempt to hide, and when people did see her, she simply waved her jaunty wave and grinned at them. Puzzled, most of them grinned back.

One grown-up said, face long in surprise, "I thought you'd decided to live on the Islands."

"Decided to come back—for a visit."

"Ah."

"Brought a friend. And I'm going to introduce her to the king."

"Ah."

When they were alone again, Kinchen said, "You *decided* to live on the Islands?"

"Well, I did agree to trade myself."

"Not a trade if the other person was stolen," Kinchen muttered.

"I *know*. Which is why we're undoing it." Caesar waved at a family eating dinner, who returned the gesture. "Yes, I'm back!" she called. In a lower voice than Kinchen would have thought her capable of, she added, "What I don't understand is why all the secrecy. Why doesn't the Raft King just tell people that he wants your brother to show him the way to the first world, and that he plans to go there? People would miss him for sure. But he's a grown-up. He can decide for himself, right?"

"Right," said Kinchen. She thought about how Ren had insisted on telling the story of how Raftworld came to be, how Venus had brought everyone over. He hadn't had time to tell the end of the story, but she knew the main point: Venus held all their hands, and she brought her people through the doorway and to the second world . . .

And that was it. That was the answer. Venus brought everyone through with her. That was why Old Ren told that story.

"It's not just the Raft King," Kinchen said.

"What?"

"That's why the Raft King is keeping secrets."

"You're not making sense."

Kinchen paused to organize her thoughts. "What if—what if it wasn't just that the Raft King wanted to go to the first world? What if he wanted to take all of Raftworld with him?"

Caesar frowned as if about to disagree. But then her face scrunched up in thought; and a moment later it opened up in understanding. "Oooh." She thought again. "But we don't know that for sure."

"It would explain the secrecy, though."

"True. So—everyone gets dragged to another world." Caesar wrinkled her nose. "Doesn't seem hardly fair to do that without telling them—*asking* them."

Kinchen nodded, struck with another thought. *And what about Pip? What would happen to him?*

BEFORE THEY REACHED Jupiter's house, they met up with two more adults carrying baskets of food as if heading home with dinner, both of whom said hello (with curious looks) and welcomed Caesar back (with questions in their voices). Caesar said, "We're going to Jupiter to see the new boy from Raftworld."

"They're not at home," one of the basket-carriers volunteered. "I saw them heading for the east dock when we were over that direction."

"Jupiter and the boy," added the second basket-carrier. Her voice shifted into something more serious. "They were with a couple of rowers. And the Raft King."

"*What* is he up to?" Caesar asked, more to herself than anyone else.

"The Raft King?" asked the woman. "We don't know." She hesitated, as if not sure what to say. "We were just talking about him." She held out an apple from her basket. "Supper?"

"I wouldn't say no," Caesar said, taking the fruit and biting in.

The man said, "We were talking about how he's been a great king the past few months, since his father died. But recently—well, he's gone kind of crazy."

"How do you mean?" Caesar spoke with her mouth full.

The man shook his head. He was shorter than the woman and box-shaped: wide square face, hands like bricks. "He's not even trying to solve our overcrowding problems anymore—he canceled the council meetings to discuss solutions this week and last." He shifted his basket to his other hip. "We live in a one-room apartment above a family of six. And the king cancels the meetings. Says we don't need to fix the overcrowding problem, that it will fix itself. And—well, he's just acting odd."

"And he traded you away, didn't he?" asked the woman, as if such an action had showed the Raft King was out of his mind. She handed them each another apple. The woman had very dark skin, even darker than Caesar's. With round cheeks and a round body, she was comfortable and huggable-looking. "You're a child—it's not lawful to send you off."

"I agreed to it," said Caesar, beginning to bounce on her toes. Kinchen frowned, eating her apple. Why was Caesar defending the king?

The woman's voice lowered and her hand reached out for the girl's shoulder. "Caesar. I know it's been hard for you, and your adopted family wasn't very warm—maybe too busy to really care for you . . ."

"What we mean is," the man said, "if you're coming back to Raftworld, you can come live with us. Our Ru and Soph think you're wonderful, and they'd love to have you as a big sister. Don't think you have to exile yourself to the Islands."

"The Islands aren't bad," said Kinchen, offended.

"Oh, of course not," said the woman. "But they're not home." She spoke to Caesar again. "You should know there are plenty of families that would love to take you in. That would love to have you."

Caesar blinked. Blinked again, her face blank. She stopped bouncing.

Kinchen shifted, surprised at the conversation. She'd imagined Caesar as completely alone in the world. Looking at her friend's face, she wondered if Caesar had been thinking of herself that way, too.

After freezing for a moment in thought, Caesar shook herself as if she'd just remembered something important. "Pip. We need to get to the east dock."

As Kinchen and Caesar approached the dock, they slowed down. It was almost evening, and all the fishing boats were pulled in, the area deserted except for a group of four men, two of them rowers. Though they all stood near the edge of the dock with their backs to her and Caesar, gazing out to sea, Kinchen immediately recognized the old storyteller Jupiter with his ponytail of white hair and the tall, big-shouldered Raft King with his close-cropped hair.

But where was Pip?

A finger poked her in the side, hard. When Kinchen turned to glare, Caesar, otherwise motionless, gestured with her chin. "Just past them. Is that Pip?"

Kinchen had been looking for someone standing. But Pip was lying belly-down on the dock's edge with his head and arms in the water, only his hips and legs anchoring him on the dock itself. Kinchen was thrown back momentarily to the memory of Pip floating in the pond behind the governor's house. He lay just as still now (as far as she could see). This time, he wasn't performing an entertainment for the Raft King. He was doing some kind of underwater job, something he'd either been tricked or forced into.

"That's *IT*," Kinchen yelled at the Raft King's back. Caesar jumped in surprise next to her, but Kinchen didn't take time to explain. She needed to stop this madness right now, save Pip, and get him home. "My brother isn't working for you, you—*kidnapper*."

She darted forward, meaning to grab Pip's legs and haul him out of the water. She wouldn't let him help the Raft King, not after all the king had done to them.

But as she shoved past the men to get to Pip, one of the guards grabbed her, not violently but firmly. As he held her shoulders, she screamed, more in anger than in fear. Caesar yelled something; the Raft King's voice snapped out in reply; the guards spoke urgently.

And the old storyteller, above the din, bellowed one loud call. Everyone stopped, surprised, and in that moment of silence, Jupiter leaned both hands on his cane and said, "Kinchen, wait. Your brother isn't in danger. Let the boy finish his work."

"He's helping the Raft King—"

"That's right!" Caesar grabbed Jupiter's hand as if she were going to pull him somewhere. "The man who kidnapped me and stuffed me in a sack—which wasn't nice at all!" She glared at the king.

"He did what?" asked one of the guards. "Wait—*you* were the sack we dropped off on the Island?"

"He *stole Pip!*" Kinchen brought the conversation back to the most important topic. "I'm here to rescue him."

The Raft King scowled. "You're all—"

"Pip doesn't need rescuing," Jupiter said firmly. "He's got everything worked out."

"What do you mean?" Kinchen asked. How could Pip have things worked out? He could barely bring himself to talk to people.

"Wait and see," said Jupiter. "I think he's coming up."

Sure enough, Pip's hands reached up out of the water to grip the dock, his head and shoulders emerging as he scooted backward. On his knees, he sat now, heels to butt, and tossed his head back. From his hair the water flew backward in an arc, fountaining on the dock and spattering the closest guard, who jumped back. Pip rubbed his hands over his head, shaking more water out of his hair, and turned toward the guard, grinning. But when he saw more people on the dock, he froze, staring at them, his face suddenly blank.

Kinchen tilted her head so he could see the bleached stripe of hair.

"Kinchen!"

Pip's voice was happy, excited—but not relieved, which was what Kinchen had expected. "I came for you," she said. Her voice sounded almost whiny, even to herself.

Jupiter, meanwhile, hugged Caesar, slapping the back of her head gently. "Crazy person. Did you walk here?"

"Partway."

His eyes glinted. "That sounds like a story. But maybe there are other things to discuss first."

Pip rose and hugged Kinchen. Then he said to the king, "I'm going to tell you some of what the fish said. But not all of it. Because before that, we're going to talk."

PART FIVE

What the Raft King Thought.

IT MIGHT surprise you to know that while Pip was talking to the fish, his head underwater and his feet sprawled on the dock, the Raft King—standing with Jupiter and the two rowers—was not really thinking about Pip at all.

What the Raft King thought about was how he was Amelia's adopted son and how she loved him and named him Putnam. And how she deserted him. Though he'd been only five years old when she left, he could not forget that day. Nor could anyone who was there—or who had heard the story. A woman riding away on birds? Everyone remembered that.

But the other thing the Raft King pondered was a moment known only to him: a conversation he'd had with his father just before the old man had died. Putnam had asked, more than once over the years, what the fish had said the day Amelia left, when his father had dunked his head and talked with them. What were their exact words? He wanted to parse those words, to look for a clue as to what had happened to his mother and why she had left him. But the old Raft King refused to divulge the specifics. He told Putnam merely that Amelia was gone, irretrievably—and safe—and back in her own world. More than that he would not say.

Until one day, shortly before his death, when Putnam was well over thirty years old, the old man *did* say.

The old Raft King had always seemed impossibly ancient to Putnam—perhaps it was the gray head he acquired before Putnam was even born, or perhaps it was his wife's death at Putnam's birth that aged him, or maybe it was Amelia's disappearance that pressed on him. He had ruled Raftworld quietly, always asking the council for advice before making a decision and never rushing into roiled waters. He was at heart conservative, and the old ways carried weight with him. The old ways that he knew, that is: the ways of Raftworld and isolation and trading and traversing the second world and visiting the Islanders.

But shortly before he died, when the skin of his hands had turned ashy and his walking became a frail thing, he finally told his son what he thought had happened to Amelia—what the fish had told him.

"They said that Amelia's birds carried her into the heart of a storm, where there was something—a doorway—"

"A *doorway*?" The two men, father and son, walked the king's garden, the old man gripping his son's arm for support.

The old king waved his free hand dismissively. "Not a real one. Not like a wooden thing you open and shut. But something—something like Venus's. A gate, a window, something that had clicked open in the storm. And the birds took her through. The dolphins saw it; so did the sharks. A space that opened up but only for a short time.

I thought—" The old man gazed into the distance as if his rheumy eyes could make out the doorway.

"What did you think?" Putnam knew his father could easily drift into the daydreams of old age, and he wasn't going to let him. Not now that he was really talking.

"Ah. The fish told me—they said they could watch for another doorway. They said these openings occurred sometimes, mostly in storms—or sometimes in whirlpools. And when they found an opening, they could take me to it, if I wanted and if I hurried, and I could go through, too. Just me. Or all of us, all of Raftworld, whatever I wanted. I thought about it for a long time, my head stuck under the water like a crazy person. Do you remember?"

His son nodded, watching the birds flit through the oversized tomato plants. Yes, he remembered. The long moments, his father kneeling, head in the water, communing with the fish.

"And finally, I said no."

Putnam had known already, had known the moment his father said what the offer was the fish had made. But it was still a surprise to hear the words. "But—why not go?"

The old man shrugged. "It was Amelia's world she went back to. Not mine."

"How do you know that her world wasn't ours, too—the one we came from? She said there was an Africa there."

"But I never came from Africa. Venus and Swimmer did, almost two hundred years ago, with all those folks in the old story—they came through one of these same doorways, if that story is true." He sighed and looked down at his hands, now both clenching his son's arm. "Truth is, I was scared to go. I'm an old man. And as for making that decision for all of Raftworld? I didn't have the right. That kind of road, once taken, can't be retraced easily—if at all."

Putnam shook his head, half in disbelief and half in anger—and perhaps another half, if that were possible, in disgust. If he were king, he'd have made a different decision. He'd have *done* something. He'd have gone.

But that wasn't correct, he reminded himself afterward. He *wouldn't* have taken action, he *wouldn't* have gone, because he couldn't talk to the fish, and he would not have been given that choice. Even when he became king someday, he'd never have the chance to choose this path.

Unless. Unless he could find a way to talk to the fish. Or someone who could translate for him.

PART SIX

Where Everything Comes Together,
We Hope.

Summer 1978.
The Second World.

Pip's Story.

BUT FIRST: you are wondering, perhaps (I *hope* you are wondering) where Thanh is (and Sang and Mai and everyone from the little boat that burst apart in the maelstrom) and when he (and they) will meet up with Kinchen and Pip and Caesar. Because, of course, Thanh will meet up with them—otherwise why would he be in this story?

We will get to them soon.

WHEN PIP told the Raft King and the others about his conversation with the fish, he said the smaller fish had brought larger creatures—sharks and dolphins—to talk with him, and they had told him that there were indeed doorways to the first world that opened sometimes during storms. And yes, they knew how to find these doorways, which were tricky, as they opened and closed very quickly, snapping shut at a turn of the storm and moving on, only to flick open in a different location next time.

"There's more," Pip said slowly to the king. "But first we have to talk."

"You gave your word," Jupiter reminded the king.

"Keep your promise," said Caesar.

The king folded his arms across his wide chest. "Fine. Talk."

The guards tipped over a small rowboat that had been dragged onto the edge of the dock for repairs. Jupiter sat down on this makeshift bench, resting his cane against his knee. The king did not sit. Their raft rocked gently, and a seagull hopped on the little boats tied off it, looking for a crumb. The guards stepped back and politely pretended not to be listening.

"You can't drag everyone into the first world," Caesar said.

The two guards edged closer.

"You don't have the right to do that," she continued.

"I'm the king. Of course I have the right."

"The right to make such a big decision for all of us?" Jupiter asked mildly. He sounded as calm as if he were asking what time it was or if he might have a cup of tea.

"What's this about dragging us into the first world?" said the first guard.

"You have no idea what you're talking about," the king said to Caesar and Jupiter and the others. "I'm going to solve all Raftworld's problems. Overcrowding? Fixed. We're going to actually *find* Africa—instead of just looking for it as we've done all these years. And we'll live there."

"We've been looking for Africa?" asked the first guard. "I mean, I know it's the *story*, but . . ."

"I thought it was a metaphor," said the second guard. "It's real?" He sounded excited.

"It can be a metaphor and also be real," Jupiter said. "And we *are* overcrowded." He looked up at the king from his seat on the overturned boat. "You could take your idea to the people—ask them what they want. And as a people, we could consider this solution." He added, gently, "That *is* your job as Raft King, after all—to help the people make big decisions."

"But the people might not agree with me," said the king. (Caesar nodded vehemently.)

"They don't know what's best for them," the Raft King said.

"People need to choose for themselves." It was the first chance Pip had to squeeze in his words. Everyone else was so quick to talk. He said it again, louder. "People need to choose for themselves."

Everyone stared at him, a sea of faces that all looked the same—and all confused. Pip focused on Kinchen—*white hair stripe*—and forced himself to keep talking.

"What I mean to say is that people need to live their own lives and make their own choices. Even if they make the wrong choice or they aren't as good at living their lives as *you* would be at living their lives." Pip stopped, scared. He wasn't a good speaker. He'd never talked to a group of people like this before, and he was worried he'd said something silly—or something they would misunderstand. But there was more. "One thing I like about being here—I mean, I like Tathenn, too—but one thing I love about here is that I get to make my own decisions. Even if they're wrong. I like it. And I don't recognize everyone, but I can tell people that—like I did with Jupiter—and it will be okay." He was talking only to Kinchen now, willing her to understand. Things had to be different from now on, and she had to know that.

Kinchen blinked rapidly, several times, like she had to clear dust from her eyes. Then she nodded. "I'm sorry," she said in a low voice. "I've done everything wrong."

"No! You're a great sister. I missed you horribly. And Old Ren. And—home. But I want to live differently than we did. I don't want to hide from people." He took a deep breath. "I want to learn how to talk to people and understand them better. And I want to talk to more fish. They have pretty good ideas sometimes." He grinned, suddenly happy. "I want to travel and meet sea creatures all over the world. I've already made a good start."

"Not much yet," the Raft King said. "You Islanders need to take more trips."

"Maybe you can help him with that," Jupiter said.

"So you'll agree not to drag everyone through the door-way with you?" Caesar asked.

The Raft King lowered his head. "I'll take it to a vote. As Jupiter suggested."

There was a pause as everyone thought about a vote and what that might mean. Caesar started bouncing, face screwed up in thought. Kinchen frowned as if trying to think of some way a vote might be a bad thing.

"That will be good," said Jupiter.

Pip agreed. And now, he thought, he could tell the rest of the news. "The fish said more. They said that there's a door stuck open. Right now."

The Raft King sucked in his breath loudly. Caesar stopped bouncing.

"Not stuck open." He paused, trying to think of the best way to explain. "*Held* open."

"Held open by what?" asked Kinchen.

"The fish said—they said there's a sea monster sitting in the doorway."

For the first time, Jupiter looked surprised.

Caesar gasped. "*Another* monster?"

The Raft King clapped his hands. "That's perfect. An open doorway. We can go back and forth as much as we want." He stopped and thought. "As long as the monster isn't vicious. And stays in the doorway. Or maybe we can find a way to prop the door open."

Jupiter was already shaking his head. "The two worlds are separate for a reason. A door shouldn't be kept open between them. It's not natural."

"What do you mean, not natural? People have gone between the two worlds before." The Raft King swelled to fill his cape.

"Yes, but it's always been a one-way trip."

"Not for Amelia."

Jupiter said, "A fluke. Not something to be tried lightly."

"If a magic door is held open, it's not magic anymore,"

Pip said. When Jupiter nodded at him, he continued. "If the door is open and it shouldn't be, then we should try to close it. I think I could talk to the monster and ask it to shut the door—I've talked to sea monsters before. Well, one sea monster," he amended. *This might even be the one I'm looking for. Her.*

"Close it *after* I go through," said the Raft King. "Because I am going through." He cut his hand at Caesar in a don't-talk gesture, then turned to Jupiter. "I'll take my idea to the people—and I won't take Raftworld with me if they don't want to go. But I'm going through no matter what. I'll find Amelia and Africa."

Jupiter studied the king for a moment, then nodded. "That's fair. I'll call for a meeting. And I'll tell the people what happened here and what we talked about. I'll tell it fairly. And people can decide if they want to come with you or not." He bowed his head to the king. "Will that be acceptable?"

"I suppose," said the king.

A DAY and a half floated slowly by, water without current, while they waited for all the people to hear the news and vote on what they wanted to do. Meanwhile, Caesar and Kinchen rested, and all three of the children told their stories to one another. Pip was pleased to hear that his old friend the Kraken had helped Caesar and Kinchen reach Raftworld; Kinchen was less pleased to hear that Pip had been good friends with the Kraken and she'd never known about it.

"What other secrets do you have?" she said in a grumpy tone. They sat in Jupiter's house, where they were all temporarily staying, even though it was crowded. Now, they were sitting cozily on floor cushions. Caesar ate green bread by the slice, while Kinchen and Pip leaned back against the wall.

Pip shrugged, not sure how to answer. "It wasn't a secret. It was just something I hadn't told you. I thought—" He stopped, uncertain how to proceed.

"Thought what?"

"That you weren't interested in underwater stuff."

"Or maybe he thought you'd feel bad," Caesar said with her mouth half full. "Because you don't have the same gift. That's how my adopted family was—they didn't like me going out walking, because they couldn't walk. They were jealous."

"You think I'm jealous? You both think I'm jealous?" Kinchen sat forward, angry.

Caesar stopped chewing, swallowed, coughed several times, and then said, "No, of course not."

Pip stared.

"I'm not jealous!" Kinchen said. She slapped her hand on the table.

"No," Pip agreed slowly. "You're not. I never thought so. But you are left out sometimes. Me and Ren, and now Caesar. You feel left out. And I'm sorry about that."

Kinchen looked away from them. "Pass the bread." She carefully cut a slice and ate it. No one spoke. Finally she said, "Maybe a little. Maybe a little left out."

Pip scooted close and put his arm around her shoulder. "You are the best big sister," he said. "I mean it. The best big sister I've ever had."

She stuck out her tongue at him. It was greenish.

Caesar laughed and took back the loaf.

MEANWHILE, JUPITER retold the story of what had happened many times, to many different groups of Raftworlders. And the outcome of it all was that the people decided not to go with the king into the first world. It was a hard decision—many people wanted to go, to travel someplace entirely new, to embark on a grand adventure; and most people wanted to visit the land their ancestors had come from. But a one-way trip, with no return? Jupiter made it clear that the doorway would shut once they went through it. Eventually, everyone decided to stay. Every person. After two hundred years, the second world was their home, they told Jupiter. They loved it here, even overcrowded, and they were sure they could find a solution that didn't involve permanently leaving.

Jupiter reported back to the Raft King. The king didn't believe Jupiter, so he went to talk to some of the people himself. And he got the same answers. "I'll talk to everyone one more time," he told Jupiter, "when we find the doorway, and it's time for me to go through. I'll see if anyone changes their mind then."

Jupiter nodded.

Pip could see that the Raft King still believed people would choose to go with him through the doorway. And maybe some would—but Pip could see that Jupiter doubted it.

He was worried, though. What if he, Pip, found out where the doorway was, revealed its location to the Raft King, and the Raft King took them all through it anyway? Pip told Jupiter his fear that evening as the two of them walked home from their meeting with the king. No guards followed them, as Pip was no longer a prisoner.

"He could *try* to take everyone through," said Jupiter, pushing a broken branch out of the path with his cane. "But the guards and rowers don't want to go. And the rowers run the hydraulics. So . . . unless the king can run all four engines on his own, it won't happen."

"The rowers will disobey him if he tells them to take Raftworld through the doorway?"

"Of course. We *voted*." Jupiter stopped in the narrow path to face Pip. "The king only rules because the people let him. That's how it works." They resumed walking. "I think it's safe to tell him how to get to the doorway."

The next morning, Pip put his head under the water and got directions from the fish. The rowers clicked on the hydraulic engines, turned Raftworld, and headed for the stuck-open doorway—and the sea monster that was holding it open.

2

What They All Saw.

BUT THE NEXT AFTERNOON, when Raftworld drew close to the stuck-open doorway, they saw something very strange indeed. A group of people, six of them, maybe a family: two men—one injured—and three younger people, one carrying a baby on his hip. All holding hands, or arms around shoulders. Walking on the water.

Walking like angels—like refugees, like survivors, like miracles given bodies. Walking on the water.

3

Kinchen's Story.

KINCHEN SQUINTED to see better. In the family that walked on the water, the skinniest boy—or maybe a girl? with a bloodstained bandage on her head—held the hands of one boy and one man. The other man, short and stocky, a bandage around his ribs, walked with his arms slung over the lean man and the sturdiest boy—the one carrying the baby. The boy with the baby and the other boy, the shortest, on opposite ends of the line and with free hands, waved.

At the king's command, the Raft's engines slowed and stopped. No one spoke. They'd never seen such people before.

When the family was close enough, Kinchen could see their pinched faces lit with joy and, behind the joy, exhaustion. The tall, lean man called loudly but not in a language Kinchen could understand. The sturdy boy translated in heavily accented English. "Please help us."

Caesar jumped up and down, calling, "Of course! Come over! Hello! Welcome!" The family stepped aboard the raft and collapsed, all of them, on the dock, Raftworlders talking and running errands and bringing food and blankets and fetching the doctor.

"How did you *do* that?" Caesar asked the boys a few minutes later, as she and Kinchen dished up bread and stew for the wanderers. "Walk on the water? Which of you has the magic?"

The shorter boy pointed at the bigger one, who had raggedy short hair and a bright red shirt and who shrugged as if to say, *It was nothing.*

Jupiter knelt in front of the baby—really a toddler—with a soft inner slice of bread.

"What's wrong with the baby's foot?" asked Kinchen. It was twisted inward in a half circle.

She realized immediately she'd asked a rude question, but the smaller boy answered anyway. "She was born that way. We were hoping she'd have an operation to fix it, but . . ." He shook his head. "She's called Turtle." There was surely more to the story, but the boy sounded too tired to say more.

Jupiter cleared his throat. "Why don't you younger three and the baby all come with me to my cabin? The older folks will be a while over your injured man."

"Will he—be okay?" asked the bigger boy. "I'll stay with him." His English was musical and harder to understand than the shorter boy's.

"He'll be fine, I think. The doctor says it's a clean cut and will fix him up. The other gentleman—"

"Uncle Truc," said the smaller boy. "The injured one is Uncle Hung. They're brothers."

"Well, your uncle Truc will stay with his brother. We'll eat and rest, and when we return, Hung will be all stitched up and ready for you to visit." Jupiter squinted at the boys.

"Let's get you out of the sun for a bit. And sitting on some cushions. And make you some tea."

"Hold on a minute," said the Raft King. "Hold on. I have a couple of questions before you go."

"Questions can maybe wait," said Jupiter.

"No," said the Raft King. "Details can wait. These questions are quick, and they can't wait. I mean to say: *I* can't wait." He turned to the uninjured man, the man called Uncle Truc, and bowed in greeting. "I need to know if you're from Amelia's world. Do you know Amelia?"

The tall, lean man shook his head, holding out both hands, and the smaller of the two boys answered instead. "Uncle Truc doesn't speak English. But I'm pretty sure he doesn't know anyone named Amelia. I mean, our world is a big place. There are probably lots of Amelias. I'm not sure we're from the world you're looking for anyway. But we're definitely not from here."

The bigger boy nodded, bristly hair standing straight up on his head. "Different water." He mimed drinking and looked like he wanted to say more but wasn't sure of the words.

"This world I'm asking about," said the Raft King, "is the first world. The one with Africa in it. The one with Amelia in it."

"We do have an Africa in our world," said the smaller boy cautiously.

The Raft King jolted, as if he'd hoped for this answer but not expected it.

But Caesar clapped her hands to her face. "Then you *are* from the first world! That's wonderful! Our king wants to go there."

The boy said, "We're not from anywhere near Africa, though." He paused. "You know it's a whole continent, right?"

"Do you know Amelia?" the Raft King asked again. He shifted his robe back on his shoulders to gesture at the sky. "She could fly. Here, she was carried by birds, but in your world she flew inside a big engine. She was paler than you, with red hair, and she flew a machine in the clouds. She was my adopted mother. From your world. She went back there when I was a boy, and we never saw her again. She was famous. She was the first woman to fly around your world. Or she would have been, if—"

But the boy jerked to his feet, his face slack with surprise. "Amelia?" he said in a foggy voice. "*Amelia Earhart?*"

4

Thanh's Story.

THANH'S FATHER had told him about Amelia Earhart—and
he'd later studied her story in one of his dad's books. She was
the famous red-headed woman pilot, an American, who'd
tried to fly around the world. She and her copilot had disappeared over the Pacific Ocean—forty years ago—and had
never been seen again. They were dead. They were dead.

Before telling about Amelia, Thanh asked what the king's
story was. He listened to the old man, Jupiter, retell how
Amelia had arrived by accident, in a storm, how she adopted
the king when he was a baby and lived on Raftworld, and
how she finally departed one day in a flurry of feathers. She
must have come over to this world, he thought, when she
disappeared from her own; and when she left Raftworld to
return home . . . she didn't make it. She must have died in
crossing back—or just after crossing back.

Carefully, with concern for this purple-caped man who
had known and loved Amelia when he was a child, this man
who'd been Amelia's adopted son, and remembering his own
parents' deaths, Thanh told his story. He told the tale well—
remembering and telling was his talent—and he felt his gift

keenly here, as if what he was doing were actually important and worthwhile. He was giving an answer to someone who longed for one. It wasn't the answer the man wanted—the Raft King's adopted mother was dead, she'd never made it back to the first world—but it was an answer nonetheless and the knowledge would provide some small amount of comfort.

When he finished talking he sat back on the floor and bowed his head at the broad-chested, purple-caped man. "I'm very sorry, mister," he said.

"Putnam," said the man. He seemed lost in thought. "Call me Putnam."

Putnam? Thanh sat up straighter. He knew something. There was a little more to the story. "She named you," he said, and the man, startled, nodded. "She named you after her husband in our world. Putnam. She named you after someone she loved and missed."

The man stepped back. "I did not know that." He cleared his throat. "What—what was he like? This Putnam?"

Thanh didn't know, except that he was Amelia's husband and very rich. And also: "He was a publisher." The man looked confused, so he added, "He made books. Stories."

"She did love stories," said Putnam.

"And you," said Thanh. "Definitely *and you.*"

AFTER PUTNAM bowed his thank-you to Thanh and walked unsteadily off alone, the old black man with the white hair made a second offer of tea and shade and cushions. Thanh felt his little pool of energy—the nugget that had kept him walking for hours with no land in sight—he felt it swoosh out of his body. He didn't think he could walk as far as anyone's cabin.

But this old, old man held out his hand and smiled, and when Thanh grasped it, he felt he could travel a little farther. "This way," said the man. "I'm glad to see you speak English."

"I studied it," said Thanh. "So did the girls, but not as much as I did."

"The girls?" The old man's eyebrows rose, and then his face cleared. "You must have different hair customs than we do. I thought that one was a boy." He tipped his head back toward Mai.

Just behind them, Mai drawled, in Vietnamese, "I'm a success!"

"She was trying to disguise herself as a boy," explained Thanh. "She's happy to hear that she fooled you." He paused as they negotiated some children's toys spread over the path. "My older sister was disguised as a boy, too."

"That one?" asked the old man, glancing back to Sang, who was now carrying The Turtle. "That one was less successful."

Thanh looked back. Sang was wearing her own shirt again—the man's shirt having been torn into ribbons to make bandages for Hung. Her hair, raggedly cut and longer than Mai's, lay flattened against her head. But under the bandage and the dried blood and the grime, her face was delicate, and her long lashes drooped on her cheek as she whispered to the baby. Their mother's necklace glittered around her throat. "We're done pretending now, I think," said Thanh.

They entered the old man's cabin, and he fed them some fresh strawberries and green-tinted bread—*but don't eat too much*, he warned them, *or you'll be sick*—and they drank tea and sat on cushions. The Turtle stood on her good leg, hitched herself onto the padded bench, and promptly fell asleep, sucking her thumb.

Three kids about Thanh's age had followed them into the house. They sat against the wall, watching. Two kids looked like siblings (one boy, one girl—the girl with a bright white stripe in her hair, the boy small with huge, unblinking eyes), and one girl was darker-skinned like Putnam and the old man—with dozens of long braids down her back. She seemed to be made of movement, twitching and tapping her leg. No one spoke for several moments as Thanh, Sang, and Mai ate.

Then the old man asked their names and introduced himself as Jupiter—which Thanh had already heard. "That's a name in our world, too," said Thanh. "There's a lot of stories about Jupiter."

The old man grinned. "I don't doubt it. And I'd love to hear about them later. And to hear how you received your training."

"Training?"

"As a storyteller," Jupiter said. "It's clear you've studied under a master. Are you apprenticing to be a storyteller for your country?"

Thanh shook his head. "I don't know what you mean.

We don't have storytellers. I mean, stories aren't important enough for someone to be an apprentice—to study them . . ." The girl with the long braids was violently shaking her head at him and drawing a line across her throat—the universal shut-up sign.

Jupiter watched him closely, smiling a little. "We'll talk more about it later. I may . . ." He trailed off, staring into space, his face suddenly lighting up as if an enormous idea had just occurred to him. "Huh. I may have some work for you here." He grasped his cane, his hand shaking. "Meanwhile, *I* have work to do." To the braided girl and her companions he said, "I'll tell people about the arrival of these sea-walking folks. Why don't you all rest here? I predict a feast tonight, and you'll want some sleep before that."

After he left, Thanh and Sang and Mai looked at one another. Thanh could see that Sang was on the verge of tears. Everything was so new, and their old world was so far away. And they were all so tired.

The braided girl scooted her cushion closer to them. She introduced herself and her companions: Caesar, Kinchen, Pip. "Caesar's a boy's name," Thanh said—and then realized he'd been rude.

But Caesar didn't seem to mind. "Used to be, when a boy had it. But now I have it, it's a girl name. Don't you think?"

Thanh nodded. And he introduced himself and his companions: Sang, Mai, and of course The Turtle, asleep. They ate and drank some more; then Mai folded herself into a mound on the floor and began snoring.

"She's been worried about Uncle Hung," said Thanh. "And she's done all kinds of work to save us. She's the one who got us here." He told them briefly what had happened, which meant talking about the war in Vietnam and about his mother's and, later, his father's deaths, and so many other things as well. (Trying to make himself sound good, he skipped over the parts where he messed up, got kicked out of school, and lost his temper on the boat.) Caesar and Kinchen asked questions. Pip mostly listened, watching with his big eyes as if trying to memorize Thanh's face. When Thanh got to the part about Mai walking on the water—a gift she'd had only an echo of in their world, valuable as that echo was— Caesar nodded as if she understood.

"That makes sense," she said.

Sang poked Thanh and motioned. Her English was poor, and she was embarrassed to ask the question herself. But he knew what she wanted to know.

"The thing is," Thanh said, "can we get back? To our world, I mean?"

Caesar tilted her head to the side, her braids swinging. "You want to go back to that war place?"

"It's not just a war place. It's our home. And Uncle Truc and Uncle Hung—they have wives and children back there."

Sang nodded. "Yes, home."

The three Raft children looked at one another for a long moment. Finally the one with the white hair stripe, Kinchen, said, "Normally the answer would be that you can't go back. For a long time everyone thought there was no way back. But the fish just said today that the door is stuck open." She shook her head. "I'm not telling this right."

"The fish?" said Thanh, feeling stupid.

"Door?" said Sang.

Mai snored and turned over on her cushion.

Haltingly, Kinchen, Caesar, and Pip told Thanh and Sang about the doorway and about how they were trying to find it. "So that we can close it," said Caesar firmly. "The Raft King—that's Putnam to you—says he wants to go through to your world. And you all can go through, too. But after that, we're going to get that monster to move and we're going to shut the door."

"Somehow," Kinchen added, as if admitting that making a sea monster move sounded like a crazy idea.

"Jupiter says that leaving a door like that open is a bad idea," said Kinchen. "And he's right. I've been thinking about it. What if your pirates came through?"

"And even though the second world is huge," Caesar said, "it's mostly water. There aren't any islands big enough for a country—except theirs." She jerked a thumb at Kinchen and Pip. "That's why our country is a raft. And we're overcrowded."

"We can handle a few people coming over once in a while," Kinchen added, "but we can't have all your people heading here every time you have a problem over there. There isn't room for all of them."

"But mainly," Pip said, "it's a magic door. Magic doors shouldn't be propped open."

Sang nodded, able to understand more than she could say. "Beautiful door." She swooshed her hands up and down to show how it went from the ocean floor to the sky.

Looking around the cozy cabin, Thanh thought how many people might come here if they could cross back and forth easily, whenever they wanted. This place seemed like a good world: a lot less packed than his (even Raftworld's crowdedness didn't seem bad to him compared to stories he'd heard about Saigon—or pictures he'd seen of New York or other busy cities in his world). And peaceful. And here there was sweet water. How long they could have lived in their little boat if it had floated on sweet water!

Without an open doorway they would have died.

As if she'd read his mind, Sang said in Vietnamese, "If the doorway stays open, how long until some rich, important country or company finds it—and goes through—and takes everything in sight? How long before they come here and try to conquer everyone? Start a war?" Her voice was reasonable, but her words had bite. "We got lucky."

Lucky because a doorway cracked open. A magic door that only unsealed in rare instances, with storms and desperation. "I see what you mean," Thanh said.

When Mai and the baby woke up—at almost the same time—they all scrounged up some more bread and ate again. Then they walked to the hospital building and found Uncle Hung reclining on a bed, propped with pillows, a clean white bandage around his side. Uncle Truc lay in the bed next to him, snoring almost as loud as Mai had been snoring earlier.

"I'm getting better," Uncle Hung said, smiling. And suddenly everyone felt just fine.

Before the dinner that night the old man, Jupiter, asked Thanh, since his English was best of the group, to tell the story of how they arrived. Thanh thought for a moment about what to say. He could remake his whole history—be a hero, or at least be as brave and hardworking as Mai. Then he shook himself. What was he thinking? The story was the important thing; what he wanted was simply to tell it truthfully, to help everyone understand who he and his people were and where they were from.

He stood at his table and faced the Raft King and all the people. And he told them—he told them the truth. He told about Vietnam—how beautiful the river was in the evening, how the rice smelled in the fields, how the buffalo shook their shoulders when the flies were thick, how the rain fell in monsoon season—he told it all. Then he told about leaving this wonderful home, starting with the war itself and moving to his mother's death and then his father's, and from there to his and Sang's life afterward, with some focus on how he'd been kicked out of school and how bad he was at rice farming. He told of their escape and how he forgot the food and knife and clothing. He told of the trials at sea and how he lost his temper and how Uncle Truc forgave him. He told of how Mai was a natural sailor and he a poor one, and how they eventually became friends. And finally he told of their salvation through the open doorway. He told everything about their trip: how he failed, what he feared, what it all felt like. He told, in other words, the story you read earlier, even the parts that made him look bad.

"This world," he said to the people. "You call it the second world. But second isn't less than first. This world isn't an exile. Some of my people want to go back because they have wives and children waiting for them. If they didn't, they might want to stay here, where they've drunk sweet water and escaped death and received the hospitality of others who arrived so long ago. This is a place for starting over. A good place."

After a moment of silence, Caesar whooped, and then everyone clapped and cheered. When Thanh sat down, Jupiter spoke to him in a quiet but firm voice. "Son. Our world needs a storyteller when I'm gone; and we don't have anyone with that gift. I'm asking you to consider it. Be my apprentice. Then, someday, be our storyteller."

"But—I'm so scatterbrained," Thanh said, surprised. "And I forgot all the supplies when we left our village. And I yelled at Uncle Truc. And I'm a terrible sailor. Did you not hear those parts of the story?"

"None of that matters for this job," said Jupiter. "You tell the truth. And on top of that, I like you. Think about"—he leaned forward—"becoming my adopted grandson *and* my apprentice. I'd adopt your sister, too. She'd like it here. We'd find a job for her—a place for her to fit in." He paused. "I never really wanted to be a father—I was too busy all the time—but I have long wanted to be a grandfather."

Thanh was stunned. Someone *wanted* him? And had a job for him to do—something he'd be good at? He couldn't think how to reply. "Sang—she wants to be an artist."

"She could certainly try that out. You think about what I said." Jupiter squeezed Thanh's shoulder, heaved himself to standing, and hobbled away.

"Did he say what I think he said?" asked Sang in Vietnamese. "Did he just invite you to live here forever?"

"You, too," said Thanh.

"What does *apprentice* mean?" She stumbled over the English word. When he explained, she studied his face. "Do you want to stay?"

He shrugged. Several people came up to introduce themselves and compliment the storytelling, and the moment was lost. But he kept the question in his heart. What might it be like to stay here? And to be good—really good—at something useful? And would Sang want to stay?

And what about Mai?

AFTER THE STORYTELLING, the people took one more vote, at the Raft King's request, on the issue of the moving back to the first world. Like the first time, everyone voted to stay in the second world, their home.

Mai went out walking on the water for hours—"practicing," she said, glowing, when Thanh asked her what she was up to.

At the dinner, Jupiter made public his desire to adopt Thanh as his apprentice and grandson—and to adopt Sang as well. He told the people at the table that he'd offered Thanh an apprenticeship, to be the next Raftworld storyteller.

Thanh sat silent, not sure how to respond yet, while

people around the table congratulated him and Jupiter and told Thanh how wonderful life was in their world.

Sang, who'd been chatting with the young woman next to her all evening, their heads bent over the table as if they were studying together, looked up at her little brother with bright, lantern-lit eyes. She'd understood what Jupiter said, and she leaned forward to speak to Thanh in Vietnamese.

"We should stay." Sang pointed at Jupiter with a pencil she'd picked up somewhere. "I asked him earlier today if there were people here who did fancy sewing. And painting. And he said yes." Sang gestured to the young woman seated next to her, the one she'd been murmuring with. "Jupiter introduced me to Chika. She's an artist." Suddenly Thanh realized that the two girls hadn't only been chatting all evening. On the table between them was an open notebook, with pages of shiny paper that looked like they might be waterproof. Small illustrations dotted the pages, some of them in Sang's intricate style, and some in a bold, spare sketching that must be Chika's.

"You've been drawing."

She nodded. "Chika said she's never seen pictures like mine. She wants to know how to make them. And I'm going to learn from her. Thanh," she said, her eyes shining, "we have a future here. Both of us."

Thanh turned to Jupiter and spoke in English. "I think we'll stay."

5

Putnam's Story.

As THEY ATE their late dinner that evening, all in a festive group, Putnam sat to the side quietly. He didn't eat. He listened and thought.

After hearing the boy Thanh's story, and after asking him about his world and finding out they would probably not be given Africa—or even a part of it—for their own, the Raftworlders had taken a formal vote, finalizing their wishes. And—not astonishingly—they did not want to go to the first world.

Putnam wasn't surprised; he could see which way the current moved. But he didn't know what to do. And he didn't know what to think. He was an adult, but he felt like a child yet again, like a part of him would always be a child, stuck in the day that his mother left. Amelia would never be back. She was gone forever—a possibility that he'd never, ever believed. She had seemed like someone who couldn't ever die. In his mind's eye her hair still flamed, and her lean, strong body vibrated with life.

She had not broken her promise. She had died.

• • •

Putnam, lost in his thoughts, sailed back to the present just in time to hear Thanh agree to stay and become Raftworld's next storyteller. He smiled and nodded—truly happy that Jupiter's apprentice problem was solved, and happy to think that Thanh and Sang—nice kids, both—would be joining Raftworld. Not that any of this would solve the overcrowding problems.

Jupiter was speaking to Sang and Thanh. "You both have gifts," he said. "But even if you didn't, you'd be welcome here. You'd find your calling eventually."

Next to Putnam, the Island girl Kinchen lifted her chin, a light in her eyes, as if this meant something to her. Putnam felt his own mouth tighten. He didn't have a *calling* to be king if he couldn't even lead his people home. He wasn't much of a leader.

The older man, Hung, stood up, hand on his bandaged side for support, and cleared his throat several times until everyone looked at him. He said something in his own language, indicating Mai. Putnam turned to Thanh, who translated. "This child," Thanh interpreted, "Mai, is gifted at everything. And she has magic in this world. Strong magic."

Mai lowered her eyes.

"This should be her world. She should stay here, too." Thanh's face lit up as he translated.

Mai looked at her uncle, and her face brightened, slowly, until Putnam thought her skin was glowing. She ran both hands through her short hair, which spiked out from her head, and spoke in English. "*Yes.* I love this world." Then she turned to the stocky older man, speaking in her own language again. Even without knowing Vietnamese, Putnam knew what she was asking her uncle. "But—what about you?"

Hung shook his head and answered in a gentle voice. Thanh translated, but Putnam understood the main point even without his help. "I can't tell you how much I'll miss you. But I need to go back. And so does Truc. We need to reach land in the other world—so that we can save our families someday. Get them to safety."

Holding his toddler in his lap, Truc nodded. "Same for me—in how much I'll miss you and Sang," he said to Thanh. "But my wife is waiting for me, and it sounds like this is our only chance to go through this doorway. Yes?" he asked Jupiter.

At Thanh's translation, Jupiter nodded.

"But this girl should stay here," said Hung. Turning to Mai, he added, "It's not sure we'll make it to land over there. And if we do, it's a refugee camp for years, and then maybe, if we're lucky, a move to a new country. But here you're already in your new country. Your home. You've bypassed the camp. You'll have a good life here. And magic. And you'll be with Thanh and Sang."

Hearing Thanh's translation, Putnam thought, *Here you are already in your new country. Your home.*

Then he realized Jupiter was looking at him, Putnam, as if he were someone in charge, as if he were expected to say something. He cleared his throat. "You are all welcome here. Anyone who chooses to stay."

No one except Jupiter seemed to hear Putnam speak, and Putnam realized his words, right at this moment, weren't important. He could say them again later, when people wanted to listen to him. Jupiter gave him one quick, almost-fatherly nod and then both men turned back to Mai and Hung.

Mai stared at her uncle. She stood up, making them almost the same height—the tall girl and the short, stocky man.

"You'll miss us," Hung said a little gruffly, "and we'll miss you. But I think this will be best—the best life for you. So you should take it. I need to go back—and Truc, too."

Truc added, in a low voice to Sang and Thanh, "We've talked this over, Hung and me. My heart breaks to leave you two, my almost children. But your lives will be better here. You—you should stay." He rose, picked up the toddler, cradling her bent foot, and walked off into the night, away from the feast. Sang followed him. Thanh took a few steps, then turned back and sat down between Putnam and Jupiter. "I'll stay in case you need translating," he muttered. Putnam nodded, grateful. Jupiter gripped the boy's knee.

Hung spoke to Mai. "It's best if you stay." In his tough, wide face, his eyes shone with tears.

Mai nodded. "I know. It feels right. But—I'm going to miss you." And her face, always so clear and calm, crumpled.

Hung put his arm around her in a sideways hug and pulled her head toward his shoulder. They walked off a little way, murmuring.

Thanh left, following after Sang and Truc and the baby.

Putnam pondered it all. The two men and the toddler were going to go back. But Raftworld would not follow.

Someone asked Jupiter what they'd do now—now that they weren't going back. Jupiter glanced at Putnam, who shook his head. He didn't know. He didn't know.

"We learned to live on a giant raft—our ancestors *built* this raft," said Jupiter. "We'll figure something out again, and adapt again. We can do it." His glance flicked again to the Raft King; but Putnam did not answer.

He was still thinking.

He could go to the first world, of course, by himself. He could depart with the other travelers—Truc and Hung and the toddler. They'd probably welcome his company and his help on the voyage. He was a good sailor, after all.

But the problem was, he wouldn't find Amelia there. And he wouldn't be leading his people home.

And he could never come back.

Putnam hadn't spoken after the formal vote was tallied; he had simply nodded. And he didn't say anything now, either; he just continued to nod as people talked around him. After dinner, he walked away from the lantern light to think, still nodding.

The hydraulics chugged, and Raftworld moved closer to the open door, following a trail of bright dolphins through the moonlit night.

6

Caesar's Story.

JUST AS the sun rose bright and clear the next day, the dolphins stopped leading Raftworld and simply began circling. Raftworld's hydraulics stopped pumping and the nation stopped, people gathering on the dock and even setting out in little rowboats to try to see the doorway.

They were still some distance off. But on the horizon, if you squinted, you could see something. Beyond where the dolphins congregated and occasionally leapt, a patch of sky hung down like a strip of curtain that wasn't *quite* the right color or texture. And if you threw back your head with your mouth open (which Caesar did, several times, braids dangling down her back), you could taste something in the air that was not exactly fresh, but saltier, with a tang of tin.

Mai went out walking on the water again, by herself—"I want to understand how it works," she explained to Caesar.

"How the gift works?"

"Yes." She seemed serious, almost solemn.

Everything about this doorway breathed of excitement—but what Caesar wanted was home. A real just-for-herself home. It was why she'd left Raftworld in the first place. She thought of the couple with the baskets and what they'd offered. Maybe . . .

"I'm not happy about this plan." Kinchen suddenly stood next to her, hands on hips. "You and Pip and—a monster."

"Right. The monster." Caesar bounced on the balls of her feet. Bouncing made people think you weren't worried. "We already agreed."

"I know."

They had talked it over with Jupiter, deciding finally that Caesar and Pip would descend together. Though each could survive underwater, they couldn't meet with the monster without the other's help. Caesar would anchor Pip to the ocean's bottom, and Pip would talk with the creature.

"I *know*," Kinchen repeated. She had argument written on her face.

"And we think the monster might be the same one who saved Thanh and everyone with him. Probably is. And might even be *her*—"

"I know, but what if it isn't? Or what if it *is* her—and she's not happy to see us? We don't know what she's like."

Caesar had thought of all these things already. She was the one going down to meet the creature, after all, along with Pip. "Then we'll charm her with our good looks!" She bounced higher, to keep the anxiety from showing in her face. "Pip will be fine—I'll make sure of it."

"I'm worried about you both." Kinchen put a slight emphasis on the last word.

Caesar bounced a last bounce, surprised. No one had ever said they were worried about her before. Without a parent or grandparent or brother or sister—like Kinchen had, like Pip and Thanh had—she had no one who'd be sad if something bad happened to her. On Raftworld after her mom died, she'd lived with a family who'd fed her and clothed her but never let her feel like she belonged. She hadn't visited them since she got back—and they hadn't visited her. But now there was the couple with the apples, and Jupiter hugging her when he saw her; and now, suddenly, Kinchen was concerned about her. Her throat felt funny.

"Pip and I will be great." To her ears, her voice sounded a little thin. She tried to be jaunty—usually that made her feel better. "No worries. I've handled monsters before." Which was, strictly speaking, true, because she'd ridden a monster to Raftworld only a few days ago. Of course, there was the possibility that this was an entirely different kind of monster.

"I'm coming with you," Kinchen said firmly, as if arriving at a decision. "More people is better if you're meeting a monster. I think."

Caesar could tell that Kinchen wasn't going to take no for an answer. She decided she liked that in a person. Grinning, she said, "That'll be fantastic."

Pip, when informed of this decision a few minutes later, was less gracious—he seemed to think that Kinchen wanted to boss him around and protect him, and he didn't think he needed either of those things. But when Caesar insisted, he finally agreed.

And then Thanh announced that he'd come, too.

"I'm going to live here," he said as the group sprawled in the warm sun on the dock. Raftworld floated peacefully, the otherworldly patch of sky perched on the horizon in front of them. "And if I'm going to become a storyteller like Jupiter, then I should show up, if I can, for the big stories. Don't you think?" Caesar and Pip and Kinchen had to admit he had a point.

Jupiter, reclining on a bench nearby, waved one hand in the air, gesturing toward the doorway. "I'm a little old for this trip," he said. "But Thanh should go. And tell us all about it when you return."

"We're just going down to chat," said Caesar. "An exploratory mission. Figure out what this thing is, and then come back and report. Preferably not get eaten," she added under her breath.

Pip said, "Most monsters are friendly. At least, that's what the Kraken back home told me."

Hung, sitting on an overturned rowboat next to Mai, spoke—Thanh translating—"We'll say good-bye when you return. Me and Truc and The Turtle and the Raft King."

They looked around. Truc and his daughter and Sang were playing farther down the dock with a wooden doll someone had given The Turtle. The Raft King was nowhere to be seen.

"Sang? Mai?" Thanh called. "Want to come down with us? This will be your world, too, you know."

But Sang laughed. "No thanks," she said. "I'll stay up top."

"Mai?" Thanh grinned at her. "Want to see the monsters in your new world?"

Mai shook her head. "I can't sink. Remember?" But there was something more she wasn't saying. She had a look on her sturdy face that made Caesar wonder what was wrong.

7

Kinchen's Story.

HOLDING HANDS, the four dropped into the water. As before, Kinchen held her breath for as long as she could; once again she came to accept that she didn't need to breathe. She opened her eyes, stopped thinking about how her chest wasn't expanding, and looked around. Thanh, on Caesar's other hand, and Pip, on Kinchen's other hand, were already gazing around them, heads moving in slow circles as they tried to see all they could. The four bumped gently along the bottom, and swirls of sand rose up around their knees.

The water was shallow enough that they could see the enormous raft above and behind them, casting a giant square of shade at their backs. In front of them, brightness. Caesar looked around Kinchen to Pip, and Kinchen could hear Caesar's thoughts as if she'd spoken. *Forward?*

Pip stood still, moving his head slowly around as if listening for something Kinchen couldn't hear. *Yes.*

They walked away from the raft, toward the doorway. The living sea enveloped them, and the light above filtered down as through murky green glass. Tiny fish wriggled past their faces and bumped at their legs. Seaweed tickled them lightly. Jellyfish floated above, their tentacles dangling, but too high above them to cause worry. A small octopus exploded from a rock and jetted away. The four walked hand in hand in hand: Thanh, Caesar, Kinchen, Pip. Caesar breathed for them; Pip led them.

Soon they entered a valley to which they could not see the bottom. The floor slanted sharply under their feet. Pip nodded. This was the way.

Deeper and deeper they walked, away from Raftworld and down, into darkness. But strands of light wrapped around them and encircled them, until they walked in a greenish-gray haze. The sand swirled at their ankles in a comforting way; and though they knew the water must be cold at such depth, no one shivered.

No one could later agree on how long they had walked. It seemed much farther a distance than it had looked on the surface. Kinchen said they walked for hours; Thanh said only lengthy minutes. Pip and Caesar thought it was just long enough. Pip urged them forward and found paths up and down the hills, and eventually, at the precise right time, they came upon her, reclining on the ocean bottom like a craggy mountain. The sea monster.

A Kraken.

Yes, her.

THANH'S DESCRIPTION of the monster at the maelstrom had been patchy, focused as he was on almost dying. Now they all knew for sure: the monster who saved Thanh and

his people was indeed the same monster sought by her misplaced husband. She was a Kraken, in the same way that the creature back at Tathenn, living in the Odd Bay and communing with old man Ren, was a Kraken. She undulated the same ripply pattern in the water, she held her frondlike arms with the same civility, and with her giant eye, she blinked the same deep, slow blink. In her gut, Kinchen immediately knew: this was the lost wife from Venus's story, the mate who'd gone exploring and never returned.
And here she was, sitting in the doorway between the worlds, unmoving—*why?*

At the same moment, from Pip: *It's her. It's his wife.* And Caesar, whose fingers shivered in Kinchen's own: *We found her!*

Suddenly, Pip let go of Kinchen's hand and stepped away from the group. Kinchen gasped into the sea, letting a stream of bubbles loose before Pip stopped and turned back to her. She held her arm out to him. *You need to hold on.*

He floated up a few feet and hovered, treading water to stay down. *I'll be okay. And it's her. We're not afraid of her.* He swam away, small and frail-looking in the murky sea light.

Kinchen yanked the others to follow, but Caesar pulled back, standing her ground, and with Thanh to anchor her, held the group still. *We'll wait here. Really. He'll be okay. Let him be.*

While Caesar breathed for them, the other three watched Pip swim toward the monster until he was floating directly in front of one unblinking eye, his small silhouette glowing faintly against the dark pupil and iris. He bowed awkwardly in mid-water. She swirled a delicate tentacle.

Pip and the creature conversed for some time while the others waited. Kinchen couldn't hear Pip's thoughts or the Kraken's. Neither could Caesar, who thought-muttered constantly: *Can't make it out. Too far away. Must be going okay. He's doing great.* Thanh said nothing but watched intently. Finally, Pip reached his hand out to stroke the Kraken—right where Kinchen imagined the nose would be, if Krakens had noses—and the Kraken patted Pip back, one tendril arm drooping over his shoulder.

Then Pip swam back to the three who were waiting.

He took Kinchen's hand at the end of the line, and his feet bumped down to the sand. *She wants to talk to us.* Next to Kinchen, Caesar nodded and stepped forward. Thanh followed, face open in interest and awe.

And through Pip, it seemed, they could now hear her. As they drew near, the monster's thoughts gradually separated from the water and clarified, funneling through Pip into the others: . . . *had a grand adventure. All over one world and another. But now I'm old. And I miss him—*

The Kraken stopped short. *That's one of them.* A tentacle whipped out, longer than seemed possible, and tapped Thanh gently in the chest. *How are you?*

Thanh froze. He didn't answer her—his thoughts instead went to Pip. *Tell her—tell her thank you. Tell her we're all okay. Alive.*

Pip did, repeating Thanh's thoughts and sending them out into the sea.

The Kraken shifted. *Even the man who smelled of blood? Is he okay?*

Even him, said Pip. *Getting better.*

And the girl whose body longed for the sweet water, the girl who wanted to float?

She is also fine. She can walk on the water.

That I saw. After I blew everyone through the doorway. Her color shaded lighter, and her body shrugged in a sigh. *I didn't know if I should follow. If you think he'll want me back after all this time—*

He will, said Kinchen emphatically. Her words hovered around her, but they didn't *go* anywhere.

And the Kraken didn't seem to hear her. *Will he want to see me again?*

He will, said Pip, and the Kraken blinked. Pip said, *Your husband misses you terribly. He's told me a hundred times at least how much he wants to see you again. Every day. He's waiting for you. Always.*

You can take me to him? She blinked her enormous eye. *It's time for me to rest. But I want to go home first. To him, wherever he is. I'm waiting for him, too.*

We can take you there, said Pip. *But it's a long trip.*

I can't move so fast anymore. Not for so long a distance.

Caesar said suddenly—and even in water her thoughts sounded bright and bubbly—*Ah! Raftworld can help. Raftworld is big enough to pull!* She jumped, and her braids floated up around her head in graceful tendrils.

But we need to make sure the portal is shut first, said Kinchen. *The doorway. The—she's sitting in it.*

Be quiet and let me talk, said Pip. *Please.* He sounded so . . . so grown-up and sure of himself. Like he knew what he was doing. Like he wasn't scared. Kinchen remembered Caesar's *Let him be* and made herself quiet.

To the Kraken, Pip said, gesturing toward Caesar, *This girl offers her nation of Raftworld to pull you to your home— after you come out of this doorway, and the door closes.*

For a moment no one spoke. Then: *I couldn't decide,* she said.

Decide what? asked Pip.

Whether to go in or out. To stay or go. First world or second. I wanted to go home for a long time, and I couldn't find the way. Imagine my surprise when the last storm blew a door open, and I could see my way into the world where my husband might still live. I could taste the sweet water. On the surface, a boat imploded, sending its people down, hand in hand. They were drowning. They were dying; they had no one to breathe for them underwater. So I shot them back up—but to the second *world, because I saw that one of them belonged in the sweet water, and I thought that, with her, they all might survive there. And they* did. *They did survive. They walked on the skin of the water. I wedged in the door right behind them. Sat down in the doorway. Because I couldn't decide.*

She shrugged all eight shoulders. *Now I've decided. Thank you.*

She heaved herself up—only a few feet, as she shifted her weight, but the disturbance was enormous. Sand puffed up in billowing clouds higher than Kinchen's head.

The Kraken was moving. Out of the doorway. Thanh yelped: *Not yet! Tell her not yet!*

Wait! called Pip. *Wait!*

They stood for a moment in an agitation of water and sand. Small fish darted past them, flitting away from the commotion.

Then she thudded back to the ground, and the sand filtered down, golden around them. Though the water remained cloudy, they could see the Kraken again, a massive hill on the bottom of the ocean. Still holding open the door.

You want me to come or not? The Kraken sounded— amused? Irritated? Kinchen couldn't read her voice well enough to tell.

The family you saved from drowning, said Pip. *They want to return to their world. Let them through first—hold the door open for them—and then we'll come back down and you can leave the doorway and come with us. And we'll bring you to him. To your husband. Can you do that for us? Wait for just a little longer?*

She laughed, and the fish darted through the resonant water to hover around her eye like butterflies around a particularly fragrant bush. She laughed a long time, the water burbling around her. *I've been waiting this long already. I can wait a little more.*

We'll return soon, said Pip. *We need to say good-bye to our friends. Then we'll come back for you.*

I'll be here. But that family that's going through the door. They'll have a long journey to shore, and a rough one. Do they know that? Can they make it?

8

Caesar's Story.

WHEN THEY reached Raftworld, they let go of one another's hands and swam to the surface, but Caesar, who could not float, climbed the rope that had been dropped down for her, deep in thought. By the time she reached the air, shook the water from her braids, and wrapped a dry robe around herself, she felt she understood what Mai's solemn look had meant. And she suspected that Thanh did not yet understand.

On the dock, she moved to stand next to Thanh. He, Kinchen, and Pip were already wrapped in robes and holding mugs of hot tea. Jupiter sat nearby on a stool. The first worlders—Thanh's people—clustered near their new boat, a sturdy little thing filled with food and water, waiting to say good-bye. One of the king's guards was instructing them on how to use the hydraulic engine, with Mai trying her best to translate. There were a lot of gestures involved on both sides.

". . . We've never tested it in salty water like you say your world has. I don't think it will last very long in these conditions. But it should take you to land at least." Oars and a sail and fold-up mast were stowed in the bottom of the boat just in case, along with the food and water and tarps and everything they'd need.

"Before the men go," said Caesar, "I have to tell you something." She tried to talk in a low voice, for Thanh's ears only.

"What is it?" said Thanh. "Remember, Sang and Mai and I aren't going. You can tell me after." He paused at the look in her face. "Unless it's important to say now."

"It is." Caesar took a deep breath. How to say it? She didn't have the right to tell Mai's plans, but she wanted Thanh to hear her own idea. Even though he didn't know her that well yet, it might give him some comfort. And she liked him. "It's this. You and Sang don't have parents. And neither do I. And Kinchen and Pip are going to go back to the Islands to live with their adopted grandfather. So I was thinking—I was thinking that you and I could adopt each other. Like a brother and sister. Like friends."

Thanh looked surprised. "Sure. Of course." He grinned. "Mai will love that, too—we can all three adopt one another; and Sang can be our big sister. But we really should talk about this later. Unless—do you want me to ask Jupiter if you can live with us three?"

A hand descended on Caesar's shoulder, and she jerked before she realized who it was. "I have room for this one if she wants it," said Jupiter. "I'll make sure of it." He knuckled under Caesar's chin. "Good girl," he muttered.

The three of them walked back to stand by Sang and Mai and The Turtle, near the new boat. Mai put her arm around

Thanh's shoulders and cleared her throat. "You know we're best friends forever."

Thanh laughed. "Everyone's my friend today."

"I'm serious." She wasn't smiling, not even a flickering start of a smile. "You're my best friend."

"Even though I'm a knucklehead?"

"Not a knucklehead. I'm sorry I ever said anything like that. You're a great person, with your imagination and your stories, and I hope—"

But the men had finished their piloting lesson and were climbing back out of the boat; Truc helped his brother ease onto the dock. The Turtle crowed at the commotion, and the moment was lost.

As the men joined the others, the rower who'd been tutoring them on their new engine chuckled and shook his head. "Having to pack water when you travel on water. That's a crazy world you live in." They all looked out toward the odd elongated patch of light—where they knew the open door-way must be. The rower sighed. "I can't believe the king's going to go there."

"The king isn't."

Caesar—everyone—turned, and there stood the Raft King, chest thrown out, in his purple robe. Putnam. "I'm not leaving. I'm going to stay here, with my people. With Raftworld. We'll figure out what to do together."

"I might—have a suggestion," said Kinchen. Her voice carried across the dock. "A place you might like to live."

The Raft King gave her a long look. "I'll listen to all

suggestions, and we'll decide as a people. Together. Let's talk after—after our guests leave, and after we shut the door."

Kinchen nodded.

With her arm still around Thanh, Mai cleared her throat and spoke in slow, careful English. "I have to say something. Now."

9

Thanh's Story.

EVERYONE TURNED to Mai with a question on their face—except for Jupiter, who looked watchful as usual, and Caesar, who looked worried. And Thanh, whose stomach suddenly sank. He couldn't read Mai's mind, but he knew—he just *knew* something bad was about to happen. And he could almost make out what it was. He didn't look at her. His best friend—his first best friend ever. What was she going to say?

Mai twisted the bottom of her shirt in her hand until it knotted. "The boat," she said to Uncle Hung and Uncle Truc, now speaking in Vietnamese. "The long trip on the water. You can't make it with just the two of you, especially since one of you is hurt. And with The Turtle. That's crazy, even with a new boat and a new engine and lots of food and water." She nodded thanks at the king, and though he couldn't understand her words, he inclined his head.

And then, suddenly, Thanh understood.

He knew what Mai was going to say, and he knew that it would break his heart. He could see what Mai was going to do. Because he would have done it, too, if he'd had any gift for it.

Mai's hands shook as she took Thanh's palm in both of hers and looked down into his face. Her features, compact and strong, framed by the fuzz of short hair, focused on Thanh, all her light and energy aimed at him. "You have to stay. This is your home. You have a new grandfather, and you have a job here. So does Sang. But I have to go. Don't you see? They need me. I can get them safely to shore. I have the magic to keep the sea calm, and now that I know it, I can do it awake, too. I'm sure of it. I've been practicing here, focusing, every time I go out on the water, and I understand more about how it all works." Her face, calm as always, glowed—but without the growing smile—and she threw her shoulders back in an echo of the Raft King.

"No," said Uncle Hung. "Get a better life here."

"Also, I'm a good sailor, and I can help take care of the baby."

Uncle Truc didn't say anything. But he looked toward Thanh, and his long face twisted up as if he were in pain.

Uncle Hung said, "Stay here. It's better for you."

Mai stepped away from Thanh and toward Uncle Hung, hugging him gently around his taped side. "This is my choice. I choose to go back with you."

Thanh couldn't move. His throat tightened and dried, as if after days without water. When Mai looked over her shoulder at him, he croaked, "But—then we'll never see each other again." He felt like he couldn't quite understand all the ripples that were going to move outward from this choice. Like it needed to be spelled out very clearly what was going to happen. And underneath all that confusion, sitting like a rock at the bottom of his stomach, was the answer. That Mai was doing the right thing.

Mai shook her head firmly at Thanh. "After I bring everyone to land, I'll row out to sea in a little boat of my own. And I'll look for you. In every storm, waiting for a doorway to pop open, until I come through again, and I'll find you. I promise."

At the thought of Mai in a little rowboat searching for a storm and a doorway, Thanh found he could move and breathe again. His throat unthawed. She'd find a way to return—knowing her—if it were at all possible.

Then he thought about what that life would be like for her. Like being Amelia on her last trip, or the Kraken when she finally became homesick, always looking but maybe without ever finding the door. Maybe wandering forever and never finding a real home. And he knew he couldn't let her make that kind of promise, not even for him.

"Try to come back if you can," he said. "But don't spend your whole life on it. Just—maybe every once in a while, try. Okay?"

And he stepped into her open arms, and she bent and kissed the top of his head as if they were even more than friends.

Then Uncle Truc grabbed him in a bone-crushing hug, those strong lopsided shoulders pressing against Thanh for the last time. The man who'd watched over him and Sang, who'd told him stories about his father, who'd brought him along on the dangerous trip, who'd forgiven him when he messed up, who'd loved him as a son. This man leaned crookedly over Thanh, laughing and crying at the same time, telling him good-bye and that all would be well. That Thanh and his sister would have a great life in their new home. That he would always, always miss them. That they were making the right choice.

Then everyone hugged everyone they could, and Uncle Hung and Uncle Truc and The Turtle boarded the boat, and Mai stood on the water next to the boat. And they left. Mai walked ahead on the water, her last chance, and the boat followed, the hydraulic engine pumping quietly.

Everyone watching knew exactly the moment that Mai reached the doorway and stepped through, for her tall, dark silhouette sank into the ocean, and she treaded water until the boat reached her and picked her up.

Thanh watched as through a window while the boat grew smaller and smaller, farther and farther away in the first world. He didn't cry. He would do that later. For now, he watched the boat shrink through the door between the two worlds, until finally the dot that was the boat turned and moved out of the frame of the doorway, and he could see it no longer. It was gone.

PART SEVEN

Pip Again.

Still 1978.
Still the Second World.

1

WHEN THEY went back down to the Kraken, she was ready; Pip could hear her before he could see her, humming with quiet expectation.

As they drew closer in the deep water, her mountain of a body appeared like an island on the ocean floor, eye open. *Did your friends get through? Oh. I see they did.* She waved a frond at Thanh, who waited stiffly at the end of the group, face stony.

I'm sorry for your loss, she said. *It is deep.*

He raised his free hand to her.

She shifted in the sand. *I'm ready to go.*

Pip took her by one tendril, as thin at the end as a child's arm, and led her away from the crack between the worlds. He didn't pull—he didn't think it seemed dignified, and he worried he might hurt her tentacle. She did the work, pushing herself forward out of the doorway. It was a tight fit, not unlike a child shoving its head into a too-small sweater. She squeezed and groaned and wrestled her way through; and in the process she stirred up so much sand, Pip felt they were buried in it. But Caesar held on to them all, and after some moments they could see again.

I'm out, she gasped. *That was something. All three of my hearts are racing.* Then she sighed. *It's shut. I can feel it behind me. It's like a draft is gone.*

Pip squinted through the dim green light—they were so deep—and though he couldn't see a difference, he had to agree the atmosphere felt different.

The salty taste is gone, said Caesar.

Thanh said nothing—he sent out no thoughts. Pip could feel his silence like a weight, and he thought probably Kinchen could also feel it.

I'm sorry, he thought toward Thanh. *I wish it could be different. I wish people never got split up, and no one ever had to leave each other.*

I know it's not much comfort right now, said Caesar. *But you have your sister. And you have me. I'll be your friend.*

And us, said Kinchen. *Pip and I will always be your friends, too.*

Thanh's face cracked. Even in the water Pip could see that he was crying.

THE KRAKEN soon declared she'd caught her breath and was ready to move again.

If you can just get up the hill, said Pip, *we'll be at the level of the towrope, and Raftworld can help pull you. Their engines are ready.* So they crawled up the sand toward the shallow water, with many rests along the way.

When they saw the towrope dangling down, and looked up to see the big square shadow ahead of them, the Kraken rested again. *Why don't you climb up my back? You'll be much closer to the surface.*

Climb up your back? Pip asked. He'd never climbed on the Kraken at home. It hadn't occurred to him. Would that be polite?

Of course it's polite. She laughed at his accidentally asked question. (As did Kinchen and Caesar.) *It's what I was made for. I mean, eventually I become an island. Then who do you think walks on my back but you land creatures?*

So they climbed, still holding hands. The Kraken's back (or, from the Kraken's perspective, the top of her head) was almost flat—good island-making material—but her sides were steep. When Pip's feet slipped, the monster stretched a tentacle and caught him, easing him up the slope. They hiked across her wide expanse and stood, ready to swim the rest of the way up. Kinchen and Thanh would pull Caesar to the surface—which wasn't far. Pip would swim himself up. Before they pushed off, Pip bent and stroked her back. *Thank you.* And: *I'll be back soon.*

Stay.

He did. The Kraken shook, a series of ripples like a minor earthquake. Then she rose, the four children standing and swaying on her back.

2

WHEN THEY rose out of the water—like Venus and Swimmer rising from the ocean—Pip could no longer hear his friends' thoughts. But he understood the Kraken. She was happy to be going home. Still worried about how her husband would feel when they met again. But mostly happy.

And he realized he was happy, too. He'd had an adventure—without Kinchen to protect him. And she hadn't had to save him. He'd done that himself, and he'd helped others, too—dealing with the Raft King and now the Kraken. He would never recognize faces. And he was sometimes awkward. But he was good at getting along with sea creatures—and people.

The Raft King and his people stood on the dock watching. The Kraken had stopped rising when her back touched the air, so it looked as if they were standing on the water.

Pip raised his hand to the people, but mostly to Putnam, whose loss was so great.

Before he could say anything, Caesar hopped forward. "I'm sorry you couldn't find your mom back. That's awful, and we're all really sorry."

The Raft King nodded. "It's a long time ago now."

"But still new to you," said Pip. "And we're sorry."

"Very sorry." Kinchen stepped forward, too, her face firm. "But we still need to talk about how you stole my brother."

Pip almost told Kinchen to stop—that now wasn't the time, and besides, he (Pip) had forgiven the king. But his sister's tight face made him stay quiet. She'd worked so long and hard on the Islands to keep her brother safe, yet she hadn't been able to stop the king from kidnapping him.

"I had no right," the Raft King said. His powerful body sagged as he folded onto a bench someone had placed behind him. Sitting, he was the same height as Kinchen. "I knew that, too. All along. But I thought my need was more important . . ."

Kinchen waited.

"I was thinking only of what I wanted for myself and for Raftworld. And I'm sorry."

At this, Kinchen nodded. "My brother is—he's fine. You didn't hurt him."

Pip shouldered Kinchen gently. "But thank you for coming for me anyway," he said.

The Raft King held out his wide, strong hands as if he were asking for something. Pip took one hand and held it in his. Slowly, Kinchen took the other.

"Now," said Caesar, "a trip to the Islands! That'll be fun."

THAT EVENING Kinchen told the Raft King her idea about where the people could settle: on the Kraken's head. "She wants to become an island. She and her husband."

Pip, seeing where she was headed, said, "He told me once—the other Kraken did—that when they get old, they turn into enormous islands, much bigger even than they are now."

"They could be your new home," said Kinchen. "And since she spent so much time in the first world, it would feel a little like something from there. It would feel right. I think."

Everyone sitting around them watched to see what the king would say—the guards, the advisors, the storytellers, the visitors.

"*I* want to," said Caesar. "I like her. Having her—both of them—for our home would be amazing."

"I'll have to think about it," said the Raft King. Then something on his face shifted. "For myself, I mean. If others want to settle there, that'll be their own decision. I'm just not sure about myself yet."

THAT NIGHT as they ate a snack in Jupiter's cabin before bed, Pip said to Kinchen, "That was a good idea about the Kraken, and the island." Pip and Kinchen sat at the table. Thanh and Sang, still tired, had tumbled into bed already, in pallets on the floor, and Caesar had simply tipped forward at the table and snoozed with her head on her forearm, her warm honey drink undrunk. Kinchen noted that this was a day of surprises.

Jupiter spoke from the bench where he was reclining. "It was a great idea you had, Kinchen." He peered toward her. "I have the feeling—correct me if I'm wrong—that you've been unhappy about something."

Kinchen flushed. Pip had never seen her flush before; she was always so sure of herself.

"It's just—" She turned the mug around and around in her hands. "I don't have any special talents. Like everyone else does." Her glance flicked up to Jupiter and back down. "There's nothing I'm good at."

"But you're good at *everything*," said Pip in surprise.

"I don't have anything special," she said.

"Anything magical, you mean," said Jupiter. "Or one special talent. A calling."

She nodded and looked up almost with relief on her face. "You understand."

"I do," said Jupiter. "But you're wrong." He held his hand up to stop her replying. "What I mean to say is, most people don't have magic like Pip or Mai or Caesar. Only a very few do. Most people don't have a special calling to be a story-teller, like Thanh does, or like I did. Most people are like you—or like Putnam. Good at some things. Medium-good at other things. Maybe not so good at other things. But not an obvious remarkable ability at anything. And that's okay."

"Like Putnam," repeated Kinchen. She didn't look thrilled at the comparison. But she didn't object, either.

Pip cleared his throat. "Besides, I think you might have a calling for something. You had a great idea for where Raftworlders could live. And you stood up to the governor and the Raft King when they were doing something wrong.

And you always want to take care of people and make sure they are okay. Have you thought of going into government someday?"

Jupiter laughed, a rich warm chuckle, the kind that you produce when suddenly everything is perfect. Kinchen joined in. Caesar woke with a snort and started laughing, too—without, it seemed, even knowing why—and the sound filled the cabin, waking Sang and Thanh just in time to share a bedtime snack with their new family.

THE VERY next day they began towing. The Kraken paddled, too, but she needed help to reach any speed. She was, she said, exhausted from years of searching for the doorway—and days of holding it open. Raftworld's engines stuttered along under too much weight; as Caesar explained, they were moving against the currents and the prevailing winds now—not something Raftworld would normally do—to get back. The journey took over a week.

As Raftworld towed the Kraken back to the Islands, the adventurers spent time exploring and meeting people. Pip missed his own country, and Kinchen said she did, too, but they both loved Raftworld's hanging gardens and the pots of dense, lush plants and the almost-tame songbirds that fluttered among them and the chickens that strutted in the little yards. They loved the music and storytelling that took place after supper every night. They attended the school—the first time either of them had tried it—and joined the other children in learning basic hydraulics and drumming and knitting.

And Pip made a decision he'd been thinking about for a while. He'd spent so much of his life feeling like he had a problem that he needed to hide. Now he thought: *It's just something different, something that makes me who I am.* He told everyone he met that he had an eye problem, that he couldn't recognize them and never would. It was like being blind without the blindness, he said. From then on, when people walked up to him, they generally told him who they were; if they forgot, he asked. Even Caesar took to announcing herself, though with her swagger she didn't really need to: "Pip, it's your buddy."

Kinchen kept her white hair stripe; she said she'd had it so long she didn't want to get rid of it. And Pip didn't want her to, to be honest. It was good to have someone you could know immediately, without ever being told. Especially if that someone was your big sister who'd gone partway across the world—farther than ever before—to find you and bring you home. Even if you didn't need saving; even so, that kind of sister was a good sister to have and to see and to recognize.

Pip and Kinchen did love Raftworld; but it was noisy and so crowded everywhere. Sometimes they needed to get away to somewhere more like their home with Old Ren, not so closely pressed with so many people.

At these times, Kinchen would climb on a roof and sit as close to the sun as possible, above the crowds. Sometimes Pip and Thanh climbed up with her, and Kinchen and Pip would explain what it was like to live on the Islands, so that Thanh would know. Kinchen told about the day they drank tea at the governor's house and the Raft King took Pip away. Pip told about the governor and her deep, strong voice. They both told about living in the woods near the caves with Old Ren. Thanh asked a lot of questions about Ren, like he was trying to put pieces of a puzzle together and something didn't fit.

Pip began to wonder about Ren, too.

WHEN PIP needed to escape from all the faces, he dove into the water and swam out to the Kraken and rode with her. She'd release one of her eight tentacles from the towrope and curl it out for him to sit on, and like a prince of the ocean he'd float just under the surface in her arm, safe in a world where he recognized everything he met.

On one of these rides, he said, *Tell me something about yourself that no one else knows.*

She thought for a long time. *My name.*

He realized then, in surprise, that he'd never asked her name. He hadn't thought about it. The other Kraken, her husband, had never suggested she had a name. Or that *he* had one, for that matter. And this was something no one knew? *No one knows your name? Not even your husband?*

She shook her head—which in her case amounted to agitating her whole body. The towline tightened and loosened rhythmically, and Pip considered that Raftworld was probably feeling a minor quake.

The sea monster said, *We were the only Krakens in the world, so there was no reason for names. We called each other*

Sweetheart. My particular name I gave to myself, much later. It's a crazy one for a sea monster. She paused, suddenly shy. Her craggy skin shaded in what he thought might be a blush.

What is it? he asked gently. *If you don't mind telling me.*

I named myself after a place—a place in the other world where I long lived. Shores full of fish and magnificent sands and the most brilliant people: souls composed of sinew and light. I lived off their shore long ago, and I watched them and loved them. A few of them could even walk underwater and talk with me. I loved those people, and I left only after they were stolen away from me, stolen on ships that stank of death. She shrugged several massive shoulders, causing Pip to bob up and down with her thoughts. *My name. Africa.*

PART EIGHT

The Rest of Venus's Story.

THIS WHOLE BOOK, *this entire tale, is the rest of Venus's story. You get that, right? This is all her story.*

PART NINE

What Happened to Venus. The Details.
Because You Might Insist on Knowing.

1782 and Following.
In All the Oceans of the Second World.

THERE WERE long years of travel before Venus finally regained land. Her brother, Swimmer, led Raftworld on its search for Africa, zigzagging around the globe. He grew taller and bulkier and quieter, and eventually he became their first king; but he never found a doorway back to their homeland. At his deathbed the regret had etched itself into the lines on his face, and even his family ranging around his bed (his wife, his three half-grown children, and Venus, who had not married) were unable to ease his pain at passing away without having girdled the ocean and led his people home.

In their travels, the Raftworlders had stopped at tiny islands dense with trees and plants and birds, and from these beginnings the people built Raftworld into a beautiful place. Their many languages melded slowly into a tongue they called Homeland. They sailed all the warm parts of the world. They never, however, returned to the island where Uncle Caesar and the scarred woman were buried; that place was so insignificant that even had they spotted it in the distance, Swimmer wouldn't have stopped there. He had always looked for something bigger.

They had found their Kraken friend and the islands of Tathenland—ruled at that time by two women—early in their travels, and as it was the only peopled country they ever discovered, they returned to it periodically for visits, remembering and practicing their English with the islanders. Every time they sailed into the harbor at Baytown, the Tathenlanders—as alone in the big new world as the Raftworlders—concocted a party that lasted for days. The two peoples traded stories and goods and artistry and technology. Early on, Venus learned to spin and knit from some women on the Islands—though, lacking goats on Raftworld, she couldn't complete much work until the next time Raftworld returned to Tathenland and she traded for more wool.

The years went by, long travels over the ocean punctuated with brief visits to Tathenland. Slowly, Venus could feel old memories—of life before Uncle Caesar—wanting to come back again, but she tamped them down. Kept them quiet. Kept moving, as Swimmer wished.

After her brother's funeral, Venus sat and thought to herself—as she had more and more with the passing years— *What if I stand still? What if I let myself remember everything?* The next time Raftworld stopped at Tathenland, the shiny new Raft King eager to trade and move on, still searching for a mythical magical land, Venus thought, *No.* Just that: *No.* She stepped off the raft to shore; she met people and traded stories and acquired more knitting tricks; she relearned how to walk on land; she dug her fingers in the dirt; and when the time came to leave, she did not climb back on the raft. She decided to stay. And finally, to remember.

The new Raft King was angry at Venus's desertion, but

only until someone young and strong from Tathenland volunteered to take her place, to travel with Raftworld around the globe. Then the Raft King agreed: a person should be allowed to trade herself away if she so desired. And likewise the two co-governors of Tathenland agreed: as long as all the lives were willingly given to the new place, the trade was good. Venus nodded and said the words that all volunteers from that point forward took as their own, as part of the ceremony of the exchange: *I trade myself willingly. I say good-bye to my beloved old home, which I will never forget, and open my heart to my new.*

WHEN VENUS decided to remain on solid ground, the two middle-aged female governors of the Islands shook her hand and invited her to tea the next day. As they sat at the table and poured her a cup, they flickered like shadows of each other. One governor was dark-skinned, one light—the dark one just a few shades paler than Venus herself, and the other a blanched cousin to the captain and crew that had held Venus in the slave ship so many years ago. The one was the daughter of people who'd lived here nearly forever, according to their story; the other, descended from a shipload of English convicts who'd been blown through to the second world in a storm only a few years before Venus herself had stepped over. The two governors moved their hands above the tea set in jerky unison. They ruled together.

That was the oddest thing about the world here: that it was ruled in tandem, by these women. Not that women couldn't rule—of course they could, as she well knew from stories Uncle

Caesar had told—but that these two, so dissimilar from each other, would *want* to work together. It occurred to Venus as she watched the two women that perhaps she could have done more for her people after she'd brought them through the deep. Perhaps she shouldn't have stepped back from leading with Swimmer, even though their ideas were so different. She'd had thoughts about how they could have settled somewhere, on land, but she'd kept her thoughts to herself and lived her own quiet life. Maybe she should have spoken.

While the governors brewed and poured Venus more cups of hot tea, they told her—their country's first immigrant in decades—about the Islands. Tathenland boasted three pubs and a library (a collection of handwritten books by an Englishman, now deceased, who'd been a famous author back in his old country), along with a mill and shops and a church and even a small stable of horses. And a storyteller, and talented fisherfolk and goat-herders, and several skilled herbalists. There was music. There was dancing. There were scientific discoveries. There was art, including a statue of great historical significance.

"A statue?" Venus already knew much from her earlier visits to the Islands, but the statue she had never seen. "Where? What's its significance?"

The governors glanced at each other—significantly, it seemed. The darker woman said, "It was once a man—a real man. After he did some terrible things here . . . he turned to stone."

The other woman added, "That's the power of the land here. And the gift of some of the people who understand the land—to make things like this happen."

Venus nodded. "I see."

"You know about power like this? Power to do things—magical?"

"I've heard of it." But she didn't volunteer her own gift, which was her secret to keep. "What did he do that was so bad?"

"Terrible things," said the first governor, shaking her head. "Betrayal and murder and lying."

"And oatmeal poisoning," added the second, her pale face suddenly intense.

The first governor rolled her eyes and muttered to Venus, "Don't ask." She paused, thinking. "Though to be turned to stone: also terrible."

The second governor said, "He deserved what he got. And since turning back would take a drastic change of heart, he'll be a statue forever. Biscuit?" She held up a plate.

The first wrinkled her brow but didn't say anything. Venus took a cookie.

After tea, the governors brought Venus to a place near the docks, to a round dais, on which stood the statue, pitted and scarred with age and weather.

"We need to get it out of the elements," said the first governor.

"But no one wants to take it," continued the other. "Too much responsibility."

"Nice statue, though," the first said. "Been altered over the years; whenever it needed repair the artisan tweaked it a bit. The sneer is gone." She turned to the other governor. "Remember that sneer?"

The statue was made of soft gypsum, almost translucent, much weather-damaged. The woman who'd kept it in repair over the years—and slowly eased the face's scorn into a smile—was now dead, and there was no one else capable of such detailed stonework.

Even dented and dinged, it was the most beautiful sculpture Venus had ever seen. Not that the subject of the carving was himself handsome, for he was not. A white man with hawkish features like the slavers', he was everything Venus found ugly; and he was craggy and pitted, badly aged. But he was so *real*, and his face so full of joy, and his hands open in front of him—tossing bread to songbirds, maybe.

Venus understood what the governors were asking without asking. She didn't know why they wanted her for this job, but she knew why she agreed: it would be quiet and peaceful work, and a statue would be just the right person to keep her company.

After a few weeks of walking all over the outskirts of town, Venus adopted a puppy and built a cabin. She chose a spot outside town and near a big bay, a location close enough to walk in for supplies and trading, but far enough away to be deliberately lonely. The cabin faced a large cave, dry and high-ceilinged. The governors moved the statue into the cave and named her its caretaker.

Venus was content. With her knitting she had work enough to support herself; and with the dog and the statue, she had the companionship she wanted: a snuggler, and a listener who never talked back. Eventually she abandoned the house, left it to fall into disrepair, and moved into the cave with the statue. During the long winter nights she dug into the recesses of her memory, and she told her two quiet friends her own story as well as stories about the others she'd traveled with: her brother, Swimmer, her uncle Caesar, the scarred woman, the man who'd been eaten by the shark, the slaver captain, the leering Mr. Stubbs—everyone she could ever remember meeting.

And she remembered. In the quiet of the cave she finally let everything lost come back to her. As the memories trickled into her conscious mind, she told the statue and the dog about the first slave ship, the one before Old Caesar, and about being stolen from her parents. She told about her parents—how her mother had welcomed the sun every morning, how her father had hugged her every night, how much they had loved her. Every part of her life had a story. And Venus wanted the stone man—white like the slavers—to understand. She wanted him to be sorry for what his people had done, even though she knew stone couldn't apologize, and anyway, his own offense had been something quite different. Still, it helped to talk, and the dog at least listened, her sad eyes blinking.

The little dog grew old on these tales; and so, after a time, did Venus. The stone man of course did not age, growth not being in the nature of statuary. Venus could have sworn in the dim light of the cave that his face acquired wrinkles as time went on. And laid over the joy, a look of tenderness. But surely that was merely the grime collecting from her cooking fire.

Shortly after moving into the cave, she discovered an old

acquaintance in the nearby bay: the Kraken, the one who'd met her people at the tiny island after they crossed over, the creature who had first convinced her that they had entered a new world. The one who'd been looking for his wife. She sat on the beach and gazed at him whenever he emerged. Once in a while he wiggled a tentacle as if he were waving. She waved back.

Years passed. When she was very, very old—when she was ancient and had outlived all her kith and kin except the statue and the Kraken—she awoke one morning and felt her life ebbing out of her. She was dying; and she knew it. It occurred to her that she might take a walk, use her gift one last time. She rose and removed her shawl; she wouldn't need it. She patted the statue and thought fondly, *Good-bye* and *good luck*. And for good measure and just in case he needed it: *I forgive you, Renard. I can't speak for anyone else, but I forgive you.* And because she could not help herself: *Come back someday and do some good in the world. Make amends. Ren.* She ended with her nickname for him, and a last pat on his forehead. Then she paused outside and cleared the twigs off the dog's grave.

The way to the beach was difficult. She was so old, and so far down the path to death. It took hours to make her feet move as she wished. She leaned on a cane and rested every few steps. But eventually she left the land behind her. She dropped the walking stick in the tide and stepped out to sea. As she walked deeper, she moved easier. The water felt astonishingly warm, and the sea ahead of her was green and infused with light. The sand swirled slow maelstroms around her ankles.

She walked toward the Kraken, who did not hide from her. *In all my travels, I never found your wife,* she thought, willing him to understand despite her deficiencies with the language. *I'm so sorry.*

He blinked his brilliant eye, as if to tell her everything would turn out all right in the end.

AFTERWORD

SOME YEARS AGO—never mind how long precisely—I began writing a book that would eventually contain sea monsters. But the sea monsters weren't yet in the book. I was still looking for them.

They turned out to be Kraken, and they showed up, the first time, when I ran out of things to say and didn't know where the story was headed. What should Kinchen and Pip and Caesar *do*? My notes at this point say, "Add in some Kraken??"

The truth is, like many authors, I don't know where I'm going, exactly, when I draft a book. I make many wrong turns before I find my way. I navigate by stars that are constantly shifting. But from the start, the story was about Kinchen and Pip and Caesar, and a giant raft, and islands. (Thanh came a little later, and I was so happy to see him!)

From the start, I knew the book would also, somehow, be about the *Zong*, a ship I'd read about while teaching college literature courses. I had no idea yet what the connection was between the *Zong* and Raftworld, but I trusted that something would emerge as I wrote and rewrote. And sure enough, there, suddenly, fully formed, stood Venus. She was walking out of the water, holding her brother's hand. And Old Caesar was standing on the shore, dropping his kindling in surprise.

Let's talk about the *Zong*. I'm guessing you already know something about the other real events this novel is built on—the Vietnam War, Amelia Earhart's last flight—but the *Zong* is a story that is relatively unknown today. And it is, at heart, where *A Crack in the Sea* really began.

The *Zong* was a real slave ship. Originally a Dutch vessel, it was bought by a group of businessmen operating out of the giant slaving port of Liverpool, England, in 1781. On the west coast of Africa its newly appointed captain, Luke Collingwood, loaded the ship with 459 Africans and headed toward Jamaica, where the plan was to sell these people, make a lot of money, and return to Liverpool to start the process over again.

But during the voyage, several very important things threw off those plans. First, both crew and enslaved Africans became sick; soon, people were dying. Second, the crew was plagued with problems: the captain himself was sick, the first mate was temporarily placed in the brig, and passenger Robert Stubbs was likely stirring up trouble. Third, the boat overshot its destination—maybe because the captain was sick or the first mate was in the brig—and sailed far past Jamaica, adding about a month to their travel time. Because of this navigation mishap, the *Zong* also may have run short of food and water.

It's not clear exactly who gave the order to throw people overboard to their deaths—the captain died only a few days after reaching Jamaica, so he never told his story; the crew and sole passenger told different versions of what happened; and no one asked the surviving Africans what they thought. It is clear, however, that *someone* gave the order, on November 29, 1781, to throw fifty-four ailing women and children overboard to drown.[2] Then on the first of December, the crew threw overboard forty-two men, chained together. Shortly after that, they threw over twenty-eight more—and that same day, another ten jumped to their deaths, for a total of 133 deaths (one man climbed back on board).[3]

Then what happened? When the *Zong* returned to her home port, her owners in Liverpool tried to collect insurance money for the dead Africans—just as if they'd lost barrels of sugar or crates of fancy lace or any other merchandise.

The insurance company didn't want to pay, and the case went to court. English antislavery activists—abolitionists— heard the story, and they showed up at court, arguing that the Africans had been murdered. But in the eyes of the law, slaves were not people—so they *couldn't* be murdered. The case against the *Zong*'s owners failed, because as the court noted, throwing slaves overboard was, in legal terms, "the same as if horses had been thrown overboard." The owners had the legal right to do what they did.

Some British people were horrified. The *Zong* case is

2   The women and children were, according to the crew, shoved out of a window one at a time. They were not tied or chained together. This detail I have altered in my novel.
3   The exact number of people killed was disputed—the insurance company eventually agreed to 122 plus the ten jumpers—but the basic facts of the case were never questioned.

considered a turning point in antislavery history because it received so much publicity and because white people in Great Britain began to consider the deep evils of slavery. It would be almost another quarter of a century before slavery would end in England (and far longer before it would end in America); but the *Zong* pushed people in that direction.

And the *Zong* is the heart and soul of my book. This is not to say that Thanh isn't important—he is, hugely important—and so are Kinchen and Caesar and all the others. But for me, the story first became alive with Venus—with my feeling that she *had* to escape, somehow, from this terrible historical fact, this thing from which, in real life, there was no escape.

Here, then, is one of the key differences between a fantasy novel and real history, something I wrestled with the whole time I was writing this book: in the second world of my novel, some of the people from the *Zong* manage to survive and make a new life for themselves. But in real life, after months at sea in horrendous conditions, 133 people from the *Zong* were really thrown overboard, and they really drowned. They died. They all died. There is no changing that fact, no matter what a novelist might wish.

And when we widen our lens to see the whole ocean, the facts are incomprehensibly grim. Reliable estimates suggest that the number of people enslaved in Africa and brought to the Americas by way of the Middle Passage stands at somewhere around 12.5 million (though some estimates range much higher). Most of these people did not escape—there was no friendly portal waiting to take them to another world.

The boat journey from Vietnam to surrounding countries in the 1970s and '80s was also terrifying—and many people did not survive. Entire boats disappeared. No friendly sea monster showed up to blow people through a doorway.

So why did I write the story as I did? Because I believe that stories can show us many things, including how bad things can get; and sometimes, stories can show us how things could be better than they are right now.

The *Zong* slave ship—and slavery in Britain and America—are history. They are officially over. But that doesn't mean racism has disappeared. And slavery still exists in other places in our world. Meanwhile, people the world over are forced to leave their homes by war and by persecution and by natural disaster; and sometimes they arrive at a new home only to find that they are unwelcome.

In light of all this pain, what can a fantasy novel offer? It can ask us to consider alternatives and possibilities. What if we lived in a world where people didn't die in chains, where people didn't drown trying to escape from war and persecution, where somehow love, like magical water, surrounded us whenever most needed and held us all up? What if we lived in a world where kraken weren't terrifying monsters—but simply people we do not yet know? A world where we could be bigger than we are, and where we could always offer a home to the stranger and the dispossessed? Where every new unrecognized face could one day become the face of a friend?

The truth is, we do live in a world where these things are possible. We simply have to choose to make them happen. And sometimes, I think—I hope—a book can help us see that, and have courage, and take action.

SPECIAL THANKS

A DEEP, deep thanks to the following astute readers: Swati Avasthi, Valerie Geary, Lynne Jonelle, Gabriel Kellman, Rafael Kellman, Todd Lawrence, Megan Wagner Lloyd, Anja Löder, Xuan Thi Nguyen, Parker Peeveyhouse, Tran Thi Minh Phuoc, Anne Ursu, Stephanie Watson, and John Yopp. And of course Tricia Lawrence, my wise, endlessly energetic, and always-encouraging superagent. Hugs to you! Thanks to EMLA more generally for being an agency defined by its deep care for its authors. And thank you, Dennis, for always answering questions so patiently.

Thanks to Anne Klejment, Xuan Thi Nguyen, Thanh Pham, Yen Van Pham, Tran Thi Minh Phuoc, and Sang Tran, for generous and kind help on understanding details about Vietnam, and especially thanks to Yen Van Pham for helping me understand what one's country really is; and Xuan Thi Nguyen and Tran Thi Minh Phuoc for expert cultural and historical advice. All mistakes are, as always, my own.

Thanks to Kathy Coskran of the Malmo Artist Colony for hospitality and peace, year after year. Thanks to Therese Walsh and *Writer Unboxed* for sending me to the first WU Un-Conference and welcoming me to your community. Thanks to the Minnesota State Arts Board (and its Legacy Grant) for financial support while I drafted this novel. Thanks to The Loft Literary Center for so many years of nurturing, and in particular to Jerod Santek, formerly of The Loft, for being exactly who he is: kind and wise.

Thanks to the University of St. Thomas for awarding teaching release time and a sabbatical during which I was able to draft and revise. Thanks also to so many UST students who've written and struggled alongside me—especially those English 326ers who giggled with me at my bad outlines into which I inserted sea monsters whenever I ran aground: you know who you are.

An enormous hug and thank-you to my brilliant, thoughtful, and kind editor, Stacey Barney, who has the best phone laugh ever. And thank you to Kate Meltzer, Cecilia Yung, Annie Ericsson, and everyone at Putnam.

Yuko Shimizu, the art is amazing. Thank you.

Hugs to Swati for talking me through it all and to Anne for insisting everything would turn out okay in the end.

Finally: thanks, as always, to my beloved children for driving with me to crazy and carting me back home with a story. Let's do it again.

A Brief List of Further Reading for Kids and Adults

Frederick Douglass, *Narrative of the Life of Frederick Douglass*, 1845.
An amazing narrative by one of America's best writers, about
his escape from slavery, both physical and psychological.
Tom Feelings, *The Middle Passage: White Ships/Black Cargo*, 1995.
Virginia Hamilton, *The People Could Fly: American Black Folktales*, 1985.
Thanhha Lai, *Inside Out and Back Again*, 2011.
Thanhha Lai, *Listen, Slowly*, 2015.
Tran Thi Minh Phuoc, *Vietnamese Children's Favorite Stories*, 2015.

Further (Adult) Reading Recommendations

For More on the Middle Passage and the *Zong* Slave Ship:

Olaudah Equiano, *The Interesting Narrative of the Life*, 1789.
Equiano's narrative of his enslavement and redemption,
including a possible firsthand account of the Middle Passage.
Marcus Rediker, *The Slave Ship: A Human History*, 2007.
James Walvin, *The* Zong: *A Massacre, the Law & the End of Slavery*,
2011.

For More on Escaping Vietnam After the Fall of South Vietnam, and Life in the Mekong Delta:

Mary Terrell Cargill and Jade Ngoc Quang Huynh's anthology,
*Voices of Vietnamese Boat People: Nineteen Narratives of Escape
and Survival*, 2000.
Jade Ngoc Quang Huynh's memoir, *South Wind Changing*, 1994.
Nguyen Ngoc Tu, *Floating Lives*, 2014 (English translation). An
evocative short story collection set in the Mekong Delta.

Turn the page to read an excerpt
from the companion novel

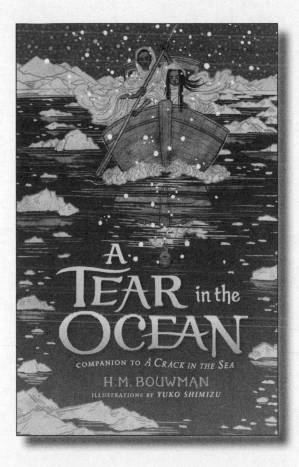

A **TEAR** in the
OCEAN

COMPANION TO *A CRACK IN THE SEA*

H. M. BOUWMAN
ILLUSTRATIONS BY *YUKO SHIMIZU*

1

*P*UTNAM WATCHED a tattered girl about his own age at the edge of the bonfire. For the past hour, she'd hovered in the shadows just outside the glow of the flames. Her face would pop into the light briefly, then snuff itself out again, only to reappear several moments later, then disappear, like a candle being lit and immediately blown out.

She'd been circling the fire, when Putnam, looking for the best spot to listen and watch, noticed her. But she stopped moving about the same time he did, not quite across the fire from him. As he listened to Jupiter, the storyteller, entertain the people with a funny tale about the time long ago when they tried to grow mangoes on Raftworld (sadly, there was not enough dirt for the trees to root in), Putnam's eyes flicked again and again to the spot where the girl's face would suddenly jut out of the darkness and then fall back into it. She didn't seem to realize she could be seen, and no one but Putnam noticed her.

Part of the reason she stood out to Putnam so much was her obvious wish not to be seen. Putnam understood that desire; he was trying to stay out of the light, too. Everyone expected so much of him—the Raft King's son! the next king of Raftworld!—and sometimes he just needed to get away. Maybe this girl had some of the same feelings. Maybe *her* so-called friends were always following her around, too, hoping for favors and being nice to her because of who her dad was.

Or maybe not. Putnam squinted at the girl through the smoke. An Islander, she had the lighter brown skin and straight hair and stocky body that was the classic Tathenlander look. But unlike the other Islanders, she wasn't spiffed up, wearing her best clothes for the party; she acted as if she wasn't even supposed to be at the party.

She made Putnam think of the story the Island's former storyteller (now dead) had told the last time Raftworld had visited the Islands, when he'd been only two—ten years ago. He didn't remember the actual words the Island storyteller had used, of course, but Jupiter had retold the tale since then: a poor orphan girl who'd been forced to work for her rich, hateful stepmother and who, when the prince threw a party, snuck in and eventually captured the prince's heart. Except—Putnam reminded himself—that girl had been given a ball gown and fragile gypsum slippers when she snuck into the ball, and this girl was here simply as herself. She wasn't likely to win a prince's heart the way she looked and acted.

He smiled at the next thought: technically, he supposed, he was the prince in the story. Though no one called him by that title, he was in fact the Raft King's only child. So if he were to follow the story's plot, he should chase this girl down and grab one of her shoes . . . if she *had* shoes . . .

The girl materialized one more time, the firelight playing on a set of bruises on one side of her face. Jupiter had moved on to a more serious story: how the Raftworlders' ancestor Venus escaped from being enslaved. And this time, as Jupiter the storyteller explained the moment of decision, the choice Venus made, the tattered girl emerged and didn't snuff right back into darkness. This time her face stayed in the light, entranced as she was by the story. And there was something in the fire's glow that made her look—not pretty, no, nor healthy nor well cared for—but full of determination and spirit and energy. Just for that moment.

Jupiter's story ended, and she vanished. Vivid in the fire's flickering light one moment, gone the next.

A big hand descended on Putnam's shoulder, and for one brief second he thought it was the girl, coming after him instead of waiting for him to chase her down and steal her shoe. But as soon as that thought flitted into his head, he knew it was wrong. First of all, the hand was too large and heavy.

"It's time." His father, of course—tall, thin, and a little stooped, in the dark red cloak he wore for official events, his graying beard closely trimmed.

Putnam nodded. He already stood in the back of the crowd; he didn't even have to jostle anyone to leave. For a moment he wondered what it would be like to just vanish, like that girl.

"Are you coming?" asked his father. "Your first Session. Let's not be late."

Putnam nodded again and hurried after the old man.

THE TRADING SESSION—usually just called "the Session"—was the biggest meeting in the entire world, which wasn't saying much, as the world was small, at least where people were concerned. The Session, which lasted for several days with long breaks for the delegates to attend parties and socialize, happened every decade or so, whenever the floating nation of Raftworld arrived in the course of its usual travels to the islands of Tathenland and the big island of Tathenn and its capital city of Baytown. Then the Raftworlders and Islanders got together for a week or more of parties and storytelling and singing . . . and trading. The Raft King and the Island's governor—and other important people—attended meetings, exchanged important information, made deals. This year, the Raft King had said that now that he was twelve, Putnam was old enough to go to the meetings. As if that was a privilege. It *was*, but all the other delegates were grown-ups. And the entire meeting was *talking*.

Putnam sat in the back corner of the room next to a convenient tray of cookies, rather than at the delegates' table, which was only big enough for the eight women and men—four from each country—who ran the Session. He was supposed to be listening and learning. He nibbled and made crumbs and tried—he really did—to pay attention.

But the day had been long, and his mind wandered, and after an hour or more of discussions of flour and wool and embroidered cloth and hydraulic engines and so many other things, his eyes drooped. Just before he slid into deep sleep, he remembered himself and snapped back, shifting suddenly in his chair and crumbling the cookie still clutched in his hand.

Eight heads rotated toward him, conversation stalling for a moment. "Sorry," he muttered, feeling foolish, as they turned back to discussion. He knew he should be listening hard at his first Session, maybe even saying something important—but barring that, at least he should *look* like he was listening. He pinched his leg, hard, and sat up straighter, shoving the broken cookie into his mouth and chewing vigorously.

And the pinching and chewing helped. He felt less tired, at least for the moment.

Until he realized what the Session leaders were talking about now: the ocean. A cloud of gloom settled over the room, and Putnam could tell everyone had been thinking about the water long before the topic was introduced. It had been turning salty—slowly, steadily—for some time. But no matter how often Raftworld advisors told the king, he brushed it off. Even when his own son brought it up, the king refused to discuss it. It was in their imaginations, he said. It would get better on its own, he said. It was a normal fluctuation, he said.

In his corner, Putnam sat up straighter. Maybe now his father would be forced to listen.

"There's no doubt at all in our minds," one of the Islanders said stubbornly to Putnam's father. "You don't see it as much because you're always moving around."

"You make it sound like *moving around* is a bad thing. What are you trying to say about us?" asked a Raftworlder, one of his father's advisors.

"Now, that isn't what's meant at all," said the governor in a soothing voice. She was much younger than Putnam's father, who'd been old already when Putnam was born. Tiny compared to Putnam's father, she sat straight in her seat, as if trying to look taller. Her dark braids wrapped around her head like a crown and shone in the light.

She continued. "We're only saying that we *see* the changes more, situated as we are in one location. In the past few years, the fish have been leaving us, heading north. The algae is dying. We know that our capital is better off than other places on Tathenn—it's much worse on the southern shores. We can't ask the fish like you can"—she paused as if waiting for the king to say something, but he didn't speak—"but even so, we can read the water pretty well. The changes aren't good."

She waited again, then said, "What did the fish say?"

"They didn't answer any questions."

The young governor's face fell.

"The water's going bad. You can taste that yourself," added one of the governor's advisors, folding his arms over his chest and nodding at the pitcher on the table.

Several Raftworlders leaned forward to add their thoughts. One said, "It does seem worse the farther south we get. When we were north earlier this year, remember how fresh—"

Putnam's father held up his long, thin hand, and everyone stopped for the Raft King to speak. "The water here has changed, it's true. I can tell from our last visit that it's different. Kind of salty, yes?" The governor's advisor nodded, as did the other Islanders in the room. "But what you have to ask yourself is this: is it maybe just a natural swing in the order of things? Or maybe because of something you've done here on the Islands?"

"And it's affected the entire ocean?" asked the governor. "Your advisor just said the water is different the world over."

The king shrugged, his face blank of expression. "He said it *seemed* that way. And other times it seems fine. We need to study it more to be sure. That's my suggestion: that we form committees. Maybe you Islanders can take samples and track any changes over time—compare data for a few years and see if it's really getting salty and, if so, how bad it is. And when Raftworld travels, we'll take samples at key locations as well, so that the next time we stop at those places, we can also compare."

"The next time? You mean ten years from now, when you circle back?"

"It's not always ten years. There are some places we visit every five or six years. It really depends."

"But the water's gone from good to bad in just a few years. And you're arguing for a decade of testing," said one of the Islanders, a gray-haired woman who looked about as old as the king. "Before we even do anything."

The Raft King paused as if thinking about his answer, and then nodded. "Raftworld moves, but we move slowly. It's what has kept us safe all these years. We don't rush."

Putnam, sitting off to the side with the cookies, could see the looks on the Islanders' faces and in their stiff shoulders and bodies: frustration and worry. He could see, more faintly, similar looks in the Raftworlders' faces—everyone's but his father's. This idea of moving slowly was . . . too *slow*. Obviously something needed to be done, and everyone but the Raft King was ready to do it.

"If we don't take action . . . ," said the young governor of the Islands. She didn't finish the sentence. She didn't have to. They all depended on the ocean—Raftworld and Tathenland— for food, for water. For everything.

One of the Raft King's advisors broke the silence. "Well, this is a topic we should return to. Tomorrow morning?" She stood, stretching her lower back and smiling a little too big. "There is, after all, a party tonight to attend."

Others stood, too, but not the young governor, who spread her hands on the table, palms down, almost as if the table were trying to fly off. She didn't smile, either. "We're not done here."

"We'll talk about it again." One of the governor's own advisors, an elderly man who wore the old-fashioned Island clothing even down to the luck pouch around his neck, patted her shoulder. "Tomorrow, when we're fresh."

Everyone filed out of the room except the governor and her elderly advisor, his hand still on her shoulder. Putnam, following the others out, turned in time to see the governor look up at the old man, her face strained.

"We'll *talk* tomorrow," she said.

"And then do something," her advisor said.

"Sure," she said, unconvinced. "If we stall long enough, pretending nothing is horribly wrong and forming *committees*"— she said the word as if it tasted bitter—"it will be just as bad as if we ignore it altogether. The sea is *dying*. And then we die, too."

The old Island man's hand flexed in a tight grip, then loosened. He smoothed her hair down, as if he were her father and she a young child. It occurred to Putnam that maybe he *was* her father. "I know," he said in a low voice. "If Raftworld ignores the problem, we'll have to figure it out on our own."

"The problem is coming from the south. We need explorers, scientists, *people*—to sail south, find out what's causing this. Fix it."

The old man nodded.

"But without ocean boats or seafaring folks—"

"I know."

"We needed Raftworld. They were our best hope, and they're saying no."

"It does sound that way. But maybe tomorrow . . ."

At the same moment they seemed to realize Putnam was still there, and as they turned to him, he muttered, "Excuse me," and stumbled out of the room.

Was this what a Session was? A place to avoid the real problems of the world? And was this who his father was? Someone too slow-moving or too scared to jump in and fix things?

PUTNAM CAUGHT up to his father as the older man neared the large tent that had been set aside for him. When Raftworld visited, the people of the Islands built tents for them

to stay in, dotted all along the beach, large and elaborate and brightly colored inside and out.

The Raft King's tent, once you were through the door flap, was lofty enough for a tall man to stand and reach for the ceiling without touching it, and it was hung with tapestries depicting many scenes from Island history: the original Islanders and their close-knit fishing villages; the three ships that capsized there hundreds of years ago, bringing so many immigrants from the other world; the fever, a few decades later, that killed off so many of these immigrants and their descendants; the nation that emerged from this and other disasters to become the Tathenland they all knew today. There was even a panel of cloth that showed Raftworld visiting, bringing goods to trade and occasional volunteers to move to the Islands.

Placed around the interior of the tent were a portable stove for heat, benches and pillows to sit and sleep on, and blankets to fight off any chill. Draperies could be closed for privacy—Putnam's own room was a curtained nook toward the back of the tent, also filled with pillows and cushions. Once he'd gotten used to the earth not moving beneath him, he liked it. A lot.

The Raft King turned to Putnam, and Putnam felt a surge of anger: how ancient his father was! And how set in his ways! He'd always been so large and impressive—but now, suddenly, he seemed shrunken. There were wrinkles around his eyes, and the gray was migrating up from his beard and invading his temples.

"What is it?" the old man asked mildly. He held the flap open for Putnam to enter, gesturing for him to go first.

Except for them, the tent was empty. "What's wrong?" the king asked. "Something's bothering you."

"The meeting," said Putnam. "People are worried about the ocean. And you're not doing anything."

The king smiled. "At least I need never fear that my son will hold things inside and not tell me what's bothering him."

"I'm serious."

"So am I. But, you want to know what I'm going to do." He sat on a padded bench and tapped the seat next to him for Putnam to sit.

Putnam stayed standing. When was his dad going to admit he was wrong and offer to take action? Everyone always said how thoughtful the king was, how good he was at listening to everyone, and Putnam used to think these were compliments. But now he knew: his dad was stalling. It was humiliating to have people think that Raftworld was a nation that didn't *do* things, that ignored problems. A nation that just floated at sea.

His father shrugged. "We're going to move carefully and deliberately. As we always do.

"This is an emergency."

"It's not."

"The Islanders can't move north when the water gets bad in their country. And it'll become an emergency for us, too, eventually. Because eventually *all* the water could go bad. Don't we want to fix it before that happens?"

"We don't know how to fix it. Whatever you mean by *it*."

His father was so irritating! Putnam again felt the hot embarrassment of overhearing the governor's conversation with her elderly advisor, and the advisor's promise to do something even if Raftworld wouldn't help.

They probably thought he was just like his dad. Unwilling.

No, Putnam thought. *Raftworld* will *help. But—*

"You said the fish didn't answer."

The Raft King's face shifted, for a quick moment, into something that looked like stubbornness, and then it was gone. He looked at the floor, avoiding his sons eyes.

Oh. "You didn't ask them," said Putnam, "because you didn't want to know. That's it, isn't it?"

The Raft King didn't answer. His jaw twitched. Then he said, "Things are complicated, son. Sometimes it's better not to ask questions."

Suddenly Putnam understood. "You didn't *ask* them. But the fish *told* you anyway, didn't they?" He could hear venom dripping from his voice, and he didn't care. "They told you the sea was dying. They told you to go south and fix it. *Didn't they?*"

"Son—"

"Did you even ask them for help? For more details so you could fix things?"

"They said it was something terrible! In the deep south! The ice! We can't fix that!" The old man took a deep breath. "I'm sure given time, things can fix themselves." But there was a note of pleading in his voice. "Our country is doing fine right now. We should . . . just keep going as we are. Don't rock the boat."

It was like a punch to the gut. His dad *was* the do-nothing politician he seemed to be. Putnam hadn't wanted to believe it. "How can you be king and not fix things?" He felt his fists curling and uncurling on their own. "You are a terrible king," he said.

His father's head snapped back as if Putnam had punched him, too. Then he took a deep, long breath, almost a sigh. "Show respect, young man."

Putnam glared.

Carefully, slowly, the Raft King unclasped the red cloak and hung it on a hook. Sitting on a brightly embroidered bench beneath the tapestry of Raftworld visiting Tathenn, he leaned forward, elbows on knees. "We might . . . discuss . . . issues in private, but you will not disagree publicly with me at the Session. We present a united front. Remember that tomorrow. Or don't come to the meeting."

"Even if I'm right?"

"Your job is to listen and to learn, not to speak publicly against the king."

"Then I won't be at the Session." Wishing he had a door to slam, Putnam yanked the tent flap aside and left.

His father, cautious as always, didn't follow or call after him.